SHERLOCK HOLMES
IN RUSSIA

SHERLOCK HOLMES IN RUSSIA

Edited and translated
by
Alex Auswaks

With an introduction by
George Piliev

·ROBERT HALE · LONDON

© Alex Auswaks 2008
First published in Great Britain 2008

ISBN 978-0-7090-8007-7

Robert Hale Limited
Clerkenwell House
Clerkenwell Green
London EC1R 0HT

www.halebooks.com

2 4 6 8 10 9 7 5 3 1

Dedicated to all aficionados *of the Sherlock Holmes canon*

Typeset in 11/15pt Palatino
by Derek Doyle & Associates, Shaw Heath
Printed and bound in Great Britain
by MPG Biddles Limited, King's Lynn

CONTENTS

INTRODUCTION

A Study in Russian

In the official biography of Sherlock Holmes, written by his Boswell and loyal friend Dr Watson, there is only one mention of the great detective's arrival in Russia. In *A Scandal in Bohemia* we are told that he visited Odessa in connection with 'The Case of the Trepoff Murder'. But in the short passage offered to the reader below, light is cast on certain circumstances of another, longer and less well-known trip, which the Baker Street consulting detective undertook to this distant and mysterious but, nonetheless, wonderful country. Paradoxical as it may sound, this journey was simultaneously virtual and real. The information concerning this visit is fragmentary and most of it has vanished in the mists of time. But the circumstances of this visit do excite curiosity, are not without interest and, surely, are worth a few pages and minutes of time. And so. . . .

12 December 1893. Tuesday. St Petersburg. Let us imagine a clear winter's day. Our boots crunch the white snow, the frost crackles and bites, but the cold air is filled with sunshine and laughter. The streets and boulevards of the city of Peter the Great are filled with happy, merry, passers-by. They are all smiles and full of the joy of life, because the New Year is nigh. The New Year in Russia is a very special festival, joyful and unclouded, because the Russian irrational *perhaps* is as eternal as the fierce

faith in it, the belief in *perhaps* better times, a magic time of change. Why, it is part of nature! Midnight will chime, a New Year will dawn and happiness and success are on their way. In Russia, the first days of the New Year turn the most convinced sceptic into a romantic who, in the depths of his soul, believes that every cherished dream will be fulfilled. Hark to those midnight chimes!

But that will be on 31 December and this is 12 December, the honeyed eve of the festival, the festive awaiting of the festival, the anticipation of which is, at times, more pleasurable than its actual arrival.

It was on such a day that there occurred an unnoticed but a very important event. Sherlock Holmes arrived in Russia.

The immortal private detective from Baker Street, called to life by the inquisitive mind, rich imagination but, also, material needs of a modest Southsea doctor, Arthur Conan Doyle, first appeared before his readers in November, 1886, on the pages of *A Study in Scarlet*, which appeared in Beeton's Christmas Annual for 1887. But the march to immortal fame was to come only five years later. In July, 1891, *The Strand Magazine*, recently founded by the perspicacious George Newnes, published the first of fifty-six stories (known today as Sherlockiana or The Canon). This was *A Scandal in Bohemia*. Its success was phenomenal! • Humungous! Two or three more months, two or three more stories and the new literary hero had conquered the country, a lasting conquest, perhaps, forever. Two and a half years later his fame reached Russia.

This happened, as you and I now know, on 12 December, 1893. That was the day on which the fortieth issue of a popular magazine, *The Star*, came out. It was published by Piotr Petrovitch Soikin, a devoted fan of adventure stories. Soikin was the first to introduce Sherlock Holmes to Russia's reading public and, having done so, this eminent worthy continued to bring Sherlock Holmes's exploits before the public through his magazines *Nature & People*, as well as *The World of Adventure*, which were the first to publish every new exploit. From February to November 1909 Soikin brought out in five thousand pages (twenty volumes) The Complete Works of Conan Doyle and followed this up with two additional volumes.

And so, the Russian reader became acquainted, for the first time, with a Russian-speaking Sherlock Holmes in *The Speckled Band*, when *The Star* was published.

The new literary hero must have been received well, because the following year saw the publication in *The Star* of *The Adventure of the Beryl Coronet* and *The Adventure of the Blue Carbuncle*. In 1876 the baton passed from *The Star* to the popular Russian publication *Niva* (*The Field*), which hospitably opened its pages to the *Red-Headed League* and (yet again) *The Blue Carbuncle*. A year later *Niva* No. 5 of 31 January 1898, published *Professor Moriarty, The Adventure of the Final Problem*. On 23 February 1898, in Petersburg – hurrah! – the first Sherlock Holmes stories in book form, a 143-page collection entitled *Notes from the Famous Detective* and consisting of *The Adventure of Silver Blaze, The Adventure of the 'Gloria Scott'* and *The Adventure of the Reigate Squires*. In December of the same year, as part of a 12-volume free monthly supplement to the Petersburg newspaper *Dawn, A Study in Scarlet* was published in Russia for the first time. It was translated from German(!), so it wasn't entirely surprising that the hero's surname sounded somewhat Spanish, Golmez, and that he lives on Bakkerstrasse and is referred to as Herr.

Such were the steps the great London detective was to take on Russian soil. It didn't spell success as yet. Let's call it a preliminary acquaintanceship, timid, coincidental, but what is coincidence if not a rod thrown at the wheel of fate speeding towards a prepared place in the universe.

And the place made ready in Russia for Conan Doyle's brilliant creation was no less enviable than the one in his native land. What had started as a coincidence, an accident, grew to become habitual. Sherlock Holmes made a lasting entry into Russian society.

Amongst those who were first to popularize Sherlock Holmes in Russia were the brothers Panteleyeff, who published a remarkable monthly magazine, *The Herald of Foreign Literature*. Working for this magazine were the best translators of the time, able to select the best new literature abroad and bring it to the attention (and judgement) of the Russian reading public. This is why, in 1901, as a supplement to their magazine, the Panteleyeffs issued, for the first time in Russia (and very probably in the world), a three-volume edition of the works of Conan Doyle, consisting of most of *The Canon* available at the time, viz, vol. 1, *The Adventures of Sherlock Holmes. Notes*; vol. 2, *The Memoirs of Sherlock Holmes*; and vol. 3, *From John Watson's Memoirs of Sherlock Holmes*. A large number of the stories in this collection appeared in Russian for the first time, including *The Sign of Four*. This was, indeed, a unique edition but, in Russia today, there is hardly a library that has a complete set. The translations were the work of M.P. Voloshinova, to whom a very special thank you!

And so, at the start of the twentieth century, as the brilliant era of Queen Victoria was ending, the era of Sherlock Holmes was just getting under way in Russia.

While the 3-volume Panteleyeff edition was coming out in July, F.I. Miturnikoff, a Petersburg publisher, put out a 253-page *The Famous Detective's Notes*.

And so, by the end of 1901, this is the Sherlock Holmes picture in Russia: six publications in magazine form, two books and a 3-volume set.

Now this was already something, but the major breakthrough was to come in the spring of 1902 when *The Strand Magazine* was to complete the publication of, arguably, the most famous of the Sherlock Holmes adventures, *The Hound of the Baskervilles*. It was the first after an eight-year silence brought about by the 'death' of the great detective when he went over the Reichenbach Falls. In a fit of unparalleled enthusiasm and loyalty, fans besieged the English and American editorial offices of *The Strand Magazine*. The issue flew all around the world at lightning speed, by post or whatever other means presented itself. Of course, it got to Russia. The success abroad was reflected in Russia, where it swept up and down the land. Russian publishers reacted instantaneously. There is a saying to the effect that, while it takes a while to harness horses, the actual ride is swift. This is how it was with this new Sherlock Holmes. The first edition of *The Hound of the Baskervilles* came out in London on 25 March 1902 and by 10 April the Panteleyeff brothers had already received the necessary official permission from the Russian censor to publish a Russian translation. Less than a month later, the Panteleyeff brothers published, in the May edition, a new, fairly exact translation of it. One thousand copies were set side and sold in book form in June. A third edition of three thousand was published in September by D. Yefimoff's publishing house in Moscow.

The success of the story (read Sherlock Holmes) amongst Russian readers was breathtaking and saw the start of Sherlockomania. Publishers began to publish anything they could lay their hands on and, during the short period between the summer of 1902 and the end of 1903, a score of books emerged. Incomplete data, just for the five years between 1902 and 1907, shows that no less than twenty publishers issued Sherlock Holmes. As regards the actual texts, one has to admit that, on the whole, the translations were weak, many were garbled, with bits and pieces of their own manufacture thrown in by translators. Few were worthy of the original. Amongst those that were an exception to the general rule, was a four-volume edition from V.I. Gubinsky entitled *The Adventures of the Detective Sherlock Holmes*, which came out in Petersburg between 1902 and 1905. Every volume had a print run of 3,500, considerable for

Russia in those days. This edition went into three further print-ings in nearly double figures. A particular feature of this edition was that it was the first illustrated edition, showing the canonical 'portrait' of Sherlock Holmes by the German painter Richard Gutschmidt. The illustrations were taken from the 3-volume 1902 German edition published in Stuttgart by Robert Lutz Verlag.

In December, 1893, English and American readers were in a state of shock to read, in *The Adventure of the Final Solution*, of the premature death of Sherlock Holmes at the Reichenbach Falls. Russian readers did not register the same sense of loss and shock because they had become acquainted with Sherlock Holmes later. Despite this, when Sherlock Holmes miraculously survived and returned, the interest and affection displayed was no less considerable than elsewhere. His triumphant return was now greeted with no less acclaim in Russia than abroad. *The Adventure of the Empty House*, which records Holmes's return, appeared in New York in *Colliers Weekly Magazine* on 26 September 1903, and already on 13 November of the same year, Soikin, in his magazine *Nature & People* published a translation.

The 'resurrection' of Sherlock Holmes only increased the sensational excitement in connection with him. New publishers, their finger on the public pulse, published Conan Doyle's stories as soon as they appeared. For example, between January and September, 1904, the Panteleyeff brothers, in their revamped *New Magazine of Foreign Literature, Science and Art*, published twelve of the thirteen stories which later became the collection known as *The Return of Sherlock Holmes*. Except that this time, Russian publishers decided to forestall events. The first edition of this collection of stories came out in New York in February, 1905, but in Russia it was already out in October, 1904 (but with-out *The Adventure of the Second Stain*).

The name of the private detective from Baker Street was not just a matter of renown, but it came to be used as a common noun. For three decades, a synonym for the word 'detective' had been

Monsieur Lecoq, agent of the Criminal Investigation police from the works of Emile Gaboriau, but now it became the eponym (and is still so to this very day), Sherlock Holmes. He cast a spell over the hearts and minds of thousands of Russian fans. He was no longer a creature of his creator, but now belonged to everybody, a supranational phenomenon. Wildly successful plays were staged of his exploits, little boys imitated him, adults tried to imitate his methods, he was parodied, his name graced signboards and goods labels. And everyone read accounts of his adventures, even members of royal families. The diary of the last Russian emperor, Nicholas II, records that he read the following (in the original) to his family, *The Valley of Fear, The Hound of the Baskervilles, A Study in Scarlet, The Adventures of Sherlock Holmes*. The Emperor read so-called 'continental' editions, published in English in Leipzig by the heirs of Baron von Tauchnitz. Today they have become price-less collectors' pieces, though at one time the ones that got to Russia were sold abroad for pennies by ignorant and uncultivated Bolsheviks. Today they are safeguarded by the library of the University of Minnesota.

Sherlock Holmes became more than a literary hero. He became virtually real, an outstanding contemporary, a great expert in crime detection, a psychologist of great depth and a zealous man of science. There is an unusual brochure by the psychiatrist Michael Mayevsky, *Conan Doyle: The Adventures of the Detective Sherlock Holmes*, Vilna, 1904. The psychiatrist had made a detailed study of the Sherlock Holmes stories, a detailed analysis of the psychological and professional aspect of the detective's personality, examined his work methods in detail, and their underlying scientific basis. He pays particular atten-tion to his powers of observation, logic, deductive and inductive thinking, how he comes to make correct conclusions. 'These stories,' writes Mayevsky, 'represent a eulogy in praise of logic, in honour of man's acute powers of observation, trained by considerable human experience ... an example of penetration into a single chosen sphere of knowledge ... clearly, precisely and entertainingly set out ... a collection of ... subtle and witty intellectual conclusions.' Holmes, says the author of the brochure, might be an amateur in his profession, however 'by no means a dilettante, but a scholar of depth'.

However, other times were approaching; mass culture had arrived and in 1907, in Russia, a Sherlock Holmes to whom Sir Arthur Conan Doyle had no connection, was fated to appear.

Roman Kim, a wonderful Russian writer, who also popularized detective fiction, has a story, *The Case of the Murder of the Great Detective*, (1966). It tells a story which ostensibly took place in April, 1906, on the estate of Conan Doyle. This is the plot. Once, his mother appears without warning, accompanied by an unknown young American lady. His mother explains that the lady is Aurora Killarney, that she teaches algebra in a Philadelphia suburb, and that she is a great fan of Sherlock Holmes. The old lady adds that Aurora persuaded her to introduce her to her son and they both intend to stay with him the whole of the coming week. In the course of that week, a series of mysterious happenings occur and there are a number of conversations the substance of which Conan Doyle cannot comprehend at first. In the end, it transpires that during Conan Doyle's absence (which was a carefully put-up job), someone had gone through his study, rummaged through all the cupboards and examined all his manuscripts. Conan Doyle is perplexed, but at the end of the story, two days after the uninvited American guest has gone, he gets a letter from her which explains everything. It transpires that Aurora worked for an American publisher. In the wake of the success of 'Dime novels' featuring Nick Carter, which is published by their rival, they had decided to publish their own series. But, so as not to have to publicize the name of an unknown detective, they had decided to give him the world famous name of Sherlock Holmes. There was, however, one thing which stood in the way. Sir Arthur was not to kill off

Sherlock Holmes as had already happened once. To ensure this, Aurora was despatched across the ocean. Meeting Mrs Doyle, she had charmed her with her incredible knowledge of Sherlockiana and told the old lady the dreadful (untrue) secret, that rumour had it that her son planned to kill off Sherlock Holmes for the second time, and this time for good. Mrs Doyle, who had always been against her son's intention, got terribly angry and accepted the suggestion made by the American to search the writer's study and find either the proof or disproof of this dreadful rumour. Mrs Doyle, under an invented pretext, sends her son and his secretary away. She lets in the wily American and stands watch at the door. When Aurora has completed her search, she gives Mrs Doyle the dreaded news: Conan Doyle, in fact, has a story all ready in which the great detective perishes right under the eyes of his friend, Dr Watson. Moreover, he dies a terrible death. Mrs Doyle nearly faints, but now she must carry out the last item in the plan laid by the crafty American. The mother must make Conan Doyle swear under oath never to kill off Sherlock Holmes. This is done. Now the American publisher can be easy in his mind. Conan Doyle's Sherlock Holmes will live and, thereafter, their own Sherlock Holmes can flourish.

There is no way of telling whether any of this is true and, if so, is this how it all took place? Was it the plot that worked?

Conan Doyle's literary agent was the exceptional A.P. Watt. It is unlikely he would have allowed this. But whatever it was that occurred, a False Sherlock Holmes appeared up and down Europe, especially in Germany. Dime novels became all the rage in Germany and, very quickly, this example of mass culture spread like a tidal wave to Russia.

This is described by Kornei Chukovsky, the classic Russian children's writer. He was a great fan of English literature and Conan Doyle. In 1916, he was in London, where he met Sir Arthur and even strolled along Baker Street in his company.

(Much, much later, in the war years and their aftermath, when there was little or no detective literature in Russia, together with the Soviet publishing house Children's Literature, Chukovsky popularized Conan Doyle. In 1959, he introduced Sherlock Holmes anew to a fresh generation of readers. He edited and wrote a new introduction to a 623-page collection, *Notes About Sherlock Holmes*, still in print to this day.)

The success of mass culture was described by Chukovsky in his book, *Nat Pinkerton and Contemporary Literature*, (St Petersburg, 1908) as a thoroughly unwelcome phenomenon. 'This invasion, this wave, this flood.... Our intelligentsia suddenly vanished ... for the first time in a century our youth had neither "ideas" nor a "programme" ... in art, pornography reigns, and in literature, riff-raff have taken over ... some primitive has appeared out of nowhere and has swallowed up, in a year or two, our literature and art.'

Chukovsky referred to mass culture as the literature of a multi-million primitives. In 1907, a new deity appeared, namely the Russian equivalent of the American dime novel, which had appeared in 1860 and became particularly popular with the dawn of a new century. These, known as 'penny novels' (from the Russian word for grosh, the equivalent of a penny) had come from Germany. They then began their existence in Warsaw (in Polish, Poland being part of the Russian empire) and then, in the autumn of 1907, penetrated the heart of the Russian empire. It all began in September, early October. In that short interval, the first of several detective series appeared: in Petersburg, *Pinkerton, Ace Detective*, also in Petersburg, a Russian novel in separate parts by an anonymous author, *In the Trap of Crime. The Murder of Countess Zaretzkaya*; in Warsaw, a long, sensational novel based on the notes of the famous German agent of the CID, Gaston Rene and also in Germany, *Sherlock Holmes; His Sojourn in Germany or The Secret of the Red Mask* And, again in Petersburg, a series of forty-eight stories appeared in booklet form under the general title,

From the Secret Documents of the Famous Detective Sherlock Holmes.

This new Sherlock Holmes, as Chukovsky so aptly noted, 'took away from the [original] Sherlock Holmes his violin, threw off his shoulders the last that was left of Childe Harold's cloak, took away all human emotions and notions, gave him a revolver and said, "Keep on shooting and let there be lots of blood. If you shoot, shoot them dead ... you'll get paid for your heroism. And no need for your Baker Street, get an office." Kornei Chukovsky's bitterness was genuine. The False Sherlock Holmes of anonymous writers did not have an iota of the human feelings for which the real Sherlock Holmes was liked so much. But, points out Leonid Borisoff, who wrote Conan Doyle's biography in Russian, 'in contradistinction to Nat Pinkerton, the authors of the Holmes stories, sometimes even educated writers, wrote better'.

The success of these penny dreadfuls was phenomenal. For an entire generation of Russian boys, these cheap booklets were the brightest events of their childhood and boyhood. Unsurprisingly, the demand grew to become a phenomenon on a national scale. In 1908, these Russian equivalents of penny dreadfuls increased to unprecedented numbers. Entertainment, the Petersburg publisher, alone issued 3,334,000 copies. It ranked third in the number of publications amongst 140 publishers. In 1908, a book exhibition in St Petersburg maintained that in that year Russia published 12,000,000 of these 'grosh' (i.e. penny) booklets. Individual booklets had print runs of 75,000 and even 200,000. And this at a time when the average print run for a book was not above 3,000 copies. Following the first Pinkertons and Sherlock Holmes, there appeared immediately in Russia Nick Carter (the American Sherlock Holmes), Lord Lister (the Police Terror), Jean Lecoq (the first living international detective), Bill Cannon (the famous American Police Inspector), Vidocq (the famous French detective), Harriet Bolton-Wright (woman detective), Treff (Russia's top detective), Count Stagart (German detective), Ethel King (female Sherlock Holmes), Avno Azeff (anarchist detective), the nameless detective of the Black Hundreds (the notorious anti-Semitic gangs) and many, many others. Their name is legion. Smart publishers and smart writers all used famous detectives and non-detectives, literary heroes and real people, turning them into the heroes of their penny dreadfuls, trying to turn a penny out of a big name. Of course, one of the most popular 'victims' of their trade was Sherlock Holmes.

Today, major Russian libraries haven't a hundredth of all such literature published in Russia. This is why it is impossible to account for the number of Sherlock Holmes series. But from what we know now, of major series (i.e. five or more issues) in 1907–1910 there were more than a score. The most famous, with the greatest number, was N. Alexandroff's publishing house Entertainment, which was in the vanguard of mass literature and the main supplier of penny dreadfuls. From 5 April 1908 to 3 April 1910, Entertainment published twenty-eight Sherlock Holmes stories, whose combined print run came to 2,261,000 copies.

Some stories were translated or home-made, but whether the authors were Russian or foreign, the action was always abroad. But very soon Russian authors began to display a new method of 'borrowing' someone else's hero. They 'sent off' the great Baker Street detective (or was it his 'double?') to far-away Russia! What could be simpler! Now Sherlock Holmes speaks Russian fluently and conducts his investigations in different corners of Russia!

It all began on 19 January 1908, when the Petersburg newspaper *Stock Exchange News* began to publish Sherlock Holmes in Petersburg by an anonymous author. This was followed by three more Holmes' stories. Their success was to come when they were reprinted as a supplement to *Stock Exchange News*, being part of the magazine *Ogoniok*. The first issue (of 23 March) contained *Sherlock Holmes in Moscow*. The introduction read, in part, 'The manuscript arrived under somewhat mysterious circumstances. "I am sending *Sherlock Holmes in Moscow*, a narrative of his Moscow adventures, by registered post", read the unsigned telegram.' A later issue carried an indignant letter from Sherlock Holmes to the editorial board of *Ogoniok*. In it, he demanded that the anonymous author must be stopped. The success of the hoax was palpable. There even arose a case, *Sherlock Holmes vs. the Magazine Ogoniok*, which many readers accepted as genuine. But S. Propper, the publisher of the magazine, achieved his aim. The popularity of the magazine grew. It also set a precedent. Now it became permissible to 'transplant' Sherlock Holmes to Russia and for his services to be commissioned by Russian clients. And so it went on and on. . . .

The poor devil from Baker Street, against his will, covered the length and breadth of Russia! Russian authors 'despatched' him to Petersburg, Moscow, Odessa, Baku, Simbirsk, Penza, Novorossiisk, Tomsk, to small provincial towns and even the villages of the vast Russian empire. But, unlike the penny dreadfuls, these nearly always carried the author's name, sometimes only a pseudonym. And another distinction, now these were not short stories but longer works, novels and even plays. The literary level of these creations was not high, but there were some examples of quality. One example of the latter was *Sherlock Holmes in Penza*, in the April–May, 1908 issue of *Penza News*. Another example was *From the Memoirs of a Resident of Petersburg*, about Sherlock Holmes, containing *The Three Emeralds of Countess V.-D.*, by someone called N. Mihailovitch. This deals with the unknown circumstances following the epic struggle between Sherlock Holmes and Moriarty, when Holmes disappeared over the waterfall. Mihailovitch tells us, for most of that time, Holmes was in Russia, where he lived as William Mitchell. The plot deals with the mysterious murder which took place in Petersburg. The story was not without a curious addition. It includes the presence of the daughter of Arsene Lupin! This sort of thing did happen frequently enough when the character of one detective novel could become simultaneously Sherlock Holmes and Nat Pinkerton and Nick Carter and Arsene Lupin.

There were many stories of a 'Russian' Sherlock Holmes. Presented in this volume are two by P. Orlovetz. From his surname we might surmise that he came from the city or region of Oriol. He was a prolific writer, author of novels and novellas, short stories and children's stories. Little is known of him.

But the most popular and most prolific was P. Nikitin, whose stories are presented in this volume. His span of literary activity was very short, from 19 July 1908 (the publication of the first collection, *The Latest Adventures of Sherlock Holmes in Russia. From the Notebooks of the Great Detective*), till 30 May 1909 (when the last collection came out, *On the Track of Criminals. The Adventures of the Resurrected Sherlock Holmes in Russia*). In less than a year altogether, P. Nikitin published four collections. In the intervals between their publication, the entire cycle appeared (on the analogy of penny dreadfuls in separate small booklets but in a much more attractive format) in two series, *The Latest Adventures of Sherlock Holmes in Russia*, and *The Resurrected Sherlock Holmes in Russia*. All in all, Nikitin published twenty-one stories.

P. Nikitin may have been the most prolific and interesting of the authors of Sherlock Holmes pastiches, but, sad to say, we know absolutely nothing about him. Who was he? Where did he spring from?' What does the initial 'P' stand for? Peter, Paul, Policarp? Not one writers' reference work, not a single encyclopedia, nowhere is his name to be found. We don't even know whether Nikitin is his real name or a pseudonym.

Time has not preserved either any information about him, or his books. The Russian National Library in St Petersburg, Russia's major library, has only one set of his stories. How gratifying, therefore, that the name of this deserving but forgotten writer now returns before the reading public, and so much more gratifying that it is to the readers of that country whose great representative he extolled and which he probably never visited.

But now, a century later, he returns there by way of his works, returns to invite 'his' hero's fellow countrymen and all English readers everywhere to that distant and mysterious Russia which, once upon a time, took to its heart that great recluse from Baker Street.

George Piliev
Moscow

George Piliev is an author, editor, bibliographer and historian of the mystery genre.

1

THE BROTHERS' GOLD MINE

P. Orlovetz

I

This incident, illustrating the extraordinary perceptiveness of
Sherlock Holmes, took place some ten years before the Russo-
Japanese War, so disastrous for Russia.

Having visited all the major centres of European Russia,
Sherlock Holmes decided to visit Russia's possessions in Asia,
which he had wanted to see for so long. I must confess that for
me, Siberia represented an especially interesting part of the
world. Legends and the most incredible stories were rife in
England about it.

Hence, it was not surprising that, no sooner had Holmes
mentioned his desire to travel there, not only did I joyfully agree
to accompany him, but in every possible way urged our departure. I was afraid he might change his mind or become occupied
by fresh cases which were offered from all sides in Russia.

Sherlock Holmes certainly understood what I was trying to do
and scoffed good-naturedly at my impatience. Nonetheless, this

impatience worked on him. And so, he turned down several lucrative but not very interesting cases, purchased the necessaries for a prolonged trip, and laid preparations for it. When at last the Siberian train left the station at Moscow, I breathed joyfully, now that my long-held wish was to come about.

The Volga River flashed by, the steppes of the Ufim province lay behind, for several hours we took in the splendid views of the Ural Mountains and then the train swept into the Siberian vastness.

Despite our expectations, we did not encounter polar bears anywhere, nor wild natives of whom French tourists wrote that they devoured not only each other but even their own children. It turned out to be like any other land mass, except that it was slovenly, muddled, sparsely inhabited, in places covered by impenetrable coniferous forests known as the taiga, which knew no boundaries and stretched as far as the Arctic Ocean.

But what surprised us most of all was the Siberian peasantry. Not only were they not downtrodden like the peasants of central Russia, they were richer and certainly more sure of themselves.

As regards education, Siberians were well ahead of their fellow citizens in the provinces of central Russia. Holmes's explanation was that, for several centuries, the Russian authorities had settled exiled elements here. A mixture of political exiles, criminals and Cossacks (resettled here in his time by the then governor-general, Count Muravieff-Amursky) had created a very special population.

The political exiles, intelligent and educated, former criminals, creative and entrepreneurial, and freedom-loving Cossacks had intermarried and passed on their characteristics to their descendants. Thus, a new sort of people had come into existence, infinitely superior to the inhabitants of the central provinces. What is more, the bureaucracy was few and far between. And so, a down-trodden and humiliated population had become proud and independent, able to stand up for itself. Their qualities displayed themselves when the Russo-Japanese War broke out and Siberian troops showed their mettle.

At the time of which I write, the Trans-Siberian Railway had not yet been completed. Trains went only as far as Zima station, after which the bones of travellers were severely shaken by horse-drawn carriages as far as Stretensk. From Stretensk, further progress was by ship on the Amur River.

It took us eight days to get to Zima station. It was another two hundred versts to Irkutsk, i.e. a hundred and thirty miles. We just about managed to get there in one piece, every bone in our bodies aching from those damned post chaises. When we finally made it to Irkutsk, we decided to rest there.

We were interested in this city, close to so many gold mines, and decided this is where we would become acquainted with life in Siberia. We found a hotel room and settled in.

Soon enough, an incident occurred through which we were to become closely acquainted with the local gold mines and the way of life connected with them.

II

Sherlock Holmes and I had long since abandoned any attempt at travelling incognito. And since Russians as a people are curious by nature, there was no shortage of gawkers around us. Sherlock Holmes's fame had penetrated Siberia and, wherever we would go, we were surrounded by curiosity seekers. There were even those who, for no apparent reason, invited us for a meal, probably to see for themselves the eating habits of an English detective.

So it wasn't surprising that, on one occasion, sitting in our hotel room, we heard a knock on the door. In answer to our invitation to enter, there did so a well-dressed, purple-nosed robust man.

'All the same, I do beg your pardon that, so to speak, I intrude and etc.,' burst forth from him in a deep bass. As is customary with Siberians, his speech was peppered with 'all the same' and 'as it is'.

'How can I be of service?' asked Holmes.

'Have mercy on my plight and help me all the same,' he said. 'I am one of the owners of the so-called Brothers' Gold Mine and I am here to seek your help.'

'Do sit down, please,' Sherlock Holmes invited him. 'I have time to spare and there is no need for you to hurry.'

'All the same, thank you,' bowed the man.

He ran his hand through his beard, then through his hair and sat down. 'As it is, the surname is Hromikh. We are two brothers, Sergey and me. I am Piotr Haritonovitch,' he said giving his name and patronymic in the Russia manner. 'That's why our mine is called the "Brothers' Mine". The mine is quite a distance from here, all the same, the road is bearable, the gold takings are good, and the equipment as good as possible. All would be well, if it weren't for the thieving. As it is, this thieving has developed so systematically and on such a scale that we hardly make ends meet. We have our own spies in the mine and they assure us that most of the gold is stolen and then smuggled out by our very own manager, a fellow named Zinovy Andreyevitch Seltzoff. But we can't believe this to be so. On two occasions, driven out of our minds by what was happening, we intercepted him along the road as he was leaving and found not a grain of gold. As it is, our situation is dire, and we would ask you to take up our case. We are prepared to pay you a third of the value of the stolen gold, if only you were to find out how it is done.' He fell silent and gave Sherlock Holmes a beseeching look.

'How far is your mine?' asked Holmes.

'Just under eighty miles.'

'And how many roads lead to it?'

'As it is, just the one.'

'Is there a place for us to stay?'

'As it is, of course!'

'Excellent,' said Sherlock Holmes, 'though I have to admit that I take your case mostly for the opportunity of visiting a gold mine and becoming acquainted with its running.'

'Oh, if only you knew how grateful I am,' exclaimed our visitor. 'Well then, do let me express my appreciation by inviting you to dine with me.'

We accepted. A room was specially set aside for us in our hotel and to the amazement of Mr Piotr Haritonovitch Hromikh we changed for dinner. Over dinner, as was to be expected, we discussed the matter freely.

'How long ago did you begin to notice the theft of the gold?' asked Holmes, by the by.

'That's the whole point. Strange as it may seem, large-scale theft began three years ago, just when we appointed the new manager.

'And the thieving is from the office?'

'Oh, no,' exclaimed the mine owner. 'That would be daylight robbery. All the same, what I am speaking of is only of contraband.'

'Explain yourself.'

'This is how it works. All the mined gold has to be handed in to the office. Once the sand has been washed, the gold that remains is handed in to the office, nor can it be stolen from the equipment used for washing. But in addition to gold grains obtained by washing sand, there are also gold nuggets to be found. These nuggets are of differing sizes, some several pounds in weight, and they are found by labourers in trenches from which they dig out gold-bearing soil and transfer them on to wheelbarrows for washing. These nuggets are easily detected by the naked eye. The labourers may pick them up manually, but are obliged to place them in containers handily kept there. For these nuggets they are rewarded with a bonus of two and a half roubles per zolotnik of weight, i.e. just over four and a quarter grams. But, despite the most vigilant attention of the supervising staff, all the same, they still manage to steal nuggets and swap them for alcohol. The nominal price of gold is five and a half roubles per zolotnik. The men who steal this gold are pursued by the administration by every possible means, and if any is found when they are searched, it is confiscated. Our spies tell us that the manager himself buys up the stolen gold from the men and manages to get it out of the mine. He gives the men alcohol, confectionery and other forbidden stuff.'

'Then how often does this manager leave the mine?' asked Holmes.

'Once only, at the end of the work year,' said Hromikh.

'At what time of year is that?'

'Late in the autumn, like now.'

'So he is ready to go.'

'As it is, yes.'

'Has anyone told on him this year?'

'Yes, but my own opinion is that this is done to deflect suspicion. We were told this year that whoever stole the gold has bought forty-five Russian pounds of it in weight. Our gold is of superior quality and the treasury values it at 19,600 roubles per forty Russian pounds. This means that 22,000 roubles worth must be smuggled out. We think that the supervisor of one of the trenches actually buys up the gold and managed to deflect suspicion by having us think it is Seltzoff.'

'Very likely,' said Sherlock Holmes thoughtfully and poured champagne into his flute.

III

We parted long after midnight, having decided to set out in two days time. In the meantime, we explored the city.

On the appointed day a comfortably spacious carriage called for us. We set off for the mine with Piotr Haritonovitch Hromikh, taking with us the barest necessities and leaving the rest of our luggage behind. Every fifteen miles or so fresh, well-fed horses replaced the ones driving our carriage. In no time we were at the Brothers' Gold Mine. Here we were given a couple of rooms next to the quarters of Piotr Haritonovitch Hromikh and on the very first day met the entire administration. Our real names and professions were not revealed and we appeared to be tourists travelling to explore Siberia.

Early in the morning we rose at the same time as the workers when the siren sounded and made our way to the trench and machinery where we assiduously studied the mining operation. At the same time, I noticed how carefully Holmes watched the manager as well as members of the administration.

Daily, as soon as work ended, Sherlock Holmes used to vanish till late at night. The result of his walkabout was that no worker could visit any member of the administration without Holmes noticing.

One evening Holmes approached me, saying, 'My dear Watson, the time has come for us to meet the mine detectives who do the secret watching.'

'Why, have you noticed something?'

'There are one or two things,' he answered. 'I have a feeling that Piotr Haritonovitch isn't quite right when he says that the men who watch secretly are wrongfully trying to implicate the mine manager. I watched him for several days and noticed a very clever manoeuvre on his part.'

'Namely?' I prompted.

'I noticed that he stopped for longer to watch work in progress where gold was densest. Let's assume this is normal practice, but then he always finds an excuse to send away the supervisor on the spot. Of course, this shouldn't be surprising either, as the manager is more likely to see something than a supervisor tired from a day's supervision, but, in fact, this is not how it is. The labourers steal nuggets so skilfully that the attention of the supervisor has to wander for only a brief moment and the nugget vanishes. And our manager frequently pays no attention anyway. But then, late at night, two labourers he places at the best spots visit him.'

IV

That very evening we dropped in on Piotr Haritonovitch.

'May I meet your so-called investigators?' asked Holmes with the touch of a smile.

'Of course,' was the answer. 'Do you wish to see them here?'

'Are there many?'

'Not really. Only two.'

'Then let's have them here,' said Holmes with a nod.

Piotr Haritonovtch Hromikh went off and was back twenty minutes later accompanied by two ordinary mine labourers.

Holmes asked him to leave us alone with these investigators, which the owner did. He then proceeded to cross-examine the two men. From what they said, Holmes learned that the manager bought gold only from two workmen. These two workmen, in their turn, bought up stolen gold from the rest of the mineworkers in exchange for spirits given them by the manager. The whole operation was carried out so carefully that there was no evidence leading to the manager. As regards how much gold was stolen, this could only be established by the number of drunkards. At first it was thought that the gold was traded with spirits traders, but then it transpired there wasn't a single one anywhere near the mine. And despite that, mine workers were drunk on this mine more often than elsewhere.

Further investigation led to the conclusion that the stolen gold was most likely gathered up by two labourers. This was done so cunningly that their identities could only be guessed at by the ingratiating manner shown them by their fellow-workers. As to how the gold was handed over and paid for, that was never detected. This is why there was no direct evidence against them. Several sudden, unexpected searches brought no results.

In the meantime, it was noted that these two workmen were in the manager's distinct favour and often visited him. The manager made no attempt to conceal this favouritism. He said the two are exemplary workers, behave well, work better than anyone, don't drink, have a positive influence on everyone, settle all minor disputes between the men and the administration which inevitably arise given the difficult existence in the mine.

Holmes heard them out with considerable attention.

'You say that the number of drunkards or the amount of spirits consumed is an indication of the approximate quantity of alcohol stolen to be traded for stolen gold, is that not so?' he asked when he had ended his cross-examination.

'Yes,' said one of the investigators. 'We keep a precise record of everything.'

'Then why isn't the administration coming down hard on those most often drunk and cross-examining them specifically?'

The two investigators exchanged ironic looks. 'Any mineworker would rather hang than reveal the source of forbidden drink,' answered one of them.

'Wonderful!' said Holmes. 'And how much stolen gold do you think the manager has put away.'

'According to the sums we have done, approximately forty-eight Russian pounds. But it is possible he may have somewhat more. We can't account for every bottle of spirits.'

'When is Seltzoff going off?'

'In three days. The work in the mine ends tomorrow and the caravan with mined gold goes off. Seltzoff has to stay another two days to submit all accounts and pay off the workmen.'

On this our conversation ended.

V

We returned to our quarters. For a long time Sherlock Holmes paced back and forth silently, deep in thought.

'No, he wouldn't trust that much gold to anyone else,' he said at last, stopping by the window. 'He is a single, lone man, has nobody close, and he has to take his treasure away sooner or later. The only question is this: will he take it with him now or hide it and return for it later.'

'I think it is the latter,' I said.

'It all depends on how cautious he is. A thief always feels that he is being watched,' said Holmes. 'And I am prepared to stake my head that Seltzoff realizes he is being watched, especially given that he has already been searched. Only, he relies too strongly on his own cunning. If that is so, he will try to carry the gold with him, because he realizes clearly enough that a second opportunity might not arrive. Moreover, a return when the season is over would attract suspicion. It would be impossible to do so secretly, because there will always be someone around and if nobody is working, all the more reason to notice someone around than when work is in full progress.'

I couldn't but agree with this line of thinking.

We began to wait patiently. Day and night, we took turns to keep Seltzoff under continuous scrutiny, except when he vanished inside his own quarters.

The next day the caravan left with the owner and the gold. Before he left, he revealed our true identities to the mine guard, asking him to give us every possible assistance.

Another day passed.

The manager made preparations to leave. His spacious leather-curtained personal coach was brought up to his quarters and his things brought out and placed in it.

'We have to give the appearance that we are leaving,' said Sherlock Holmes as evening fell. He spent some time in discussion with the mine guard.

We dropped in on the manager, thanked him for the hospitality we had been shown, and announced we were leaving that day.

'We could travel together,' proposed the manager.

'Oh, no, thank you,' answered Holmes. 'As it is, I cannot forgive myself for having stayed today.'

A hardly perceptible ironic smile appeared on the manager's face. We left him and immediately ordered a carriage to be prepared for us. Two hours later we were off with the mine guard.

But we had hardly gone five or six miles from the mine when Holmes ordered the coachman to turn off at the next crossroad, and a quarter of an hour later we were deep in the thick coniferous forests of the taiga.

'Let him get ahead of us,' Holmes explained. 'An attack from the rear invariably works better. We'll fall upon him as soon as he gets to the first post house to change horses. I doubt if an ordinary but carefully conducted search won't produce the requisite results.'

We spread out felt matting, wrapped ourselves in warm blankets and slept the night in he forest. We rose with the dawn. The sun had most probably already risen, but in the deep gloom of the taiga it was still dark.

VI

Our bivouac, which gave all the appearance of a robber encampment, was a mere two or three hundred paces from the main road. Every little sound would penetrate the deathly silence of the taiga, more so the rumble of wheels and the beat of horses' hoofs. We left our horses behind and the three of us crouched behind bushes, near enough to see anything moving along the highway.

Everything was quiet till one in the afternoon, but then my ears detected some sort of sounds in the distance. I glanced at Holmes. He was already on the alert. The sounds increased in volume until, at last, the rumble of wheels and the beat of hoofs increased in volume.

A few minutes and a troika, the carriage driven by three horses, sped past.

The coachman was on the coach box. The manager inside. He had flung himself back in his seat, apparently dozing away as if he hadn't a care in the world. He didn't even look in our direction. Looking at him, nobody would imagine a man with anything but a clear conscience.

When his carriage had passed us a mile or so, Holmes threw himself into ours, motioning for us to follow. We sped in the path of the vanished manager, afraid we wouldn't catch him in time at the next post house where he would change horses.

Mile after mile flashed past. Our troika made a sharp turn and through the forest we spied the post house. With horror we saw that the manager's troika had nearly completed the change-over of horses. Another minute and we would have lost him, but just in time, as his coachman was clambering up to take his seat, our troika, horses foaming at the mouth from exertion, drew up beside him.

'Mr Manager, I must detain you for just a minute,' said the mine guard, approaching him.

'Is anything the matter?' asked the manager in surprise. And turning towards us, he said jovially, 'I never thought I'd overtake you! Wherever did you get stuck? Surely not in the taiga!'

'I'm afraid we got slightly involved in hunting,' said Holmes.

'And that is to be commended. At least the mine guard will be able to carry out his errand.' The sentence was uttered with the deliberate intention of delivering a little sting. A malevolent look appeared for a moment in his eyes. 'Now, sir, I am all ears,' he turned to the mine guard.

'Permit me to search you.'

'Me!' The manager burst out laughing. 'Do you really still think that I am carrying away my employers' gold. In any case—' He shrugged. 'The laws of the taiga are rough, and anyone who has fallen into it must be reconciled to them. Do your duty, sir. I am at your service.' He and the mine guard went into the post house.

'Oh, what a rogue!' Sherlock Holmes exclaimed merrily. 'I am prepared to wager anything that he guessed our identity all along. He's laughing in my face.'

'So I see,' I said.

And as if to confirm our words, the manager suddenly sprang out of the post house. 'Gentlemen, aren't you joining us? No need to carry on with your comic act, no need to conceal your real profession. Do come in, Messrs Detectives!' he yelled at us.

'If that is so, of course, there is no need for us to hide who we are,' said Holmes with a smile. 'Come along, Watson.'

We went in and began the search. But Seltzoff had absolutely nothing except for a cotton-lined heavy coat whose pockets were empty and a suit in whose pockets all we found was a wallet and a few letters.

We went outside. We ransacked his entire carriage, the suit-case and the bundles. A feather would not have escaped us. But, despite all our efforts, we found nothing. There was no gold.

Holmes took me aside and said softly, 'My dear Watson, there's one place which we haven't looked at so far.'

'And that is—'

'It could very well be that the gold is in the axle or the shafts, or sealed inside the carriage walls. But it has been hidden so craftily that no outward inspection will reveal its presence. Somehow or other we must deprive him of his carriage and see how he reacts to that.'

'That shouldn't be too difficult. Break the axles and wheels.'

'Hmm, that's not too subtle,' answered Holmes. 'It must be

done in a way that is not apparent. I'll take him inside the post house. Let the mine guard take over. He must order the coachman to break down somewhere along the way.' He thought for a moment and added, 'Towards which end, it would help to saw through the axle just a little.'

VII

Saying this, he left me and walked towards Seltzoff. Seltzoff followed his movements with irony in his eyes. Holmes asked him to return with him to the post house, leaving me alone with the mine guard.

Left one-on-one with this keeper of law and order, I passed Holmes's instructions to him. He nodded his head to signal his willingness, called over Seltzoff's coachman and began to explain to him what had to be done.

For my part, I promised the coachman a reward of fifty roubles if he could bring the manager's carriage into a state of utter disrepair and explained that this was being done for the good of his employers. Needless to say, the coachman readily agreed to everything. 'There is a steep incline not far from here and where it turns there is a mileage pillar,' he said. 'Ride into it at full tilt and the carriage will disintegrate.'

I got a little saw out of my suitcase and quickly filed under both axles. A few minutes later Holmes and Seltzoff emerged. Holmes apologized for having caused him so much inconvenience and did it with such patent sincerity that the mine guard and I couldn't believe our ears. He even appeared to have made friends with the manager.

We all sat down to breakfast together, drank a bottle of champagne and decided to drive to Irkutsk together. We stowed away our luncheon baskets, took our seats in our respective carriages and set off. Seltzoff went ahead and we followed. Sherlock

Holmes never took his eyes off the troika ahead of us. And now, at last, the steep incline the coachman had told us about appeared.

As soon as we got to the top of the incline, the horses of the leading troika began to play up. No matter how hard the coachman tried, he couldn't control them. The sweating horses reared up and raced down. Seltzoff was terrified. But he leaped up, seized and pulled at the reins of the horse on the left. This worked somewhat. Their pace lessened but was still somewhat strong.

The coachman panicked as the troika flew towards the mileage pillar. But just before the mileage pillar he apparently came to himself. The troika zigzagged. The horses escaped the impending disaster, but not the carriage. There was the sound of a terrible crack. The horses came to a halt. The coachman went flying head over heels off his seat. Seltzoff was thrown on the back of one of the horses.

'Bloody idiot!' he exclaimed angrily getting off. 'Thank heavens they are right behind us, otherwise what would we do between two post houses!' He was walking round his coach, shaking his head in distress.

Our troika stopped beside him and we got down and expressed our sympathy.

'What's there to grieve over,' he answered sadly. 'I'll have to abandon the carriage. You, gentlemen, will have to be somewhat a little squeezed.'

'Of course,' exclaimed Holmes, 'but surely you don't intend to abandon such a carriage!'

'What am I supposed to do about it, carry it? It will be a lucky find for someone who might even be grateful for such a find.'

The trap hadn't worked. Seltzoff's things were stowed in our carriage and, taking only his horses and their harness, we set off. But with five people, the load was too much.

'I suggest we take turns walking,' said Holmes.

We agreed to do so. It was decided that two would sit inside and two would go on foot and change over every three miles or so. Holmes and I were first to set off on foot. Having walked the agreed distance, the manager and the mine guard walked and we sat in the carriage.

It was cool and Holmes and I had not tired. Not so Seltzoff. At first he strode along boldly. But just over a half mile on, he was perspiring and his face was red. The next half mile or so he desperately tried to appear as if his energy had not deserted him. But yet another half mile or so and he announced he couldn't walk so much as he wasn't used to it and, besides, his feet were hurting.

'Strange,' said Holmes with a smile. 'At work you were on your feet all day and you weren't tired, and here you become tired.'

'Strange, indeed! I was thinking along those same lines myself,' said the manager.

The ironic look in his eyes had vanished and was replaced by a look of alarm.

At this moment Holmes shouted at the coachman, 'Halt!' Seltzoff shuddered imperceptibly.

Holmes placed his hands on Seltzoff's shoulders and said frostily, 'Well, Mr Manager, sir, you laughed at me in vain. Putting anything over Sherlock Holmes doesn't come easily. Give me your coat.'

'But I'm cold,' muttered the manager.

'In that case, force will have to be used,' exclaimed Holmes and nodded at the mine guard.

It took a moment to strip Seltzoff of his coat. Holmes took the coat by its collar and was just about to lift it with his outstretched hand.

'So you've got me then,' Seltzoff growled angrily.

'I don't understand,' I said. 'What is going on?'

'Oh, it only came to me because he was getting tired,' Holmes explained, smiling. 'The gold is in the heavy cloth of the coat. In its raw state, before it has been worked on to be hardened, gold is pliable and soft enough to be rubbed in its entirety into heavy material. It becomes a fine dust and, as such, it virtually dissolves into the cloth and vanishes. That is preceisely what this gentleman did. He rubbed the gold into the cloth and then all he would have to do to recover the gold is to burn off the cloth. But he wasn't able to do it, and from this moment he is under arrest.'

We set off again, this time with Seltzoff tied up, though to keep him warm, we gave him another coat to replace the one we had taken away.

Forty-seven pounds of gold were recovered from it.

2

THE RAILROAD THIEVES

P. Orlovetz

I

The story of how the gold stolen from the Brothers' Mine was found spread like wildfire throughout the whole of Siberia. Sherlock Holmes's name was passed from mouth to mouth, while tales of his exploits were so exaggerated that he became some sort of mythical hero. Often, he had to listen to the most incredible stories about himself, with which we were entertained on trains by fellow passengers who did not know our surnames. Holmes was terribly amused and entertained by such stories.

The following case occurred half a year after the withdrawal from Mukden, in north-east China, of troops who had participated in the Russo–Japanese War (1904–05). We were on our way to Harbin, also in north-east China, from where we intended to go to Vladivostok, Russia's port on the Pacific Ocean, and then to return to European Russia via Khabarovsk, Blagoveschensk and Stretensk. This route would enable us to visit all the principal cities of Siberia.

On a grey September day our train stopped at Baikal station, named after the great Siberian lake on which it stood.

The stopover was a long one, so we got off at the station to have lunch, to taste the famous Baikal salmon, extolled by Siberian exiles.

We had eaten this fish and the ghastly soup that was on the menu, when a cavalry captain, and officer of gendarmes, sat down opposite us. He looked at Holmes, and his brows puckered as though he recalled something.

Sherlock Holmes also looked at him and suddenly smiled, 'I think you and I recognize each other, Captain,' he said, raising his cap. 'I had the honour of seeing you half a year ago at the headquarters of the Moscow police. As far as I remember, you were summoned in connection with counterfeit gold five-rouble pieces!'

'Quite so!' said the officer and saluted. 'It took me a while to recognize you, but now I do. Aren't you Mr Sherlock Holmes?'

'Yes!'

'And this is your friend, Dr Watson.'

I bowed.

On the one hand, Sherlock Holmes wasn't shy or withdrawn when he met someone. On the other, he didn't like to draw public attention to himself, which would have happened if anyone had heard his name pronounced aloud. So he suggested we adjourn to a separate little table in a corner of the station buffet.

A waiter moved our food and cutlery and we took up our new places.

'You've been transferred here from European Russia?' asked Holmes.

'Yes, four months ago,' said the cavalry captain.

'And if I am not mistaken, your surname is Zviagin.'

'Absolutely right!'

'And are you satisfied with your new appointment?' asked Holmes.

'Not particularly.'

'Boring?'

'Oh, no! The problem is that pilfering on the railroad, and especially on Siberian railways, is on such a monumental scale that not a single consignor can be assured his consignment is safe. I was assigned to investigate this phenomenon but, alas, I reckon with horror that I cannot cope with it.'

'Really!' Holmes gave an ironic little laugh.

'There is so much pilfering and it is all so cleverly organized, I'm simply lost as to which one to investigate first and how!'

'Have you any idea of the monetary scale of the pilfering, say in one month?'

'Oh, yes!'

'And, as a matter of interest—?' asked Holmes.

'Well, for example, take July. One hundred thousand roubles worth of state-owned consignments haven't reached Manchuria and Harbin stations. Private cargoes worth seventy thousand never reached their destination.'

'I say!' exclaimed Holmes, taken considerably aback.

'This may seem considerable to you foreigners,' said Zviagin with a little laugh, 'but in Russia, and especially here in Siberia, we are quite used to such sums.'

At this moment, another officer of gendarmes came up to Zviagin.

'From whence?' asked Captain Zviagin

The newcomer named one of the larger Siberian cities.

'Passing through?' asked Zviagin.

'Yes, I took some leave to get about a little.'

They exchanged a few words and the newcomer left.

'There's a lucky fellow,' sighed Zviagin.

'Who is he?' asked Holmes.

'Security Chief for his city. A year younger than me, a mere twelve years on the job, gets a salary of six thousand a year, plus another thirty thousand expenses for which he doesn't have to account.'

'What!' Holmes asked in total shock. 'Thirty thousand a year for which he doesn't have to account!'

'Yes!'

'For what purpose?'

'Finding spies, etcetera.'

'Dammit, my dear Watson,' exclaimed Holmes, absolutely stunned. 'What would our Parliament have to say if presented with this sort of thing!'

He turned to Zviagin again and asked, 'Can one security department in a provincial town spend that on political investigation?'

'Some have more,' said Zviagin coolly.

'I've never heard of any such thing,' said Holmes, now thoroughly embarrassed. 'One would think half your population are political offenders. But . . . if that's so, the term loses its meaning.'

'Not entirely,' Zviagin answered with a smile. 'In any case, talking to a foreigner about this is a waste of time. You do things your way and we do things our way.' He gave another deep sigh and lit a cigarette.

A subordinate appeared. 'Your Excellency, the freight car arrived at the next station with half its cargo missing again,' he reported. 'Mitayeff is just back from there.'

Zviagin swore, 'See for yourself. You take up one case and at the same time you are presented with a second . . . and a fifth . . . and a tenth.'

He looked at Sherlock Holmes in despair. 'I'd give half my life for your assistance,' he exclaimed and gave the famous detective a beseeching look.

The idea seemed to have lodged itself in his head and he began to beg Sherlock Holmes and me to stay for a while to put an end to these dreadful goings-on. 'You can demand any payment,' he exclaimed.

'But we're here only as tourists,' countered Holmes.

'That's wonderful! I'll show you the whole of the Baikal, the forests and bush land of the Varguzinsk taiga, and the penal servitude settlements. You'll see much that's interesting, things that you could never see otherwise when you travel by train. And what is more, we'll split the reward half and half.'

Holmes turned to me, 'Wouldn't you say it's worth thinking about, my dear Watson. What do you think?'

'It's certainly a very tempting offer,' I answered.

'But, of course, do stay on,' Zviagin kept on insistently, encouraged by what my friend had said.

Holmes was considering something.

'Well,' the cavalry captain urged him.

'It's settled! I'm staying,' answered Holmes.

'Bravo!' Zviagin exclaimed happily. 'Hey there, waiter, let's have a bottle of champagne and call a porter!'

Our luggage and other things were transferred out of our compartment and placed in the station waiting area, while we went back to our table on which champagne already foamed in tall flutes.

II

'And so, I only ask that our real names should not be revealed to anyone,' said Holmes, as he clinked glasses with Zviagin and me. 'Let your people think we are ordinary detectives you have employed. We were looking for work on the railroad, we became accidentally acquainted and you made us a tempting offer.'

'What about the railway and engineering senior staff?' asked Zviagin.

'Let them think we are your relations. We'll see how we go.'

'That's why, in the absence of a hotel hereabouts, you can stay at my place, all right?' Zviagin suggested.

'Of course!'

Our initial conversation and any further talk about the case was now over. A second bottle was placed before us. After spending about an hour in the station buffet, we moved on to Zviagin's place, put our things away and locked ourselves in with him in his study to plan what we would do.

'How often do passenger trains pass through here?' asked Holmes.

'Twice a day,' answered Zviagin.

'And freight trains?'

Zviagin made a dismissive gesture with his hand.

'When and how they please?' asked Holmes.

'Something like that,' answered Zviagin.

'Do you suspect anyone?'

'Everyone!' said Zviagin sharply.

'What do you mean by everyone?' asked Holmes in surprise.

'It's simply that I think everyone steals, starting with the bosses at the top, down to the signalman.'

'If I understand the captain all right, my dear Watson, we will have to deal with half of Russia.'

'At any rate, the whole of the railroad,' broke in Zviagin angrily.

Having got some more information out of Zviagin, we took the maps and plans of the railway system going around Lake Baikal and beyond and went to our rooms.

I must have been long asleep while Holmes still pored over timetables and maps. And though he went to sleep after me, he was already at work when I woke up. His notebook, filled with a mass of notes, lay before him.

Seeing that I was awake, he nodded his head at me and said, 'Get up, Watson. Today, we're going for a little trip on a freight train.'

'Now?'

'No, we'll spend the day examining the station and storerooms. In the evening, we'll take a little trip beyond Lake Baikal and return tomorrow.'

III

It was an exhausting day. Sherlock Holmes examined the railway, warehouses, the railway station for freight trains, and drew the conclusion that the system was chaotic enough to make stealing mere child's play. 'It would be a miracle if there wasn't any stealing,' he said. 'The first thing that hits you between the eyes is that none of the staff is in their appointed places. It's a wonder that the station manager and district manager haven't been stolen!'

'Perhaps they are not worth stealing,' I answered.

'I quite agree, my dear Watson,' said Holmes, laughing at this quip.

We took a nap after lunch and in the evening went to the railway station. The train conductors and the station staff in general didn't know us yet, so we easily got the chief conductor of the freight train to let us ride first class round Lake Baikal for less than a rouble. Holmes deliberately rode as a passenger without a ticket, because a passenger without a ticket raised no suspicion.

At ten o'clock at night the train left. It was a dark night and the huge cliffs on our right added to the gloom. Vast Lake Baikal slept peacefully between its rocky shores. In the dark, they were nearly out of sight, except for the gleam of their dark steel reflection in the water.

The train climbed uphill, from time to time stopping at gloomy stations that looked like the lair of bandits, and diving in and out of tunnels.

We stood on one of the platforms at the rear of a carriage in the middle of the train, admiring the picture of a grim Siberian night. About three hours later we arrived at a small railway station. It was about 12.30 in the middle of the night.

Our legs were tired from standing or sitting still, so Sherlock Holmes suggested we stretch our legs along the station platform. Half the lights were out, probably for reasons of economy, and it was dark everywhere. We walked up and down waiting for the departure signal.

Suddenly, a loud male voice yelled in the darkness, 'D'you hear, Burmistoff, send your locomotive to hell.'

'I'm coming,' answered a voice from the engine.

'Come on, hurry, the vodka is waiting.'

'But when will you let the train move on?'

'When we've had enough to eat, that's when I'll let it go.'

The voices fell silent.

We went up to the locomotive and saw only the stoker inside.

'When is the train departing?' Holmes asked him.

'Only after the engine driver has had his dinner,' said the stoker imperturbably. 'Didn't you see him go off to dinner with the stationmaster?'

'Did you hear that?' muttered Holmes, confused and perplexed, when we had gone some way from the engine.

'I did!' I answered.

'Is that what they call a timetable? Let's see what happens now!'

It was a long wait. The engine driver took two hours over his dinner. Eventually, very unsteady on his feet, he emerged from the station house accompanied by an even more inebriated stationmaster.

'—it's those bastards, the correspondents, I fear,' loudly resonated from the stationmaster, evidently concluding a conversation that had begun earlier. 'Earlier on, that trash never bothered coming here, it being free-and-easy enough elsewhere.

Then came the war and they were here one after another, like evil spirits.'

'Ye-es,' drawled the engine driver in his deep bass.

'But most important, you didn't know where such fellows are likely to pop up from,' the stationmaster continued. 'You even find 'em amongst the military! Turn up, sniff out and disappear.'

'You should've pushed one of 'em under the wheels . . . like it was an accident.'

'Brother, you won't get hold of one of 'em. Too quick, and they always come on a passenger train. How can you tell 'em for what they are? Just as well they don't rummage about on freight trains or we'd be back in no time on just our wages.'

'Bloody swine!' swore the engine driver.

They moved towards the locomotive.

'How about one for the road?' suggested the stationmaster. 'A little cognac?'

'Why not!'

'Hey, there, Ivan,' called out the stationmaster. 'Cognac and glasses here!'

The two friends disposed themselves on the grass and a few minutes later started drinking again.

We hid behind a carriage and listened.

'How many carriages did you take?' we heard the voice of the stationmaster.

'From Aberyantz?' asked the driver.

'Yes.'

'Two,' said the driver.

'Did you get much?'

'Twenty roubles each,' answered the driver.

'Ah, yes, he did complain to me about you. He said it's robbery.'

'Let him! The other day you showed me those carriages, so I ordered them to be uncoupled from the rest of the train. He noticed and came along. "Who gave orders to uncouple those

47

carriages? They're supposed to travel non-stop and they've been coming from Russia for all of four months. That's a disgrace!" And on and on he went. So I tell him, "The train has to go uphill and is lugging too many carriages. The locomotive will never make it, so the hind carriages had to be uncoupled." So that's why he must've come to you.'

'Yes! Yes! Well, I told him the driver knows best. He yelled and yelled, threatened to complain. But I know these merchant types. In the end he paid up.'

'Ha! Ha! Ha!' laughed the driver.

'What are you laughing about?'

'I was thinking to myself, what would a merchant be prepared to pay for a carriage full of his goods and going at normal speed, to be delivered from Moscow to Harbin in China?'

'I did try calculating it,' said the stationmaster merrily. 'According to my calculations, on top of the tariff, about two hundred roubles per carriage.'

'It used to be more in war-time.'

'Ye-es! I used to get up to a thousand. Let's knock back a few more.'

'Let 'im have it! Anyway, what we are getting should be enough!'

'Tomorrow I'll be making money out of Liu Pin Yuan's freight cars,' said the stationmaster.

'Maintenance?'

'Yes. I'll tell him they're out of order. I'll tell him that they have to be taken to the depot, but the goods cannot be transferred as the seals were affixed in Moscow. A day or so on the alternate track and he's bound to reach into his wallet. If he doesn't, I'll keep them there for a month!'

Both laughed merrily. The bottle gurgled. But half an hour later, the bottle must have been emptied and the inebriated engine driver, having farewelled his friend, clambered up into the locomotive.

The third bell sounded.

The train got under way with such a jerk Holmes and I nearly fell off the platform.

'Nonetheless ... hmm ... riding these trains is more dangerous than chasing the most dangerous robbers,' Sherlock Holmes complained.

IV

The train went off in reckless flight. Carriages shook up and down and side to side as if they, too, were inebriated, and we had to hold on to the handrails for dear life, not to be shaken off the train.

'Some way of doing things,' Holmes went on complaining. 'Any insurance company would be bankrupted if it were to insure trains and people from crashes. And what sort of administration have we here! How do you like it? To have your freight delivered in normal time, you have to hand out two hundred roubles in bribes alone.'

The sentry boxes of the railway security detail flashed past, one after another. And now, at last, the semaphore winked. The drunken engine driver began to slow down and slammed the brakes so abruptly several carriages nearly crashed into one another.

Half an hour passed.

'Dammit! This is some halt!' Holmes said indignantly. 'My dear Watson, let's ask when the train will move on?'

We headed for the station. The noise of revelry came through one of the windows, drunken singing, loud shouts.

'Will the train be departing soon?' Holmes asked some guard.

'The engine driver and his assistant have to dine first and then it'll go,' came the answer.

'What do you mean, dine!' asked Holmes, beside himself with rage. 'He's eaten more than enough at the last station!'

'Evidently not enough,' was the phlegmatic rejoinder.

'Phooey!' Holmes spat out and moved back to the train.

'I say, wouldn't it be better to get off this train for another, whose driver isn't so partial to dining out?' I advised.

'Hmmm ... I'm beginning to think the same myself,' muttered Holmes. But since no other train was available, we sat on the steps of our carriage and awaited developments.

On this occasion, the engine driver and his assistant took an hour and a half over dinner.

Dawn began to break. At last they appeared. But their appearance! The engine driver had dined so well, he couldn't go under his own steam. Hence such a glorious procession. Two guards hauled the driver, his heels dragging along the ground. His assistant followed, just about managing to place one foot in front of the other, while singing a rollicking Russian melody.

Holmes gave me a little nudge. 'My dear Watson, what do you think will happen to the train if this driver and his assistant decide to have another dinner. We may assume we won't make it to another station after that!'

I simply gestured dismissively with my hand.

'In any case, let's have a look whether one of the rear carriages has a platform. It'd be much safer if the train crashes,' said Holmes.

And so, while the driver and his assistant just about managed to get into the locomotive, Holmes and I got on the platform of the third carriage from the rear.

'Now, then, Watson—'

Before Sherlock Holmes could finish the sentence, the train gave an incredible jerk and we grabbed at the handrail.

'This is it!' I said in horror.

But to our astonishment, we remained in the same place without moving. Holmes poked his head out to see what was going on and suddenly said in amazement, 'My dear Watson, our train is gone!'

'How?' I asked in wonder.

'Very simply! The driver fell asleep and his assistant gave such a sudden start to the train that the four rear carriages broke off and remained standing with us on one of them, while the train went on.'

Pandemonium broke out at the station. It is likely that a conductor on the train noticed what had happened because, as soon as the train got to the semaphore, it stopped and began to reverse back to the station.

The now inoperative fourth carriage from the rear, with its connecting links broken, was taken out of commission. Two more mighty jerks, which nearly knocked us off our feet, finally exhausted Holmes's patience. He jumped off the train shouting, 'Get off, my dear Watson, get off quickly, before our ribs are smashed and our necks are snapped.'

I have to admit that I willingly followed his advice.

The train departed and we remained on an empty station where everyone and everything seemed fast asleep.

V

Later, we were not to regret letting that train go without us. Exactly three quarters of an hour later, it went off the rails at full speed. It had sped too quickly round one of the turnings. The guard told us that twelve carriages became debris. Several broke up and only the last five carriages survived. The train staff suffered considerable injuries. The driver and his assistant died in the accident; the stoker was badly hurt. Two conductors also died and three were severely injured.

When we heard this news, we adjourned to the cargo platform and, getting out the food we had prepared in advance, satisfied our hunger pangs, which were finally beginning to appear.

Then Holmes brought out his notebook and began to write something in it. 'I am making a note of those who, in England, would be considered criminals,' he said.

'Many?' I asked.

'I'm afraid that by the end of our travels, my notebook won't suffice,' answered Holmes and shook his head.

Some four hours later, the next goods train pulled into the station. One of the rear carriages being empty, the conductors let the public into it, pocketing the fares for themselves. This was probably common practice, because none of the station higher-ups paid any attention.

I was in total agreement with Holmes, when he said, 'It seems all Siberian railways are made by the Russian government, not for the population but for the engineers and railroad staff.'

On this second train we passed through several stations, stopping the length of time determined by the driver, though this one didn't take as long over his meals. This was a great consolation to us.

Unnoticeably, evening crept over us again. It became completely dark. Our train left some station or other and covered about six or seven miles. Suddenly, the engine began to emit alarming whistles. One after another the whistles followed turning into a frenzied wail, while the brakes pressed hard against the wheels. At last the train halted.

We jumped off the platform to see what was going on ahead. Shouts, yells and the most angry swearing came from there, and some sort of light flickered.

'What's happened?' asked an alarmed Holmes of a conductor returning from the locomotive with a torch.

'We nearly ran into an open freight wagon,' the man answered and swore.

Soon the train moved again. In fact, as we moved forward, we saw about ten such wagons uncoupled by the side of the track. Piled sleepers lay beside them. Beside the uncoupled wagons, people with torches stood and cursed for all they were worth.

When our train had moved past this scene and picked up speed, Holmes smirked and said, 'I'm prepared to bet there's something illegal going on here, too.'

'Namely,' I prompted.

'First of all, why move sleepers by night? Next, why are ten freight cars being hauled by people when all the sleepers could be hauled on a flat-bed wagon by a locomotive?'

'Perhaps there wasn't a locomotive available!' I said.

'Now that I gravely doubt,' said Holmes with a laugh.

Mile after mile flashed by and, at last, the train stopped at a station.

Holmes suggested a break. We got off the train and stretched out on benches for first- and second-class passengers and slept soundly.

VI

Exhausted by the events of the two previous nights, we slept till about eight in the morning. We breakfasted at the station buffet and then explored the station and the area around.

There were earthen huts for building workers not far off.

It was a holiday, and the workers sat in circles by their huts, drinking tea or vodka. We strolled past responding with bows to theirs. One of the groups attracted our attention.

A man, evidently drunk, stood in their midst, addressing the others, 'I know enough to spill things on him,' he yelled. 'I don't care if he's an engineer. I'll make him sorry.'

'Fired you?' someone asked.

'You're kidding!' said the first. 'The section head told me to clear out, so I went to his superior. This is how it is, I tell him. He steals sleepers by the thousand and fires me for taking just a couple of hundred. I'll send a report to Mr Yugovitch and a copy to the Minister of Transport Communication.'

'And what happened?' asked one of the workers.

'He promised he'd transfer me to another section if I didn't send any report. They've all got their snouts in the trough, see, so they oughtn't to make a big deal out of what we small fellows do!'

'Right! Right! That's for sure!' burst out approving voices.

'See what they do when presented with some of their bloomin' wonders!' said one of the workers stepping forward. 'For example, that one engineer steals sleepers from another engineer. Say, for example, Engineer Ilya Petrovitch instructs his foreman to take ten freight wagons and load them up with sleepers stolen from his friend Feodor Nikolayevitch who runs the adjoining section!'

'The devil knows what they do under the circumstances!'

'Don't you know?' exclaimed the first worker. 'Don't you understand? Say Ilya Petrovitch stole from Feodor Nikolayevitch. Of course, that's all done to pull the wool over the eyes because, if Feodor Nikolayevitch didn't want anyone to steal from him, he'd mount more watchmen. But this is what is really going on. Feodor Nikolayevitch will now notice the theft and draw up a charge sheet in the presence of witnesses. The charge sheet will say, nicked by Chinese bandits. A detachment will be despatched and no Chinese bandits will be found, but money is sent to Feodor Nikolayevitch to replace the stolen sleepers. Now Ilya Petrovitch stacks up the stolen sleepers. Enter the contractor who supplies Ilya Petrovitch with sleepers and who is in on this. If Ilya Petrovitch steals a thousand sleepers, his contractor delivers a thousand less, but bills for the full number. Ilya Petrovitch now gets paid by the contractor. Out of this deal Ilya Petrovitch gets something, and Feodor Nikolayevitch gets something. It's all the work of Chinese bandits and they're not around! That's how it is!'

The conversation turned toward Chinese bandits.

'Do you hear that?' Holmes said with a laugh, as he led me aside. 'This is well organized, orderly thievery. I don't know what we'll uncover further, but so far I haven't yet come across a single honest person.'

We walked to the little village, consisting of a few small shops and houses.

'Shall we try that shop?' suggested Holmes.

'Let's,' I said.

We went in.

VII

Sherlock Holmes threw a quick glance round the shop and asked to be shown long underwear, singlets and boots. The owner produced all three.

'Do you have any other sort?' asked Holmes. He then rummaged through the entire shop and finally selected a pair of boots, two singlets and a pair of long underwear. He paid, picked up his purchases and we moved along to the next shop.

Once again Holmes rummaged and rummaged, but only bought two lemons.

One after another, we went through the other shops and came away with china from one, suspenders from another and in yet another, for some reason, cut-offs of materials for women's dresses.

After that we found an open field.

'Now, then, let's have a look at our purchases,' said Sherlock Holmes. He sat down on the grass and began to untie the packets we had brought with us.

'I'm wondering why you had to buy all this rubbish, for which we have absolutely no use,' I said, shrugging my shoulders.

'You're wrong, my dear Watson. This rubbish is very important for me,' and he laughed. 'Just look at this lemon, my dear

Watson. It bears the mark of the Red Cross on it. Of course, the kind-hearted donor didn't consider that his lemons would be sold in the most ordinary grocery for a few pennies, instead of getting to a wounded soldier.'

He unwrapped another packet, got out a pair of boots and pointed inside the boot leg, 'Here, look at this, with the mark indicating it is army property. Instead of going to a half-bare-footed soldier, it is being sold in a shop where even a Japanese, the country's former enemy, can buy it.'

I looked with curiosity at the samples Holmes had collected. All the time, he went on unwrapping one item after another, saying, 'A superb collection! Singlets from the Red Cross, long underwear, also, china bearing the hallmark of the International Association of Sleeping-cars, hmmm . . . undoubtedly from the train of the commander-in-chief . . . brace-bands of the 14 Field Hospital . . . Well! Well! Well!'

'It won't be easy for you to sort out this mess,' I said. 'Digging into this could take years.'

'Undoubtedly! But for me, the important thing is to locate the common thread and the dots it goes through.'

'What do you intend to do?' I asked.

Holmes thought for a minute, 'As far as I am concerned, the middlemen don't interest me, Watson. Do you see this? I am much more interested in the suppliers and that's why you and I, in my opinion, wouldn't be erring greatly if, for a while, we traded in these stolen goods.'

'How?' I asked, because I did not understand.

'We'll pick some likely place where stolen goods are in great-est demand and that's where we'll start selling.'

'In that case, our trip will have to take longer.'

'Of course! We'll send a detailed account of our intention to Zviagin, but shan't send regular accounts of progress. He'll forward our luggage wherever we need it. Do you agree with this, Watson?'

I could only shrug my shoulders. 'Why do you bother to ask for my assent?' I answered. 'You know perfectly well that I gladly follow you everywhere.'

On this we ended our conversation.

We spent the whole of the next day travelling and our choice fell, at last, on Sliudianka station. From here, Holmes dispatched a short communication to Zviagin and, in a business-like manner, we set about preparing for trade.

VIII

Approximately ten days went by. In those ten days we managed to get a few things done.

We rented a Chinese *fang-tze* [hut] and had it redecorated. The local carpenter urgently made counters and shelves, while the two of us went about suppliers, trading agents and dealers, bargaining over every conceivable kind of goods, sometimes even ill-assorted.

Before long, samples were being brought to us. Holmes took only small quantities of those goods which did not rouse his suspicion. But no sooner was anything suspicious placed before him than he took large quantities and spoke at length with the suppliers. Such deals were often accompanied by drinking sessions, during which Holmes and the seller would each put up a few bottles of champagne.

Some twenty days later, when the carpenter had finished, we started accepting deliveries in the store. Holy Mother of God, what did we only not stock! Holmes seemed positively determined to open a general store such as the world had never seen: sugar, lubricating grease, cotton cloth, calico, chintz, dried vegetables, boots, perfume, singlets, almonds, vodka, linen, dental and surgical instruments, in sum, anything that anyone would want. Merchants and agents poured in endlessly, having heard that we bought anything that came to hand.

One evening, Holmes had just begun to open a case of boots, when an Armenian named Bakhtadian dropped by. Bakhtadian was his top supplier and, in the manner of people from the Caucasus, addressed him in the familiar second person and not the polite plural second person. 'Opening up a case of boots, are you?' he asked.

'Yes, they're your boots,' said Holmes, with a smile, taking out a pair and deliberately studying the inside of the leg.

Bakhtadian laughed, 'Looking for the mark?'

'Doesn't bother me,' shrugged Holmes. 'I'll scrape it off. But how come you aren't afraid to sell them like that so openly?'

'What's there to be afraid of?' Bakhtadian asked in surprise. 'If it is the authorities themselves who do the selling, anything goes. If one had to remove seals and stamps and brands and marks from every article, it would take five years.'

'Oh, is there that much?' asked Holmes, also in surprise.

Bakhtadian merely gestured dismissively with his hand. 'Let's drink wine. We have to talk.'

Holmes stopped what he was doing and the three of us moved to the back where we lived. Holmes told the Chinese shop assistant to bring red wine and champagne. In Siberia they not only prefer these two drinks, but they like to mix them.

At first Holmes avoided any talk of business, filling Bakhtadian's glass more and more. And it was only when he saw Bakhtadian's face had turned red from drink that he let him talk business. The result couldn't have been better.

Bakhtadian came straight to business. 'You, my dearest fellow, think that I believe you wish to trade hereabouts?' he asked with malice in his voice.

'Whatever else?' asked Holmes in surprise.

Bakhtadian winked slyly. 'Then why do you buy anything that comes your way? Could it be you are sending it all to Russia, where there's a seller's market!'

'Let's say that's so,' said Holmes.

'Do you have a lot of money?'

'Enough,' said Holmes.

'Well, then, how much can you put into the business?'

'As much as necessary,' Holmes said gravely. 'If I don't have enough of my own, there's a friend.'

Bakhtadian nodded approvingly.

Later, Holmes was to tell me that all the time Bakhtadian suspected that Holmes and I were the heads of a superbly organized gang with a large capital and occupying ourselves with buying and selling stolen goods.

'Do you want to do business, then say so,' said Bakhtadian.

'Of course, I do,' said Holmes.

'Then do so! I can deliver all the goods you want.'

'From where?' asked Holmes.

'They're on offer from everywhere. From here and from Missova, from Innokentievsk, from Manchuria, Baikal, well, from every possible railway station.'

'What's on offer?'

'All sorts of goods: beds, underwear, perfumery, fabrics, sugar, candles, medicines, instruments, typewriters, printing machinery.'

'Expensive?' asked Holmes.

Bakdtadian's eyes narrowed as he looked at Holmes, 'Are you familiar with factory prices?' he asked.

'Yes,' answered Holmes.

'How much of a discount on factory prices do you expect?'

'Say, seventy per cent,' said Holmes.

'You're out of your mind,' exclaimed Bakhtadian.

'No, I'm not,' said Holmes coldly.

'Don't I have to make something?'

'You do,' Holmes agreed.

'Then what's in it for me?'

'You'll get something from me,' said Holmes.

'How much?'

'Ten per cent,' said Holmes.

Bakhtadian thought it over, 'No, they won't let it go so cheap,' he said at last. 'Pharmaceutical goods, marked underwear, boots, topographical and surgical instruments – you can have a discount of eighty per cent, but when it comes to the other stuff, up to forty per cent and with my ten per cent, that'll make it fifty per cent.'

'Blankets?'

'As many as you want, but no more than fifty per cent discount. The Chinese are very eager to buy them.'

'Well, all right ... I'll think about it. It's all far too much,' Holmes said lazily.

'Enough of this haggling! What's your price?' Bakhtadian began to insist. 'Now, then, what sort of a discount? Tell you what, with my cut, average forty-five per cent. How about it?'

'No, no good,' said Holmes. 'The goods you said they'd let go cheap, seventy-five per cent and forty for the rest. For you, without exception, ten per cent from me. If not, there's nothing more to be said.'

The haggling went on for an hour. But no matter how Bakhtadian argued, no matter how often he walked off for show, Holmes remained adamant. Not one single per cent more.

'All right, have it your way,' exclaimed Bakhtadian at last. 'But, at least, give me a small advance so I can start.'

'That's all right,' said Holmes coldly. 'After all, if you can make off with a small advance, you'll miss out on the greater amount. Here's three hundred.' He took three hundred out of his wallet and handed them over.

Bakhtadian cheered up. Evidently, there were prospects for money to be made in the deal. He called the shop assistant, gave him twenty-five roubles and told him to get three bottles of champagne. The drinking spree lasted well beyond midnight.

*

IX

The whole of the following day, Sherlock Holmes sent off telegrams in all directions. Evidently, these telegrams had the desired effect. A day later and the replies rained on us, but they were as long as letters. Reading them, Holmes smiled and kept on shaking his head.

'What's happening?' I asked him once.

'See for yourself,' he answered and handed me a stack of telegrams.

I began to read them. They were fairly lengthy and came from major companies and certain hospitals, informing us of the loss of furs and other goods, descriptions, seals and stamps marking them, the packaging, numbering on invoices and other details.

Judging from these telegrams, there wasn't a single major firm in Eastern Siberia that hadn't been robbed. The total worth of the stolen goods exceeded three hundred thousand roubles.

Holmes selected the information he needed and meticulously wrote it down in his notebook.

'Now, then, my dear Watson, half the task is done. All that's left is to identify the sellers at source and find the warehouses where the stolen goods are kept. Watson, could you possibly follow Bakhtadian, who seems to have direct contact with the thieves.'

'With pleasure,' I agreed.

'In that case, you'll have to look like an ordinary workman and be ready for some tiring work. He's coming to see me today, but by then you'll have your make-up on. Just don't go near him.'

Saying this, he put on his hat and promised to return in a few minutes, which he did.

'There you are, I've got Bakhtadian's address,' he said cheerfully. 'It appears he lives right here, at the edge of this little village, but he is seldom home. In the meantime, Watson, let's have a bite and then we'll get to work.'

We ate cold veal, roast beef and ham, drank them down with a decent amount of Lafitte, and then Holmes and I set about transforming my appearance. My new costume consisted of well-greased high boots, baggy striped old trousers, a canvas smock and a peaked cap. A few brush strokes on my face from Holmes's skilled hand and I became completely unrecognizable. I completed the change of clothes, went into the shop and sat on a sack of salt in a dark corner.

At the same time, Holmes also changed into the same sort of clothes that I was wearing, but hid them under an eastern type robe called a *khalat.*

Bakhtadian soon arrived.

He paid no attention to me but addressed Holmes as soon as he came in. 'Well, you should be getting about five chests today. The cargo will be fairly varied, because there's been no time to sort out the stuff. They go for anything near at hand. When they bring them, we'll see what's inside.'

'All right,' said Holmes. 'How late will they be delivered? After all, I have to prepare space for them.'

'Not before three o'clock in the morning,' said Bakhtadian. 'I'll be here myself by then.'

'All right! All right!' said Holmes.

'And now, I'm busy!'

'Off to where you have to go. I'm not detaining you,' said Holmes, shrugging his shoulders.

Bakhtadian went off.

Darkness was falling and half a minute later his silhouette was already difficult to make out as he went in the direction of the station.

'Quick! Go after him! Don't let him out of your sight!' Holmes shouted as he picked up his make-up box. I hurried out after Bakhtadian while Holmes, with the speed of lightning, was already working on his own face.

I followed Bakhtadian to the station. Without letting him out of my sight, I squatted down on the ground by the fence.

A lanky fellow came up. He looked as if a barber had upended a bowl on his head and cut his black hair from below it. His hands, face and clothes were so stained with coal you could hardly make out his short, black, bristly moustache. He squatted down beside me, 'How long before the next train to Manchuria, man?' he asked.

'The devil alone knows,' I answered.

'So—' he gave a melancholy drawl.

He sat beside me for a while, then turned towards me, and clapping me on the shoulder in a friendly way said, 'Not too perceptive are you, my dear Watson!'

Now I recognized the familiar voice. I glanced at him, and his filthy appearance caused me to break out laughing.

'Shhh,' he whispered. 'Don't let's bring attention to ourselves.'

At this time the depot manager went up to Bakhtadian, pacing up and down the platform, took him aside and very gravely and very carefully began to explain something to him. A third man, who looked like a foreman, joined them. While they spoke, a goods train came into the station.

The depot manager walked away slowly from them towards the stationmaster who came out of his office on the platform. The two of them together walked alongside the train, stopping at the fifth carriage from the rear. I saw the stationmaster give a nearly imperceptible nod at this carriage.

It was at this moment that Bakhtadian and his companion, both of whom had been watching the other two from a distance, jumped on the platform at the end of a carriage.

'Let's follow where they are going, Watson,' said Holmes. 'They are being very circumspect. I am sure it is the fifth carriage from the rear that the stationmaster indicated to Bakhtadian. We'll have to make sure nobody sees us. First, the other side of the train and then let's get on one of the empty platforms at the rear end of a carriage.'

We did so. We went around the train and, on the other side, began to walk beside it.

Now the third departure signal rang at last. The train began to get under way. We picked an empty platform at the end of a carriage and jumped on it as the train moved.

X

As soon as the train began to slow down before the next station, we jumped off and hid under the carriage of a train standing on the adjoining track. No sooner had we concealed ourselves when we saw the figure of Bakhtadian and his travelling companion. They marched quickly past us, stopped just before the fifth carriage from the back and, like us, hid on the track underneath the train. But the moment the third signal for departure sounded and the train began to move, both jumped on the platform of the fifth carriage. We, too, jumped up to take our former place on the platform. There were four carriages between us.

The train had moved little more than half a mile and the steep cliffs reappeared to our right, when the darkness descended, so that we couldn't even see the telegraph poles along the route. We went through tunnel after tunnel. Going through them, the din was so deafening that we couldn't hear anyone or anything no matter how we strained our ears.

But now the train began to climb uphill. The train slowed down and at the next tunnel was climbing at a crawl. But even here, despite the slow progress, the din was so great that it was impossible to hear any extraneous sounds.

As soon as we emerged from the tunnel, Holmes said to me, 'Listen, my dear Watson, at the very first stop, get off and try to get home as soon as possible. You should be able to get back by three o'clock to accept the delivery. When Bakhtadian arrives with the goods, tell him that, because of a lucrative deal, I'm away for a day or two. Tell him you can't unwrap and evaluate the goods and if he doesn't trust you, he can take the chests away till I return.'

'What about you, Holmes?' I asked.

'I'll be back in approximately a day, perhaps even earlier or later, depending on the circumstances,' he said. 'In any case, watch carefully everything going on around you.'

He gave me certain instructions and, when the train entered the station, he got off. I got off, too, but did not see him. I was lucky! The return train was standing at the station. Since it was night, nobody intercepted me and I was able to find myself a platform on a freight train. At a quarter past two I was already home.

XI

At about half past three there was a knock on the door. It was Bakhtadian with two others, bringing four chests of goods. He expressed great surprise that Holmes, whom he knew as Vedrin, wasn't home. Obviously, he wanted to get rid of the goods as soon as possible, collect his money and then he could consider himself on the sidelines. But there was nothing to be done. He didn't feel like taking the goods back, so he said that he'd be back in two days.

I spent all the next day alone, selling one or two trifles to an occasional customer. Holmes appeared at about nine o'clock in the evening. He threw off his working-man's clothes, washed the make-up off his face and threw himself hungrily at food. 'I'm sorry I didn't take a few sandwiches along with me. I had to work on an empty stomach all day,' he complained.

The fixed, preoccupied stare probably meant the day's trek

had not been in vain. He cast a passing glance at the newly delivered chests saying, 'Bakhtadian was here! He came at about half-
past three in the night accompanied by two labourers. There was
a white stain on his right shoulder.'

I remembered that Bakhtadian did, in fact, have such a stain
and it was, indeed, on his right shoulder. 'You saw him?' I asked.

'Yes, but much earlier.'

'And most likely you have found out something of great
importance,' I prompted.

'Yes, I can certainly boast of that,' Holmes said cheerfully. He
lit a cigar, stretched out his legs and began to speak, 'Of course,
Watson, you remember the moment when we parted. As soon as
the train stopped, I ran to the fifth carriage from the rear, but
neither Bakhtadian nor his companion was there. I looked everywhere, inside every nook and cranny, but it was a waste of time.
There was no doubt in my mind they'd jumped off while the
train was in motion. But when? It had to be when the train
slowed down and that could only be when it was going uphill.
There was only one steep climb before that station when the
train really slowed down.'

'That was just before we got to the long tunnel,' I interrupted.
'I think the whole tunnel was on a steep incline.'

'Quite right, my dear Watson. You are to be commended for
your powers of observation,' said Holmes. 'And so I had to
assume that they'd both jumped off either before we got to the
tunnel or inside it. If so, the question arises, why? And then
another question, why did they move from the first carriage to
the platform of the fifth, the very one on which the stationmaster and depot manager focused their attention. My first instinct
was to throw myself headlong into the tunnel but, instead, I rode
as far as the next railway shunting. To examine the carriage
while the train was standing at the station was both inconve-
nient and dangerous. As soon as the train moved, I jumped on
the platform which Bakhtadian and his companion had occu-

pied. The train moved out of the station and, as soon as we were beyond the last station semaphore, I began to examine the sides of the carriage with the aid of a pocket torch. The first thing I noticed was that there were chinks in the panelling and these chinks were not filled with paint. It was as if the panelling wasn't painted after it had been installed, but boards had first been painted and then used for panelling. In one of those panels I found a little hollow. It was as if someone had hammered in a thick nail but, before hammering it all the way through, it had been pulled out.

'I took out a steel pin I carried with me, inserted it in the hollow and jiggled it from side to side. Nothing happened. But when I jiggled it up and down, it slid deeper in without resistance. Now it became possible to remove the entire panelling and then four more, creating a wide gap.'

'This is most intriguing,' I exclaimed.

'Yes.' Holmes nodded. 'When I went into the carriage, it was half empty. There were only a few chests left, which the thieves hadn't the time to throw out before the train reached the top of the incline. I replaced the panelling carefully and, as we were going up another incline, I jumped off the train. All the way back I ran at full speed. At last I got back to the station and walked beyond. I had marked the tunnel, which was a good eight miles from the station. There were two more tunnels along the way and I walked through them without hindrance, although I came across watchmen at their entrances. But no sooner did I come to the tunnel I was aiming for than I was intercepted by a watchman, "Where d'you think you're going!" he yelled. "Don't you know tunnels are out of bounds!" I argued and swore, but to no avail. He wouldn't let me through. I had to resort to cunning. I pretended to go round and hid behind a bush on a high rock. From here I had a clear view of the watchman. As soon as I saw him go inside his booth, I threw myself down and darted into the tunnel. It was a long tunnel, I thought, a good half mile and longer.'

Sherlock Holmes paused, drank a little red wine and went on, 'I moved forward carefully, listening for the slightest sound, shining my torch on the walls and examining the sides of the tunnel carefully. Some three hundred yards into the tunnel, I came across a wagon that had been emptied and leaned up against the wall inside an archway. I scrutinized every stone of the tunnel at this point. And then I saw that four stones were not at one with the rest of the wall. They were cemented together. Moreover, they were not rock, but slabs cemented together. The four together were seven feet square. Undoubtedly, an artificial entrance way but, try as I might, I couldn't find how to get it to open. Today, my dear Watson, we'll summon Bakhtadian, settle up with him for the delivery, and go there together.'

'Do you suspect that's the hiding place for stolen goods?'

'Yes, at least for this route. Every railroad route has its own storage facilities,' answered Holmes.

We agreed on when we'd be going and lay down to sleep. Holmes slept for a couple of hours and then, having dressed in his ordinary clothes, vanished. He was back half an hour later with Bakhtadian in tow.

The three of us set to sorting out the goods Bakhtadian had delivered. The chests contained boots marked army quartermaster issue and underwear for junior ranks. Holmes assigned everything the exact factory prices and this, and the agreed percentage, was paid to Bakhtadian.

Bakhtadian promised to deliver another lot the same night, but not before four o'clock, and left. We changed swiftly into our previous workmen's clothes and sped to the station.

XII

We carried dark cloaks with us. The station was empty. The next train was due to leave in two hours and a quarter. We decided not to waste that much time, so we returned.

First we went to where Bakhtadian lived. But it was dark there, too, so we walked up and down the streets of the little village. It was in total darkness. The little village slept the sleep of the dead. At its edge we were near the Red Cross storehouse and were about to turn back, when we suddenly heard voices.

'It's Bakhtadian,' Holmes whispered. 'For heaven's sake, take care. Follow me!'

He bent low and crept to the pile of goods belonging to the Red Cross, covered with tarpaulin. Soon enough, we saw the silhouettes of three men, amongst whom I recognized that of Bakhtadian. We crept nearer, ducked under the tarpaulin and began to listen. 'You don't have much to sell, have you?' Bakhtadian was asking quietly.

'As far as we are concerned, we have army quartermasters as part of us, which means we can let you have quite a lot,' said another voice. 'Everything you take, we can show as having been forwarded but destroyed during the retreat. We've come to an agreement over this with most army quartermasters. But you have to take the stuff as soon as possible, before the commission checking on remainder quantities gets to work.'

'So where do we get the stuff from?'

'Partly here, partly in Harbin.'

'What have you got?'

'Mainly tinned goods, canvas, leather of all sorts, ready-made boots, oats, barley, flour—'

'And where do we discuss prices?'

'See me. I arrived today and I'm staying with the quartermaster.'

'Very well, but how do you aim to bring the cargo from Harbin?'

'Oh, don't worry about that. We live in harmony with the railways and share everything.'

'Very well, I'll see you tomorrow morning,' said Bakhtadian.

And evidently now turning to the third man, he said, 'And how about you?'

'The same as with them,' the third voice answered. 'There's a lot you can buy from us in the Red Cross, sugar, underwear, wine, cloth, tobacco, tinned goods—'

'Where can they be picked up?'

'Also here, then in Goon Ju Lin, Harbin.'

'No fear of discovery?'

'No fear. We're dealing with people who won't talk.' He proceeded to name names, which Holmes quickly wrote down under the light of a concealed torch.

'So how did you find me?'

'Ivan Nikolayevitch recommended you to me.'

'Yes, I was the one who told Trudin,' a third voice confirmed.

'Hmmm,' lowed Bakhtadian. 'Come to Ivan Nikolayevitch tomorrow morning, agree on a price and then start moving the stuff.'

'Done!'

We heard all three depart while continuing their conversation. We left our hiding place and began to return, but Holmes didn't go to the station. 'I have to ascertain one or two things,' he said, 'so, tonight, you're on your own.'

We shook hands and he vanished.

XIII

The following day at about noon Holmes came home excited and happy.

He said not a word, but seized a sheet of paper, dashed off a telegram and rushed off to the telegraph office.

'Well, my dear Watson,' he said, when he returned half an hour later, 'now I've got them all firmly in my hands. In three days time, all the stolen goods will be freighted from every-where.'

'You've seen something?' I asked.

'More than necessary,' said Holmes cheerfully. 'When we parted, I went to the home of the quartermaster. His orderly was outside and we fell into conversation. He told me that there was a guest, an official of the Harbin quartermaster. This official's name is Ivan Nikolayevitch Bravoff, who has been assigned a corner room with windows leading into the garden. When the orderly went to bed, I climbed up to the roof without any prob-lem and slipped into the attic through the dormer window. I found the area above Bravoff's room and drilled a hole in the ceiling. I sat there quietly without moving all night. At about eight, peeking through the hole, I saw Bakhtadian appear, then Trudin and, finally, a fellow called Verkhoveroff, an assistant stationmaster. They all began to haggle without any constraint, naming many names participating in the business, all of which I was able to write down. Amongst them were generals, and engi-neers, and agents empowered to act on behalf of the Red Cross. The discussion was so frank and open, I was really convinced that without the indirect help of such people, neither Bakhtadian, nor Trudin, nor Bravoff was in a position to do anything or would have to limit themselves to trifles. Some of those named were in such high positions, they themselves had such powerful patronage (protexia, as they call it hereabouts), that they could have any investigation or prosecution against themselves suppressed. But that, Watson, is none of our busi-ness. In three days time, the delivery to the secret depot from their nearest points begins. Then, from the furthest to the near-est, which will now serve as intermediate points. It looks as if this gang is so sure of the power of the people at the top that the members operate openly. Well, we'll see. The day after tomor-row sees the arrival of Zviagin with gendarmes in disguise.'

*

XIV

For two days we quietly held ourselves ready, continuing to watch Bakhtadian. At the end of the second day Zviagin arrived with eight disguised gendarmes. Like them, he, too, was in civvies. They went by train to the nearest station and walked from there. They arrived late at night and, so as not to attract suspicion, settled themselves in a shed in our yard.

Holmes told them in minute detail everything that had happened in the meantime. They made notes all night, but I noticed both fear and indecisiveness reflected on Zviagin's face.

We were all up early. Bakhtadian arrived at about nine. He told us that, in a day or two, he'd be delivering a vast amount of goods to us and, asking us to prepare space and money, he left.

The rest of the day I spent with Holmes at the station. Dressed as labourers, we attracted no attention and were easily able to watch four freight cars standing on the outward route being loaded in preparation for departure, while Bakhtadian and the depot manager looked on from a distance. The cargo for these freight cars was brought on Chinese carts from a small village.

At the same time, a freight train arrived from the east. The chief conductor came up to Bakhtadian and, having said something to him, poked a finger at three successive carriages at the rear of the train.

Holmes looked at them and smirked, 'They're not sealed, but are bound to have goods inside.' And as if to confirm his observation, the door of one opened and out jumped Bravoff and Trudin.

With the help of the Chinese, they began to unload the three freight cars and transfer the chests to the still-empty freight cars on the outward route which had been loaded up by Bakhtadian. There was now one long line of rolling stock.

'Let's go home,' Holmes whispered to me.

Zviagin was already waiting. He was gloomy and deep in thought.

'Captain, three gendarmes by cart to the tunnel I told you about,' said Holmes hurriedly. 'They are to take their positions at the eastern exit and, when the alarm is raised, detain everyone.'

Zviagin issued the necessary orders.

'Now, sir,' continued Holmes, 'the other gendarmes are to hurry on their carts and make haste to the tunnel. But they have to conceal themselves not far from the western entrance, so that they can see the trains. As soon as they see three flashes from a torch coming from one of the trains, they must hurry, but very carefully, into the tunnel. As for us, we have to hurry to the station.'

We checked our revolvers and new torches and set off for the station. The train, now fully loaded, stood on the outward route. The three of us hurried towards it.

Holmes left us for a few minutes and when he came back, whispered, 'There are eight of them. Four are on the platform in the rear of the first carriage and four on the fourth. There's nobody on any of the other platforms.'

The locomotive was now attached to the train and the full complement moved slowly forward. The three of us jumped on one of the end carriages and we were off. We passed a station and Holmes observed that the stationmaster let it through although it wasn't travelling by any timetable. The train wasn't even examined and simply moved on. All this was done openly.

The train went through several tunnels and then began to go uphill. Before we got to the tunnel we wanted, Holmes flashed his torch thrice.

Approaching the tunnel, the train slowed down to such an extent that it would have been possible to keep up with it at a walking pace. Then, when the last carriage had entered the tunnel, the train ground to a complete halt. We threw on our

dark cloaks and, at a signal from Holmes, jumped off our platform and cautiously moved along the tunnel.

Light appeared on the other side of the freight car and voices
could be heard. The carriage doors began to open. Someone was
issuing orders and, one after another, chests tumbled off the
trains and thudded on the ground, where they were picked up.

We crept into one of the niches and, squatting on our heels, we
watched how the work proceeded on the other side of the
wheels.

Half an hour passed. Suddenly there was a rustle from the
western side. Holmes took out his revolver, rushed off in that
direction and vanished in the dark.

Our nerves tense, we awaited the appearance of the unknown
people from the west. And then, suddenly before us, as if he had
sprung from the ground, Holmes appeared with a bunch of
people in tow. These were the gendarmes who had responded to
the agreed signal. At a signal from Holmes, they, too, hid with us
in the niche and we waited.

All of a sudden a clear voice broke the silence, 'Take the train
back. Everything's been unloaded. Too crammed to work here.'
The wheels clattered and the train began to crawl back.

We pressed ourselves to the wall, our cloaks held together to
ensure we weren't seen from the locomotive. But the driver must
have been looking the other way and never even noticed us
when the sparks from the train and its lamps lit us up. Another
minute and the train was gone. We threw off our cloaks.

It was an unusual scene that we saw! Eight people, looking
like underground spirits, were working in a darkness lit up by
crimson and purple flares. We saw how Bakhtadian moved
towards the side of the tunnel, inserted a small rod into it and
part of the wall fell back, leaving what appeared to be an
entrance. A bright light came through it and lit up the tunnel. All
eight energetically fell to shifting the chests towards it.

'Forward!' ordered Holmes.

Revolvers at the ready, we threw ourselves towards the opening. The sound of our footsteps alerted the robbers. Bakhtadian tried to make a run for the entrance that had just yawned open, but Holmes's revolver rang out and he fell prostrate to the ground.

'Don't move, if your life is dear to you,' barked Holmes loudly.

But the robbers only fired back. They had recovered, moved together and were firing as they retreated towards the east.

There came a fierce exchange of fire in this underworld domain and in the near-absolute darkness, someone must have been wounded. We heard him moan in pain. Cries intermingled with curses and gunshots.

'Gendarmes Petroff and Sidorchuk, action,' barked Zviagin.

Two shots echoed from behind the robbers.

'Don't shoot!' Zviagin shouted. The gunfire from behind them panicked the robbers. Cries for mercy came from among them. One after another, they threw down their arms and begged for mercy. With our torches on, we approached them slowly, our revolvers at the ready.

'Two gendarmes on the train and stop it leaving. One stand guard by the cargo!' Sherlock Holmes gave the order.

And turning to the robbers, he said coldly, 'And as for you, the wisest course is to let yourselves be tied up. There's more of us than you think and the eastern exit is guarded. Hurry up, Mr Bravoff, and you, Mr Trudin.'

The men from the Red Cross and the quartermaster stood silently, their heads lowered.

'Gendarmes, take them!' ordered Zviagin.

At the word 'gendarmes', a shudder went through the robber band. Up until now they must have thought they were dealing with another robber gang. But as soon as the word 'gendarmes' sounded and the disguised men moved forward, several members of the robber band raised their revolvers in a desperate resolve.

'Aha! So that's how it is!' shouted Holmes, raising his revolver.

In the same moment, seven gendarmes fired in coordination and four ruffians fell to the ground covered in blood and filling the tunnel with their cries. Bravoff fell with them. That was their last attempt to defend themselves. Their numbers down, their morale gone, the remaining robbers stood there shaking in fear.

XV

'Take 'em!' shouted Zviagin and rushed forward. The robbers were tied up in no time.

'God help us!' suddenly a desperate cry burst from Holmes. We turned to look at him. He was moving like lightning towards the entrance to the underground warehouse. He got as far as some object lying on the ground when there was the sound of a blow and we saw Holmes, his face distorted, dragging an unconscious Bakhtadian away.

'What's happened?' I asked in alarm.

'A few more seconds and this villain would have blown himself up and us with him,' answered Holmes. 'We paid no attention to him because he was wounded. He realized there was no escape, so he gathered up all his strength, dragged himself to the spot where there is a fuse coming from a mine inside the wall. I seized him just as he lit the match to light the Bickford cord. Just as well I got to him in time to prevent him blowing us all to kingdom come!'

The wounded groaned in pain.

Out of my pocket I took bandages and my campaign first aid kit with all the items needed for caring for the wounded and began to tend to them.

We left men to guard the gang and the three of us, with two gendarmes, went to examine the underground storage chamber.

The entrance was a first-class piece of workmanship. It was made up of four large stone slabs. They were fixed into a thick iron frame so skilfully that the closest scrutiny couldn't distinguish them from the tunnel walls. Once through them, we were in a vast underground grotto carved out of the rock.

The grotto was lit up by ten bright lamps, whose light fell on mountains of chests filled with the most varied goods. In one corner there was a small office desk with a thick notebook on it. Entered up in it with absolute precision were the supply and delivery of goods, with notes indicating from whom delivered and to whom sold.

'This is all we need,' said Holmes, taking the book. He turned to Zviagin, 'I've done my job. Here is a list of all those mixed up in this business. One hundred and ninety-two major figures and, as for small fry, probably ten times more.'

Zviagin took the list and with a frown began to scan it, 'These are VIPs,' he said, looking troubled and confused. 'How does one get to them?' He fell silent.

Holmes looked at him ironically. 'The root of the evil must be sought at the top of a rotten bureaucracy for which some little man is usually made to carry the blame. If in all seriousness you wish to get rid of this evil, you will only be saved by a just and correct Parliamentary system.'

'And that's already not up to me,' said Zviagin coldly.

'But, surely, the fact that such people participate in such matters proves the necessity for public control by the people and not bureaucratic control out of which these people emerged,' Holmes persisted.

'I would ask you not to say such things in the presence of lower ranks,' Zviagin interrupted him curtly and added, 'Our job is done. The sentries are in place. We can go.'

We came out, got aboard the train waiting near the tunnel and ordered ourselves to be taken back.

*

XVI

Several years have passed since then. We read the accounts of trials. We knew that the case brought to trial was subject to considerable alteration. Many, many were brought to book, but it was the small fry who paid the price, plus a few secondary officials in various departments.

The First and the Second Governmental Dumas, the Russian attempt at a Parliament, were dissolved before either could get to the happenings in Siberia and Manchuria. The Third Governmental Duma was so overwhelmed with legislation and so occupied with good intentions, that it had absolutely no time for Siberia.

3

THE STRANGLER

P. Nikitin

I

Sherlock Holmes was reading the papers when I came into his hotel room. Seeing me, he put aside the newspaper he was reading and said, 'In the sort of life we lead, either we are asked to do something or, for some reason or another, we do it of our own accord.'

'You are speaking of—' I prompted.

'I am speaking of our profession. More often than not, we are approached for assistance by others, but there are times when something crops up and investigating it is a positive joy, despite the fact that nobody has asked us to look into the matter.'

'Do I take it that you've found something interesting in the papers today?' I asked.

'You are absolutely right, Watson,' Holmes answered. 'Today's papers are full of a particularly mysterious crime committed yesterday not far from Moscow and, if you are interested, let me read you one of the accounts of it.'

'But, of course,' I answered. 'You know perfectly well that I am always interested in anything that interests you and you would be doing me a great favour if you were to read to me whatever it is that could intrigue you so much.'

Instead of answering, Holmes picked up one of the newspapers and, finding the required item, began to read out aloud.

'Last night, 25 May, at 11 o'clock in the evening, the police began to investigate a highly mysterious crime which took place near Moscow on the estate of a member of the gentry, Sergey Sergeyevitch Kartzeff.

'At three o'clock in the afternoon, Sergey Sergeyevitch Kartzeff locked himself in his bedroom to rest, as he always did after having dined at home. Normally, his valet would wake him by knocking on the door after a couple of hours. This time, despite several attempts by the valet, there was no answer. Surprised at his master's failure to respond, the valet knocked harder, but there was still no response. The valet now became anxious, ran to fetch the cook and maid, and all three of them began to beat on the door, but there was still no response. Fearing that something untoward might have occurred, they broke it down and found Sergey Sergeyevitch Kartzeff dead. He was lying in his bed, his eyes bursting out of their sockets and his face blue. The district police and an investigator were immediately sent for and on arrival at the scene of the crime pronounced that Sergey Sergeyevitch had been strangled to death. A close inspection of the scene yielded only contradictory and incomprehensible results. First, it was established that at the time the crime was committed, the room was locked from the inside, though the lock was damaged because the staff had had to use force to break in. The window had been sealed for the winter and only a hinged pane in it could be opened, so small that a seven-year-old child could hardly squeeze through it. The room was on the second floor, and it had no other openings or apertures, even through the stove. Nevertheless, the old man's throat showed clear traces of a strangler's unusually long fingers. The face of the dead man was severely scratched in several places. An examination of the window, the windowsill and the ground beneath the window showed absolutely no clues of any sort. This might have been caused by a light drizzle which had been falling that day and most probably washed away all traces. The whole house stands in its own grounds. All that the investigators found were several strange traces on the wall outside of the room in which the corpse was found. These traces, most probably, belonged to some freak of nature whose fingers were inordinately long and left such strange prints. The staff were asked whether anyone in the house had deformed feet, but they all declared there never had been anyone like that. The investigators cross-examined the entire staff. Old man Kartzeff was a bit of a recluse, they said, enjoyed managing the estate, seldom received guests, visited neighbouring landowners and got along with everyone. He treated peasants and workers kindly, which ruled out revenge as a motive. Moreover, there is one other circumstance pointing to robbery as a motive. A drawer of the dead man's desk was open and there were many papers and objects strewn all over the floor as if in haste. Asked by the investigators who had recently visited the deceased, the servants testified that since the end of winter there had only been two visitors. One was his nephew, Boris Nikolayevitch Kartzeff, who lived on his own small estate, Igralino, not too far away, and another nephew, Nikolai Nikolayevitch Kartzeff, brother of Boris, had dropped in a couple of times. The latter was by no means a rich man and occupied himself with some sort of private business in Moscow. Further inquiries established that both nephews had each spent the night in his own home. Thus the investigation has produced no results and it seems that catching the perpetrator will be no easy matter.'

'So, my dear chap, what have you to say to that?' asked Holmes putting down the newspaper.

'I can say that the perpetrator carefully considered every possible way in and out,' I answered.

Holmes nodded, 'I agree with you completely and, frankly, I wouldn't have stopped upon this crime were it not for those strange references to abnormal traces left by the strangler firstly on the neck of the victim and then by the wall in the garden below.'

'My dear Holmes, from what you have said before and your reading of this account, I conclude that you wish to take up this case,' I said with a smile. Knowing full well the character of my friend and his inordinate interest in every sort of mysterious crime, I knew Holmes could not pass up such a case.

'Do have in mind,' I added, 'that this case has intrigued not just you, but me as well. Hence, I volunteer in advance to be your assistant.'

'Oh, I didn't have the least doubt on that score,' exclaimed Holmes, gleefully rubbing his hands, 'and anticipated that you would make the offer first and since you know me so well, you knew I would get on with it without more ado.'

Instead of replying, I rose and began to put on my coat.

Seeing this, Holmes smiled and picked up his hat. 'You are an indispensable assistant, my dear chap,' pronounced Holmes with one of those good-natured glances that so gladdened me, 'and when I am with you, the work advances thrice as quickly as with any other person.'

'Just one thing,' I asked, 'are we going out of town now?'

'Yes,' said Holmes, 'I have to look at the scene of the crime and see everything for myself. That's why we are off to the Nikolayevsk station to undertake a short trip to not-so-distant parts.'

Chatting thus, we went out and hired a hackney to take us to the station. We didn't have to wait long for a local train. We were told to get off after two stops and that the estate of Sergey Sergeyevitch Kartzeff was just over three miles from the station.

II

The journey passed swiftly. Getting off the train, we hired a coach to take us to Silver Slopes, the name of the estate belonging to Sergey Sergeyevitch Kartzeff. We arrived to find everyone rushing hither and thither in a scene of total chaos. Last night's crime was still too fresh in everyone's mind and, moreover, the corpse was still there amidst the chaos and the bustle.

The investigator was there, as were the local chief of police and Boris Nikolayevitch Kartzeff, who had come from home when informed of his uncle's sudden death.

Boris Nikolayevitch turned out to be a handsome man, some thirty-five years of age, with the outward appearance of a rake and gadabout. He was tall, with dark hair, an energetic look and a muscular body. His uncle's death had evidently upset him and he now issued orders nervously and absent-mindedly.

A moment before we came in, Holmes whispered in my ear, 'Remember, Watson, we mustn't own up to our real names. Let's pretend, say, that we are real estate agents here for the purchase of the estate. Dear uncle is dead, nephews are stepping into their inheritance, and this seems the appropriate moment to ask whether they are prepared to sell as soon as it is in their ownership.'

I nodded in agreement.

Our arrival was noted. Boris Nikolayevitch approached us first, asking who we are and what is our business.

On being told we are real estate agents working on commission, he involuntarily shrugged his shoulders. 'Aren't you a little premature? You come to the funeral like carrion crows!'

Somewhat rude, but under the circumstances, still understandable. In any case, something even a well-mannered man might say. But in the confusion round the corpse, we were soon ignored. This was enough for Holmes to start investigating. He left me to myself, bidding me to keep out of sight, and left to return all of an hour later. He took me by the elbow and said, 'Let's go, my dear chap. I've done everything I needed, but for the sake of appearances, let's intrude on Boris Nikolayevitch with our original inquiry.'

Boris Nikolayevitch was pacing hither and thither, so intercepting him did not take long. But when we posed the same question to him again, he looked at us irritably and replied sharply, 'It wouldn't come amiss if you were to make yourself scarce. But just in case, leave your address.' Having said this, he looked intently at Holmes. He stared for some seconds, then his lips widened slightly in a little smile, 'Perhaps I am wrong,' he said, 'but I suspect you are not whom you make yourselves out to be. There is something about you which reminds me of someone else I came across accidentally during my travels abroad.'

For a few seconds Holmes was silent and now it was he who gazed intently at Boris Nikolayevitch Kartzeff. 'I'd be interested to know where,' he finally said.

'England,' answered Kartzeff.

'In that case, no point in concealing our identities any further,' said Holmes. 'You guessed correctly and it is a great tribute to your memory. I am Sherlock Holmes and this is' – indicating me – 'my friend Dr Watson.'

A look of unutterable joy came over the face of Boris Nikolayevitch Kartzeff. 'So I was right. The reason that I recognized you was that I saw you in London when you were a witness in an important case. But I felt too embarrassed to say so right away, and then I was completely taken aback by your superb Russian.'

He came close and shook our hands warmly.

'But since this has happened and since you are here at your own initiative, it seems fate has brought you to our help and I cannot tell you how relieved I am, knowing full well that the villain who perpetrated this foul deed will not escape you. As of this moment, you are the most welcome, the most longed-for guests in this house, and I now beg your permission to present you to our investigator and the police authorities who are here.'

Holmes bowed his consent. With an exchange of pleasantries we went into the dining-room which was full of people.

'Ladies and gentlemen, allow me to present Mr Sherlock Holmes and Dr Watson,' Boris Nikolayevitch said loudly.

Our names created a sensation. Investigators and police jumped to their feet as if we were their superior officers. Compliments rained on Sherlock Holmes's head.

'This gives us fresh hope!' was heard on all sides.

We joined the company and the conversation soon turned to the murder. As was to be expected, there were many presuppositions, but they were to such an extent without foundation that neither Homes nor I paid much attention to them.

From their conversation, we learned that several people had been arrested, amongst them the valet, cook and maid.

'Are you sure that the valet and the cook together smashed a door definitely locked from within?' Homes asked the investigator.

'Oh, yes,' the man answered with total conviction. 'There is absolutely no doubt, as you will see for yourself from so much as a glance. Only a locked door could have been mangled in such a way.'

'Then why did you arrest them?' Holmes asked in astonishment.

'More as a matter of form,' was the answer. 'I'm sure we'll have to let them go in a few days.'

Having questioned the investigator and police chief concerning certain details, Holmes asked whether he could examine the dead man's room without wasting any further time. Needless to say, the request was granted, though I couldn't help but notice the smirk that appeared momentarily on both their faces.

We all went to the dead man's bedroom. It was just as we had been told. The door was smashed in and the key still stuck from the lock on the bedroom side.

Having examined this closely, Holmes said softly, 'Yes, there is no doubt the bedroom was locked from inside and the door smashed in, in its locked form. This is apparent from the fact that the lock is twisted and the key is so jammed as a result that it would only be possible to take it out if the lock were to be taken apart.'

Having done with the door, Holmes next approached the bed in which Sergey Sergeyevitch had been strangled and, taking his magnifying glass out of his pocket, he proceeded to examine the bedclothes closely. Knowing my friend as well as I did, I couldn't help noticing that he looked puzzled as he examined them.

Some minutes later he bent down to the floor and again began to examine something the others had missed. From the barely perceptible nod he gave, he had evidently found something.

We all watched with intense curiosity. From the bed he moved to the window. Here he pottered about for quite a while. It would appear he examined every little bit, even a little spot left by a fly. Gradually his face became more puzzled and more serious. And when Holmes finally moved away from the window, I could see that he was intensely absorbed.

Questions came at him from all sides.

'Not just yet, not just yet,' Holmes said absent-mindedly as he turned to his questioners.

'Surely you don't intend to keep us in such a state of uncertainty?' asked Boris Nikolayevitch. 'We're all closely connected to each other and to the case.'

'There are certain matters it is sometimes premature to discuss,' Holmes answered.

'But at least can you not point to anything suspicious, which may be a clue?' the investigator asked impatiently.

'Yes, there are one or two things,' said Holmes enigmatically. 'But, gentlemen, I repeat that, owing to certain considerations, I must refrain from further explanations.'

Everyone shrugged at this reply and a brief look of distrust appeared once again on the faces of the investigator and the police chief.

And so silently and evidently very unhappy with Holmes, everyone returned to the dining-room. The rest of the evening passed in conversation to which neither Holmes nor I paid any attention. After eleven o'clock Holmes asked for us to be assigned a room and we retired.

III

When I awoke the following morning, Holmes wasn't in the room, although it was still early. As I had expected, he had been up at five, gone off somewhere and only returned at nine. This I found out only later from his own words. When he returned, I was awake.

'My dear chap, I didn't want to wake you,' he said. 'You were sleeping so soundly and so peacefully, I had no wish to disturb your slumber, but now that you are awake, I must ask you to dress quickly.'

Much as I would have wanted to go on sleeping, I could hardly do so in the face of his demand. I jumped out of bed, washed and we sat down to breakfast which had been sent up to our room.

'Are we leaving?' I asked.

'Not entirely,' answered Holmes. 'It is very likely that we'll have to return, but in the meantime, I'd like to accept the kind invitation extended by Boris Nikolayevitch for us to visit his estate.'

Chatting away, we drank several glasses of tea and when, at last, Boris Nikolayevitch knocked on our door, we were ready to leave.

Boris Nikolayevitch still appeared depressed, but was courteous and attentive. 'I hope you slept well,' he said, entering the room.

'Oh, yes, for which we wish to thank you,' Sherlock Holmes answered on behalf of both of us.

'Is there anything else you would like,' he asked. 'Perhaps you are used to a hearty breakfast in the morning.'

'I must confess that ham and eggs wouldn't go amiss,' Holmes answered with a smile.

Boris Nikolayevitch Kartzeff was all attentiveness and a few minutes later returned with a servant carrying our breakfast and a bottle of sherry.

Thus fortified, we thanked our cordial host and rose from the table.

'Do you wish to come with me today,' asked Kartzeff, 'or do you wish to rest a while?'

'With your permission, we'd like to accept your invitation this very day,' answered Sherlock Holmes. 'We are very pressed for time and it is very likely that we have to return to England in a few days.'

'In that case, I shall give instructions for the horses to be made ready as soon as the funeral is over,' said our cordial host.

As he was about to leave, Holmes stopped him, 'Another little request. With your permission, I'd like to see your late uncle again before we leave.'

'But, of course,' answered Boris Nikolayevitch. 'Shall we do so this very minute?'

Holmes nodded. We left our room and made our way into the hall where the funeral service was in preparation.

Approaching the coffin, Sherlock Holmes carefully lifted the muslin cloth over the face of the dead man and proceeded to examine the corpse. Several minutes passed before he tore himself away. But when he moved away, one couldn't gather anything from the expression on his face.

Then the priests arrived and the usual service for that sort of event began. The reader began his doleful chant. The priest recited the service monotonously. And all was as if it was being done on a factory floor, unhurriedly, in a fixed manner but yet to some mysterious beat. Not particularly involved in the sacred service, we each stood sunk in his own thoughts.

The service over, we went out for some fresh air into the garden round the house. The garden was over ten hectares, i.e. nigh on ten acres in area. It was fully planted with fruit trees and truly magnificent. Here and there flowerbeds were scattered from which brightly coloured blossoms struck the eye. Yellow sand neatly covered the pathways and sculptures added to the sense of proportion of this lordly manor garden. We strolled silently through the alleyways and, from the look of intense concentration on the face of Sherlock Holmes, I could sense that a secret thought had lodged like a thorn in his brain.

A half hour later Boris Nikolayevitch followed us out. After the funeral service his mood seemed to have lifted. 'I hope you won't refuse to attend the burial today,' he said pleasantly. 'We don't intend to let it drag on for long, especially as there will be no women present. I'm not particularly sentimental and am always against the dead being detained for long in the house of the living.'

'How right you are,' said Holmes. 'The presence of the dead in a home is depressing, and as far as we in England are concerned, we always try to remove the body as quickly as possible to its place of burial.'

'I'm sure you will excuse me for leaving you now,' Kartzeff apologized. 'I'm sure you will understand that all funeral arrangements are exclusively my responsibility.'

'Oh, but of course,' Sherlock Holmes nodded. 'We'll stay here while you see to your duties and I beg you not to concern yourself with us.'

Boris Nikolayevitch Kartzeff bowed himself away politely, while we continued our aimless meandering.

Several hours passed. At about two in the afternoon Boris Nikolayevitch again reappeared and said that the body would be carried out in a quarter of an hour. We followed him inside.

We saw the corpse lifted up on a long piece of cloth and, accompanied by the clergy and choir, the sad procession moved to the village cemetery.

I won't describe the details of the burial as they are too well known to all. To the sad strains of the service and the wailing of the choir, the body was lowered into the ground. Heavy clods of damp earth thudded on the coffin lid and soon it vanished from sight. More and more damp earth was unevenly heaped over the grave and then, under the skilled hands of the gravediggers, evened out into the usual tidy mound.

The last note of the burial psalm and then all those present quietly trudged away, for some reason speaking of the departed in soft undertones. Sherlock Holmes and I also returned.

The dining-room table was already set and Boris Nikolayevitch, still preserving a look of sadness on his face, invited us to partake of refreshments.

In any wake, the faces of the guests begin by looking long and sad, but become merrier as the wine begins to flow until such time as the proceedings acquire the character of a proper binge.

It must have been all of seven o'clock, because the sun was beginning to set, when the guests and clergy rose from the table. At this point Boris Nikolayevitch approached Holmes saying, 'I'm at your disposal now. And if you so wish, we can go to my place together.'

'I am ready,' answered Holmes. 'Mind you, I see no reason for staying on. What I was able to find in the dead man's bedroom has little bearing on this scene and so, having rested at your place, we still have to return to Moscow, where I hope to find more reliable clues concerning this matter.'

We didn't have much to pack. Boris Nikolayevitch gave final instructions and we got into an elegant landau harnessed to a troika, three horses harnessed abreast. The sun set completely.

The well cared for horses, energized by the cool evening air, rose to the occasion and our carriage sped merrily along the country road.

It was less than five miles to the estate of Boris Nikolayevitch. At first, the road passed through open fields in which ears of grain were like dark waves. Then it entered the forest. This was thick with fir trees that hadn't seen an axe for a long time, evidently protected for a long time by the late Sergey Sergeyevitch Kartzeff.

Now right, now left, the road wound through the dark forest lit by a patch of sky in which a myriad stars blazed. I don't know how others might be affected, but this mystery-laden road only served to depress me with its gloom.

We drove a mile and a half without encountering a living soul. There was something strange about this vast, unpopulated, silent country road which lay between the estate of the uncle and his nephew. I was unable to refrain from expressing my thoughts to Kartzeff who was sitting beside us.

'What's there to be surprised about?' he said, shrugging his shoulders. 'This is a direct road joining our two estates and since time immemorial the peasants aren't permitted to drive along it.'

Emerging from the forest, we again drove along open fields and, at last, the tall contours of the Igralino estate rose before us.

We were met by the friendly barking of dogs, but as soon as they heard their master's voice, they fell silent. Our troika rolled up to the porch. An old retainer opened the door. He bowed low to his master, cast a suspicious look at the guests, let us through inside and helped us off with our outer garments.

The house did not overwhelm us with its opulence but, notwithstanding that, a glance into any of its rooms and you would conclude that a scion of the old gentry lived here. Not only were their portraits preserved, but their way of life. The house itself was too ordinary to be described as palatial. But the furnishings in any of the rooms had been selected with remarkable good taste and were far from cheap.

'First of all, gentlemen, abiding by a purely Russian tradition, I must show you to your quarters and then share with you whatever my humble abode is rich with,' said the master of the house, cordially welcoming us.

With these words, he led us through several rooms and in one of them said, 'I hope you will be comfortable here for the night.'

The room was fairly large. Apart from two beds, there was a wash basin, cupboard, a chest of drawers, a comfortable divan and several cushioned and ordinary chairs. Needless to say, we were very satisfied with the arrangements.

We thanked Boris Nikolayevitch and followed him to the dining-room. It was decorated in the Russian style and dinner was already laid out. The cooking was out of the ordinary. Over dinner our host made every effort to appear bright and cheerful, but I couldn't help noticing that the events of the day were still with him. This was not unusual and so neither Holmes nor I paid much attention to that.

IV

'You're probably tired after such a day,' said our host to Holmes, 'which is why I don't feel I ought to tire you for long. Frankly, the day has worn me out, too, and so, if you don't wish to retire early, I'll have to apologize for leaving you to your own devices so soon.'

'I do understand,' said Holmes sympathetically. 'I, too, would like to rest. Silly of me not to have said so earlier.'

'In that case, I wish you a very good night,' said Kartzeff.

He went off, leaving us to ourselves.

Holmes shut the door and carefully examined the room and

window. This was the only window in the room and as in Russian houses it had the usual hinged ventilation pane set inside it.

'Perhaps the owner doesn't seem to be much bothered by draughts,' Holmes said as if by the by, turning the catch now this way, now that. 'It doesn't lock and the slightest breeze will blow it open.'

From a small leather case in his pocket he took several nails and nailed them securely into the frame of the window pane. After that he locked the door, leaving the key in the lock and began to undress. I did the same and a few minutes later I was fast asleep. I don't recollect whether anything happened that night. All I know is that from the look on Holmes's face sitting at the table when I woke, I could see he had spent a sleepless night.

Seeing me open my eyes, he heaved a sigh of relief and then said in a tired voice, 'Well, now, my dear chap, thank God that you're awake. This will give me a chance for a little rest. Stay awake, there's a good chap, and I suggest you pay special attention to this little window pane.'

With these words he threw himself on the bed and a minute later he was already sleeping the sleep of the dead. Thoroughly puzzled, I sat there for a couple of hours, my gaze fixed on the window, but try as I might, I detected nothing suspicious.

The sun was already high in the heavens when Holmes awoke. He jumped out of bed, washed quickly and said cheerfully, 'Well, my dear chap, I can now stay up for a couple of nights. That tired feeling is gone. Such tiredness is unforgivable and just this once, accidental.'

'What's the matter?' I asked. 'I suppose something unusual took place last night and you'll tell me what it was all about,' I said.

'You'll allow me, my dear chap, to refrain from a direct answer,' said Holmes solemnly. 'It is very likely that in a few hours you will know more than you expected, and then your curiosity is bound to be satisfied.'

We chatted about various trifles and the time passed unnoticed. At nine there was a knock on the door. The door opened and Boris Nikolayevitch came in. His eyes were baggy and his face somewhat drawn. He greeted us, asked how we had spent the night and, receiving a positive answer, appeared contented enough.

'Tea is served,' he invited.

We nodded our acceptance. Over tea, Holmes, who was at first withdrawn, livened up and jokes, anecdotes and witticisms poured from him. When we had drunk our tea, he announced that it was imperative for him to go to Moscow.

'Surely you can stay longer,' exclaimed Boris Nikolayevitch in a hurt tone.

Holmes gave a sad shrug. 'Alas, I cannot. I did warn you yesterday that it is essential for me to be in Moscow today for pressing business and I hope you remember my words. This is why I must ask you to have horses made available immediately to get us to the station.'

'Most certainly,' exclaimed Kartzeff. 'I will give the necessary orders at once.' He went off but wasn't back for some considerable time.

Holmes sat there without stirring, his head in the palms of his hands. The rest of the time before lunch and the lunch itself passed slowly. After lunch we were told that the horses were ready and, having bidden farewell to our host, we departed for the station.

V

Arriving in town, we made straight for Nikolai Nikolayevitch Kartzeff, brother of Boris Nikolayevitch and whose address we had taken.

'It seems a little strange,' said Holmes pensively along the way, 'that the second nephew didn't even wish to attend his uncle's funeral.'

'Yes, that is very strange,' I agreed. 'Could it be that we will find here some clues leading to the crime?'

Nikolai Nikolayevitch lived right on the edge of town, just before Sokolniki, so that it took a while to get to him.

Our ring was answered by a kindly sympathetic old woman, who asked the nature of our business. On being told that we had come to see Nikolai Nikolayevitch, she made a gesture expressing regret. 'Oh, what a shame, what a really great shame that you missed him,' she sighed good-naturedly. 'We live so far away, and anyone who comes gets so upset when the master isn't home.'

'And you are his *matushka*?' asked Holmes, using the Russian diminutive endearing form for mother.

'Nanny, sir, his nanny,' she answered with a warm smile. 'Brought him up as a little boy, spent my life by his side. He's such a good man, he is, and now he keeps me in my old age, where another would long since have thrown me out in the street.'

'So where's he gone?' Holmes asked.

'Why, he left just before your arrival. He just got the news that his uncle had been strangled or was it knifed, in truth I don't know which it was. His own brother didn't tell him. I don't suppose he had time, with all the stir it must have caused.'

'So how did he find out?'

'The newspaper, my dear sir. That's where he read it. It was all in the newspaper. Gentlemen, you will come in and rest a while. We may be poor, but there's always a cup of tea. Happy to share what God has given. That's how we do things. Should any friend of his not find him home, he'll always come in for a cuppa.'

'Thank you, *nianushka*,' said Holmes, addressing her by the

Russian diminutive endearment for nanny.

We entered the apartment. It wasn't very big, all of two small rooms, a kitchen and a tiny box room for the old woman. The furniture was not particularly ostentatious. There were only a few things, more the sort you would find in a country hut, anyway. It was all fairly typical of the domicile of a young artist.

In one room there was a bed, a wash basin in poor condition, several chairs, a writing desk, canvas concealed the walls. Paints, brushes and other painter's objects lay scattered everywhere.

The other room was filled with easels, picture frames with canvas stretched on them. Completed paintings and rough sketches hung on the walls, showing that Nikolai Nikolayevitch might be at the start of his career, but already showed great promise.

A great connoisseur, Sherlock Holmes examined the work of this beginner with considerable relish. The old woman was evidently very proud of her charge. She stood beside Holmes and with a smile watched him examine the work of her favourite.

'Why don't you sit down, sirs,' she said warmly. 'I'll get the samovar going. It will boil in no time at all.'

'Thank you,' said Holmes.

And shaking his head sadly, he said, 'And so the uncle dies! How come his own brother didn't bother to tell him?'

The old woman shook her head sadly, too, 'He's just a bad lot, is Boris Nikolayevitch, a bad lot. If he were a man like other men, of course he'd've told the master. I think he's got nothing inside his head except for the wind whistling.'

'A bad lot, you say!'

The old woman gestured with her hand to show nothing could be done. 'What is there to say,' she sighed. 'He's a born gambler. First he inherited an estate and a sizable capital sum. The capital sum he gambled away. He may have been a good-for-nothing, but he certainly knew how to ingratiate himself. My Nikolai Nikolayevitch was done out of his fair share because he wasn't one to bow and scrape. But the other fellow knew where and when to turn up and flatter relatives, who would give him a warm welcome. That's what happened with their grand-mother. She included him in her will and left out Nikolai Nikolayevitch!'

'And did Nikolai Nikolayevitch often visit this departed uncle?' asked Sherlock Holmes.

'On the contrary! You have no idea how often he was invited. Mind you, he did go twice, but didn't stay long. No doubt he won't get anything there, either. You'll see, Boris Nikolayevitch will get the lot.'

'To waste it on more carousing,' said Holmes sympathetically.

'For sure! For sure!' said the old woman. 'Nothing good will come out of the money that will come to him. He'll waste it on mam'selles, as he always has in the past and that's that! He did have a job, but got sacked for all those misdeeds.'

'What was the job?' asked Holmes.

'He was a naval officer. Sailed as first officer on his own ship for some time. No less than ten years. And then he was kicked out. Thank God he wasn't tried. Mind you, even then, everyone said he couldn't evade being tried but luckily for him he wriggled out of that. They must've felt sorry for him.'

She suddenly remembered the samovar and with a cry quickly ran out of the room. In no time tea appeared. We drank it with great pleasure and continued our interrupted conversation. Most of all, we spoke of Boris Nikolayevitch. The old woman spoke of him without evident rancour but in the sort of tone people use when speaking of someone of whom they disapprove.

From what she said, we pieced together the information that Boris Nikolayevitch, the older brother of Nikolai Nikolayevitch, graduated from a naval academy and had sailed far and wide on a ship which had been part of a squadron of the Russian navy. Then, for improper conduct and some sort of financial peculation, he was dismissed. After that he spent some years sailing the Indian Ocean on British ships plying between Bombay and Calcutta. Two years ago, Boris Nikolayevitch Kartzeff returned to Russia and the gossip amongst his friends was that he had been dismissed even from the ships of the private line by which he had been employed. During those two years he had managed to squander the remains of his small capital. As for the estate that had been left him, he'd brought it to the point where it was threatened with going under the hammer.

'But he's always been lucky, *batiushki*,' she said. 'Born under a lucky star, he was,' she said. 'No sooner do things get bad, then uncle dies.'

'Yes, it isn't the deserving who flourish on this earth,' sighed Holmes.

'How right you are!' gestured the old woman. 'Take our Nikolai Nikolayevitch. He doesn't get any assistance from anywhere. Pays for his own studies. Supports himself and me. Wonderful, wonderful young man! While if ever a spare kopeck comes his way, it goes to a needy friend. He keeps nothing back for himself.'

We sat there for a little while longer, thanked her for the welcome she had extended us, bade her farewell and left.

'So, what do you think of the young man?' Holmes asked me when we were outside.

'That this is not where we will find the criminal,' I answered. 'I think this is all a false lead.'

Holmes said nothing. He paced along quickly, deep in thought.

Sokolniki was not a district with which we were familiar. We soon stopped a cabbie and Holmes directed him to take us to our hotel.

'Any post?' he asked the porter.

The porter rummaged round in a drawer and handed him a letter. Holmes opened it, read the contents quickly and then, having carefully examined the envelope, handed me a sheet of paper.

'Just look at this, if you please, my dear Watson,' he said with a smile.

I read the following, 'Dear Mr Holmes, England has more than enough criminals of its own and your presence there would be immeasurably more beneficial for your fellow citizens than chasing fame in Russia. From the bottom of my heart, let me give you some good advice. Clear off home while you are still alive.'

I glanced at the envelope and saw it had been posted locally.

'Well, what do you say?' asked Holmes with a disdainful smile.

'It looks as if our presence here is upsetting someone, and it seems that the letter has some connection with the mysterious crime at the Silver Slopes estate.'

'Very probably,' said Holmes indifferently, as he climbed up the stairs. 'We've got enough time to change and get back on the train.'

'Dare I ask where we are going?' I asked.

'Oh, we have to get back to Silver Slopes and Igralino once again. Nikolai Nikolayevich going there is just the perfect excuse for us.'

Without further ado we changed and made our way to the station.

VI

Boris Nikolayevitch Kartzeff couldn't conceal his astonishment at seeing us back.

'What hand of fate brings you here?' he exclaimed, coming

out on the porch. 'I must confess I thought you have long since been in town.'

'We've been there, too,' answered Holmes, jumping from the carriage and greeting the owner. 'But we were told that your brother, Nikolai Nikolayevitch, was on his way here and since we were interested in asking him a few questions, we hastened back.'

'Not even stopping off wherever you were staying?'

'What's to be done! In our profession it isn't always possible to do as we please and it becomes necessary to accept the situation with all its inconveniences. I hope Nikolai Nikolayevitch is with you.

'Unfortunately not. He went to his uncle's graveside. But if you think it necessary, I'll send a carriage after him at once.'

'Oh, no, please don't concern yourself. It'll keep. If you were to allow it, we would like to spend the night here and go tomorrow.'

'But, of course. You know perfectly well that I am really glad of your company,' exclaimed Boris Nikolayevitch.

Chatting away, we went in and sat down at the table which our host had ordered to be laid. At about four in the afternoon, Nikolai Nikolayevitch returned.

Told who we are, he didn't mince words, 'Yes, it would be a good thing to catch the villain. I'd be the first to cut his throat with my own hands.'

The death of his uncle had clearly affected him greatly.

'Say what you will, but this murder is beyond me,' he began. 'If anyone could wish his death, it would only be the two of us, as we are both his heirs and in the will found amongst uncle's things, his entire estate is to be equally divided between us. To tell you the truth, it doesn't give me any pleasure to receive this damned inheritance, coming as it does in such a manner. As far as I am concerned, I have always been used to living within my own means since I was quite young and even as things stand, I can support myself.'

He lowered his head sadly without paying us any more attention.

Using his tiredness as an excuse, Holmes asked Boris Nikolayevitch's permission for us to retire. Our host personally escorted us to the door of our room and cordially asked whether there was anything more we required either that evening or for the night.

'No, thank you,' said Holmes and we entered the room allocated us.

It was the same room we had occupied the previous night. Nonetheless, this did not prevent Holmes from conducting the most meticulous examination which included every little thing. Glancing at the small hinged pane in the window, Holmes gave a barely concealed smile, 'Have a look, my dear Watson, at this example of gracious forethought. Of course, you do remember that when we first slept here, the pane was not secured. But now, just look at the improvements made by the host.'

I looked and all I saw was the addition of a latch.

'Well, what about it?' asked Holmes. And clapping me on the back, he said with a smile, 'I am just trying to test your powers of observation.'

I gave a surprised shrug of my shoulders, 'The latch has been repaired, that is all.'

'And that is all?

'I think so.'

'But don't you detect anything special about the new arrangement?' asked Holmes with a smile.

'Absolutely none!'

'In that case, pay due attention to the following: for some unfathomable reason, the contraption actually goes right through the pane. Hence, it can be opened and shut from inside as well as outside the room.'

'Do explain yourself.'

'Why, only that I see such a contraption in a window pane for the first time in my life.' Saying this, Holmes drew the heavy curtains over the window and lit the lamps.

It was already dark.

All was still outside, except for the soft lowing of cattle from afar. Very likely the herd was being driven to pasture.

'My dear Watson, I recommend the utmost care and vigilance tonight,' said Holmes to me. 'It is likely that the events of the night will tell us much, which is why it would be a good thing for you to abstain from sleep. Now, I suggest that you watch the inner courtyard, if you can. Actually, no. We'll go out for a little stroll in the field and then take up our watch.'

With those words he opened the door and went out. I followed. Boris Nkolayevitch and his brother were sitting at the dining-room table.

'Have you already rested?' asked Boris Nikolayevitch.

'No, we thought we'd get a little fresh air,' answered Holmes.

'Perhaps you'd like me to accompany you,' our host offered graciously.

'Oh, no, we'll find our own way. We don't intend to go very far.'

We went out and for half an hour strolled round the house. I saw that Holmes missed nothing, not the slightest detail. Soon we had gone round all the outhouses and seen where everything stood and what was kept where. An old man passed by. Holmes hailed him and proffered him half a rouble to show us the grounds in detail. The old fellow was delighted at his good fortune and couldn't thank us enough. He was a herdsman and told us he had lived there as long ago as the days of the late owner, the grandmother of Boris Nikolayevitch.

We wandered round the yard, examining whatever we saw, and eventually arrived in front of a small doorway. It was covered with metal and bolted with a large hanging lock. 'Is this also a storehouse?' asked Holmes.

The old man's face took on an enigmatic appearance, 'No, sir, not a barn. Mind you, when the late mistress was alive, oil paint was kept here for the roof, linseed oil as a base for varnish and other things. But since the new master took over, something strange seems to have appeared inside.'

'Something strange, say you?' asked Holmes. 'What could it possibly be?'

'How can I put it sir, since I don't know and neither does anyone else.' The old man lowered his voice to a whisper. 'Since the very day the new master arrived, none of us has been inside. I saw him drag in a huge chest, but nobody knows what was inside. He himself goes in twice daily, but none of us is allowed there.'

'Well, I never!' said Holmes in a tone of evident disapproval.

'Oh, yes, sir! You can hear it moaning,' whispered the old man enigmatically.

'What is it that is moaning?' asked a surprised Holmes.

'Whatever is locked in that chest. Some folk say that a man who has lost his mind is hidden inside. Someone possessed. Might be related to the master!'

'Where do you get all that from?'

'I'll tell you where from. Sometimes at night you can hear someone grunting or snarling. It is neither a human sound nor an animal's either.'

'Maybe someone got frightened and just said it,' suggested Holmes.

'Out of fright!' said the old man, this time truly aggrieved, 'I heard it myself.'

Holmes approached the door and looked at the lock. 'Yes,' he said thoughtfully, 'this is no ordinary lock. You wouldn't easily find a key to fit it. In any case, if I were to decide to open it for myself, it would take a considerable while.' He turned suddenly and looked at the big house.

I don't know what made me, but I automatically followed his

example and that very moment I noticed the figure of Boris Nikolayevitch jumping back from the window as soon as we turned around. Actually, I don't know whether this was so or merely appeared so to me, but the expression on the nephew of the dead man was on this occasion particularly strange. It seemed to me that his eyes looked at us with an unnatural anger. But all this was only momentary.

Holmes turned away calmly from the mysterious shed and we continued on our way still interrogating the old man about any old trivia. Our stroll didn't last more than an hour. When we had had enough of the yard, we went in again and this time, meeting nobody, went to our room.

VII

We had just about retired, when there was a knock at the door. It was Boris Nikolayevitch, come to ask whether we'd like to have supper before retiring for the night. He looked perfectly content to accept our refusal, wished us a good night and departed.

We began to undress, but before we went to bed, Sherlock Holmes locked the door, leaving the key in the door and, approaching the window, began to look out carefully at the grounds. He stood like that for nigh on a quarter of an hour. Then he reached into his pocket for his leather case, took out a few nails and once again very carefully nailed them into the frame of the pane.

Next he put out the light, came up to my bed and leaning down to my ear whispered very softly, 'My dear Watson, have your revolver at the ready and under no circumstances let go of it. In the meantime, I suggest that you part the curtains carefully and give your attention to anything that occurs anywhere near our window.'

We tiptoed towards the curtains, parted them ever so slightly and put our eyes to the gap. A pale moon had risen and cast its mysterious light over the park. We tried to stand so quietly that the slightest move would not betray our vigil. A considerable time must have passed. I couldn't check the time in the dark, but it must have been all of two hours.

I became bored by the long silence and finally just had to ask Holmes, albeit softly, 'What do you suppose is going on?'

'Quiet,' he said. 'This is no time for conjecture. We'll know everything in the morning.'

And once again, hour after hour stretched past. My legs became numb from prolonged standing and I lost all sense of where I stood.

Suddenly, some object appeared at the window. A pole with an attachment! Holmes indicated I was to increase my vigilance, but my nerves were already stretched taut as it was. The pole was being slowly guided from below by some unseen hand and the attachment stopped at the level of the pane.

Whoever was below came nearer and the outer latch of the pane was now in the groove of whatever was on the end of the pole. It turned. Clearly, someone was trying to unlock it from down below. But now, just as it must have happened last time, the nails that Holmes had fixed with his usual foresight, proved too much of an impediment.

Someone below was trying hard to open the pane, but it would not give way. The effort lasted for nearly half an hour. The man seemed desperate to carry out his intention but eventually the pole was lowered beneath the level of the windowsill. We heard a slight noise from outside and below and then all was still. We waited in vain while another hour passed and then moved away from the window.

'There you are,' said Sherlock Holmes, 'you and I, my dear Watson, proved to be wiser, and as it seems to me, this time escaped certain death.'

'What do you mean by that?' I asked.

'Someone was intent on opening the pane to let in a strange creature capable of squeezing through such a narrow aperture. Undoubtedly, it could not be a human being. The pane would have been too narrow.'

He was silent for a moment and then added, 'In any case, the morning brings wiser counsel, so it would be better for us to sleep. I'll tell you everything in the morning.'

I was dying of curiosity, but I knew perfectly well that Holmes would never say anything till such time as he was good and ready, and so I did not insist.

VIII

Next morning, for a change, I was up before my friend. But I had hardly swung out of bed when Holmes opened his eyes. He was a remarkably light sleeper. No matter how tired out he had been, the slightest movement served to waken him.

'Aha, my friend,' he exclaimed cheerfully. 'I'm not quite myself this morning. Surely you couldn't have wakened before me.' I gave an involuntary smile.

We began to dress. Our movements and voices must have come to the attention of the household. Hardly twenty minutes had gone by when there was a knock on the door. A servant had come to ask whether we'd like tea served up in our room.

'No thanks, my dear chap,' Holmes answered. 'We'll have it in the dining-room.'

He waited till the servant had gone before giving me a look fraught with meaning, saying 'It'll be safer this way, especially being able to see the host drink first.'

Having completed our toilet, we entered the dining-room, where Boris Nikolayevitch and Nikolai Nikolayevitch were already sitting at breakfast.

There most probably had been a slight tiff between the brothers, at least judging from the end of the sentence uttered by Boris Nikolayevitch, '—you cannot possibly lay claim to any part of the inheritance. After all, you never paid so much as a visit to our uncle and he was entirely in my care.'

'A will represents the will of the departed,' Nikolai Nikolayevitch answered coldly. 'Whether I visited him or not is beside the point. Since he left me a part of his estate, this is how it must be.'

Boris Nikolayevitch was about to say something, but noticing our arrival, broke off the conversation abruptly, greeted me very cordially and offered tea. 'I hope you slept well,' he addressed us both.

'Oh, yes,' I said. 'I slept like a log till morning.'

'And I, too,' said Holmes. 'Country air does predispose one to sleep, especially after an energetic stroll. And we must've strolled round your place at least a full hour before retiring.'

'You have such a lovely nanny,' he added, turning to Nikolai Nikolayevich.

'Oh, indeed!' answered the young man smiling happily. Evidently, he liked having the old lady praised. His face lit up with a kind and sympathetic smile. 'I do love the old lady,' he said tenderly, 'for I have neither father nor mother. She is all I have left as the only loving reminder of my happy childhood.'

The brothers reminisced about their childhood, their capers and pranks. Our presence didn't seem to divert them from their memories. However, when breakfast was over, before leaving the table, Boris Nikolayevitch turned to my friend, 'You will allow me to ask a question, Mr Holmes?'

'By all means,' came the answer.

'Forgive me for what might be considered an insolent question, but I am curious to know how far advanced is your investigation into clearing up the mysterious murder. In fact, has it advanced at all?'

Holmes gave an enigmatic smile. 'Yes, one could say that it is advancing and successfully so,' he said. 'But owing to certain circumstances I have to be circumspect and consider the time is not yet ripe for me to reveal the results. Of course, while I know I can rely on your discretion, nonetheless, an incautious word, involuntarily dropped, may serve to harm the course of events.'

Boris Nikolayevitch shrugged, 'Of course, you know best and it would be silly of me to insist. Sooner or later, however, you'll reveal all yourself, but since I do not belong amongst the ranks of the curious, I shall be silent, at least until such time as you yourself choose to share your secrets with me.'

We exchanged various trivia and then Holmes announced he had to say something to me in private. We thanked our host for breakfast and left the dining-room. We went back to our room, put on our hats and went out, following the country road further out. Holmes glanced around him, saw that nobody followed and we lessened our pace. Well over a mile later, we threw ourselves on the soft grass beside the road.

'Well, then, my dear Holmes, last night you promised you'd reveal something interesting to me concerning your preliminary findings. We are all alone here, and since we cannot be overheard, there is nothing to prevent us from speaking loudly and clearly.'

'True, true,' said Holmes and stretched himself out with evident pleasure on the green sward. 'When we set off, it was with the intention of sharing with you everything I have done up to this point. If you are ready, I'll begin.'

'Of course,' I said in joyful anticipation of a good story.

IX

Holmes stretched himself lazily, turned his head to face me and began his story.

'You probably remember, my dear Watson,' he began, 'our first arrival on the scene. As soon as we arrived at the scene of the crime, I was really amazed at the inadequate attention the investigative authorities had given the matter. It was as if the crime was of no particular interest. They didn't even bother to examine the room in which Kartzeff died. By the way, even from my initial glance at the bed on which he died, I was able to spot clues with the use of my magnifying glass and that put me on the right track. It was from that moment that I was convinced that the crime was committed not by a man, but by a beast.

'I spotted a few soft grey hairs on the blanket and the pillows. I examined them with a magnifying glass and established that they undoubtedly belonged to an animal. Then a close examination of the waxed parquet floor showed several traces of movement from the window to the bed and back again. These were long, with a narrow heel and long toes. They had definitely been made by an ape. I found the same sort of traces by the wall from which the window of the dead man looked out.

'It was clear that the ape had crept into Kartzeff's room through the window pane, strangled him, clambered up to the roof and then descended using the rain pipe attached to the wall.

'An examination of the corpse only confirmed my assumption, as there were traces of an ape's paws round the throat of the corpse.

'You know, of course, that I have often journeyed through India. I have covered nearly all the shores of the Indian Ocean, often travelling deep inland and, on several occasions, I saw the baboons which local Indians utilized for hunting. It was enough to show these dreaded animals the intended victim for them to leap on it with lightning-like agility, using their muscular paws to choke the life out of it. For some reason, these Indian baboons somehow came to mind when I looked at the scene of the crime.

'I have to admit that, at first, my suspicions fell strongly on Nikolai Nikolayevitch, of whom it was said that he visited his uncle extremely rarely and when departing never ever displayed any warmth. That's why I hastened away with you to test my suspicions. But the old nanny's account caused me to change my mind completely and all suspicions directed at Nikolai Nkolayevitch flew out of my mind.

'In fact, since then I had no doubt that his brother, Boris Nikolayevitch had committed the crime, although the latter hadn't betrayed guilt in the slightest manner. His service and dismissal from the navy and merchant marine, his poor reputation and finally his travels up and down the Indian Ocean gave rise to the first suspicions. Even then, the thought struck me that it could have been there that this sort of ape was acquired by him.

'The threatening letter which came to us in the hotel only strengthened my suspicion. That letter was a terrible blunder on the part of Boris Nikolayevitch and became the prime mover in establishing his guilt. Of course, it is possible to disguise handwriting, but I am certain that a handwriting expert will prove that it is that of Boris Kartzeff.

'And so, this was the course of my thinking: he'd lost everything in riotous living and now he couldn't wait for the death of his uncle. He knew about the will. And so, seeing that his own estate was about to go under the hammer, he decided to advance his way out of the situation.

'The fact is that from the moment of his arrival he had kept the ape under lock and key, let nobody see it, all this was a clear indication that he was up to no good. Evidently, that damned beast had been prepared for its task long before and all he had to do was point it at the victim for it to carry out its task. This is how Kartzeff distanced himself from the crime, substituting a creature that had no sense of what it was doing, thus guaranteeing his own safety from punishment.

'I fully comprehended his train of thought and action, but I have to admit that as an intelligent man he too read my mind and intuitively realized he could not escape from me. Of that he must actually have been convinced on the very first day we met, and when we arrived the very first time he immediately decided to put an end to us. You, of course, hadn't noticed that we had been assigned a room in which the window had a pane with a broken latch, nor that the room in which old Kartzeff had been strangled had a pane with a similarly broken latch.

'But on that occasion, his plan did not work. With foresight, I had nailed down the pane and for it to be opened there would have to be enough noise for us to be alerted. And that wasn't part of the villain's plan. I think you saw him in the window during our stroll last night—'

'Oh, I shall never forget that look, a mixture of fear and loathing,' I said.

'If until then I had any reservations about his guilt, all doubt vanished from that moment. And so, during the night, I waited for confirmation of my presuppositions,' said Holmes. 'In any case, there's not much more to tell you about the most recent events. You saw for yourself how an invisible hand tried to open the pane for that cursed animal to get into our room. Now, Watson, all that's left is to lure him to a last desperate step. As soon as we return, I will announce that we have decided to depart for the city and, depending on how he reacts, we'll decide what to do next. In the meantime, let us take our time getting back.'

X

We strolled back.

Boris Nikolayevitch was busy in the yard, handing out some sort of orders concerning household matters, when Sherlock

Holmes approached and firmly stated that we had to return to Moscow this very day.

A hardly discernible gleam appeared in Kartzeff's glance. But it was only momentary and, taking himself in hand, he said indifferently, 'I am so sorry you cannot stay longer, but it can't be helped. Work must come first. If you don't intend to stop off at Silver Slopes, I'll send you to the station by the direct road. I am only sorry that I cannot do so immediately. My horses are all out on the road and you'll have to wait a few hours.'

'Oh, that's no problem,' answered Sherlock Holmes.

'I'll give instructions for you to be driven to the ferry. It belongs to me, by the way. From there, the same horses will take you to the station.'

'Excellent!' said Sherlock Holmes.

We thanked him again and went inside, where we chatted with Nikolai Nikolayevitch and Boris Nikolayevitch who occasionally dropped in on us. Nevertheless, hour after hour went by and no horses appeared.

At a convenient moment, when both brothers were out of the room at the same time, Holmes whispered to me softly, 'I forgot to tell you another little detail. This morning a sock went missing. I deliberately placed my boots outside the door and stuffed my socks inside them. Tell me, why do you think a sock went missing?'

'I haven't a clue. Now why should he need an old sock of yours,' I said with a smile.

'All the same, it is a serious matter,' said Holmes. 'I am nearly certain that he needed the sock for that ape to scent.'

Dinner was served at five and went off normally. It was another two hours before the host informed us the horses were ready and awaited us by the porch. But even here there was a delay. Kartzeff examined the carriage and claimed it hadn't been properly oiled. He gave instructions for it to be oiled all over again. It was clearly a deliberate attempt to delay us further.

Night was beginning to fall when, at last, we thanked the brothers for their hospitality, bade them farewell and departed. After a mile along the road, the carriage entered a forest. Now the sun set and it became completely dark.

'Be even more on your guard and hold on to your revolver,' Holmes whispered.

As we drove into the forest, the driver slowed down.

Holding his revolver in his hand, Holmes looked back and ordered me to do the same. The precaution was not wasted. A couple of miles into the forest, Holmes pressed my hand forcefully. Leaning over the seat with his outstretched hand holding a revolver, it was as if he was expecting some invisible foe. And suddenly, despite the darkness, I saw the fairly large, dark silhouette of some strange creature. It sped along the road after us in silent leaps. I had hardly become aware of what was going on, hardly had the thought flashed through my mind that this might be the ape-strangler, when the terrifying creature caught up with us and made a colossal flying leap.

Simultaneously, our shots rang out. The damned creature crashed to the ground.

At exactly the same moment the driver tumbled head over heels off the coach-box and vanished amongst the trees. The horses surged forward, only to be stopped by Holmes's powerful grip. He quickly passed the reins to me and, revolver in hand, jumped off the carriage. He ran a few quick steps towards the animal lying on the ground and a third shot rang out. He returned dragging the dead ape along with him. He threw it in, jumped on the coach-box, seized the reins and we galloped away. We raced through the forest with the speed of lightning. The foaming horses pulled up by the ferry.

We yelled and yelled, but nobody appeared. We had no idea how the ferry operated and ended up wasting the best part of an hour in fruitless activity, jumping on and off it and then alongside.

113

'The devil!' said Holmes fiercely. 'He'll catch up with us.'

We made another desperate attempt and this time success crowned our efforts. Just as we managed to find the end of the mooring rope, we heard the sound of horses galloping, but we had hardly managed to cast off when a troika came straight for us and into the water.

Two men leaped out and before we had time to gather ourselves together, they scrambled on board.

'Aha, so that's what you are up to,' we heard a hoarse voice rage. In that moment I saw Boris Nikolayevitch leap like a cat at Holmes standing by the mooring rope. I threw myself to help him but powerful hands pinioned me.

The ferry forged ahead at full speed and there was nobody to see the life-and-death struggle being waged on board. We fought with every ounce of strength we possessed, we fought tooth and nail as we rolled over and over. In the heat of the struggle I couldn't see what was happening with Holmes. I gathered up my last reserves of strength, seized my opponent by the throat and with every ounce of strength bashed his head in the darkness against the wooden planking. He, too, made a desperate effort, slipped out of my hands to roll over and vanish beneath the waves.

I leapt to my feet to help Holmes. But it was too late. I was nearly at his side, but he was in a deathly embrace with Kartseff and they went overboard together. Holmes vanished out of sight.

I kept on yelling and screaming for him, but the river was as unresponsive as the grave. Somehow I managed to steer the craft to the opposite shore and at the first village I raised the alarm. I invoked the help of the villagers, and entreated them to find my friend.

All night and day we searched and searched. We even requested the help of the village downriver, but all was in vain. Holmes had irrevocably vanished. We searched a further five days but to no avail. I set off for Moscow, where I laid everything before the police. Soon I departed for England, grieving the premature end of my best friend.

4

THE ELUSIVE GANG

P. Nikitin

I

'Surely you notice, my dear Watson, that revolutionary times in Russia affected townspeople and citizens of the Russian Empire generally much more so than those who, up until such times, kept out of the limelight and emerged to show themselves only with the greatest care.'

'Surely that was to be expected,' I replied. 'The turmoil that accompanies revolution invariably deflects conservative elements. In their drive to quell revolution, these elements fail to see the mass of riff-raff who live by theft, robbery, burglary, blackmail and suchlike shady means.'

The conversation between us took place as we sat on a bench along the Tversky Boulevard, where Holmes and I had gone out for some fresh air.

'When I look at the chronicle of current events set out in the local press, I am simply amazed at the sheer number of daring and impertinent robberies systematically carried out in Moscow.

You would think that, having regard to the improved strength of the investigation department instituted with the first revolutionary outbursts, it would be possible to cope with ordinary crime! But it looks as if the opposite is the case.'

While he was saying all this, Holmes drew Kabbalistic symbols in the sand with his cane, while pensively looking up at the investigation department, directly opposite which we sat.

'I think that the reason is clear,' I said, 'if we take into account that at one time all the efforts of the investigation department were solely directed at ferreting out revolutionary organizations, catching terrorists and looking for forbidden literature. Until the revolution got under way, revolutionary organizations were so conspiratorial that catching them was more difficult than catching criminals.'

'But in the revolutionary period,' Sherlock Holmes interrupted me, 'the revolutionary organizations showed their cards far too openly, they operated nearly in the open, as a result of which agents of the security service were able to infiltrate them and this error they haven't been able to correct even now. It goes without saying that investigations into political affairs require little or no effort these days, but concentrating mostly on political investigation leads to the worst elements in society not being under scrutiny any more. Just look, burglaries in Moscow amaze with their unusual and systematic effrontery. Often they are carried out in the town centre in broad daylight and it is only in rare cases that the police are able to solve these crimes quickly.'

It was a hot day. Strollers filled the boulevard. Dust rose all around us. Neither Holmes nor I liked crowds, preferring more quiet places for our strolls. Which is why, when the boulevard became crowded, we exchanged glances and, understanding each other without words, rose from our bench. Exchanging conversational trivia, we were about to make our way towards

Strastniy Boulevard, when we were overtaken by a crowd of drunken hooligans. We sought refuge in a cab.

'There's no getting away from them,' said Sherlock Holmes angrily. 'In general, my dear Watson, if we were to compare Russia with England, there is much to marvel at. You wouldn't encounter a tenth of the number of beggars in London as you would here, even though the number of unemployed in London is several times greater than in Moscow.'

Saying this, he drew a cigar out of its case and threw himself back in his seat. 'When a city or a government isn't sufficiently concerned with the grey mass of people and is only interested in preserving the interests of the bureaucracy and the capitalist class, that's what always happens. The grey mass, driven in on itself, sinks like a stone in water.'

In the meantime, our ghastly cabriolet with its metal wheels stopped outside the Moscow Grand Hotel. We settled with the unprepossessing driver and went to our room.

The first thing that we saw, as we came in, was a sealed envelope placed conspicuously in such a way that we could not miss it.

'I can already anticipate something new,' said Sherlock Holmes, opening and reading it.

'Maxim Vasilyevitch Kliukin, publisher and book store proprietor, invites you, Watson, and me – to see him on an urgent matter,' he added as he finished reading the letter and placed it back on the table.

'And you, of course, are off to see him instantly.'

'But, of course. After all, we haven't done much this month and it wouldn't go amiss to give ourselves a little shake-up. Let's have a leisurely lunch and then make our way along Mohovaya Street, where he owns a store.'

We changed, went down to the restaurant, chose a table and ordered lunch.

*

II

At about five in the afternoon we came out on to the square where the Duma stands, turned into Tversky Boulevard, turned into Mohovaya Street and went in the direction of the university.

'I think I can just about imagine what they'll tell me when we get there,' Holmes said as we walked along. 'If you have read the news in the Moscow papers, you must have seen accounts of a whole number of robberies from major publishers during the last year. Kliukin's publishing house, as well as his book store, are amongst the biggest in Moscow both as regards the number of publications as well as the variety on sale.'

'He probably got taken for quite a lot,' I interrupted, 'but it seems strange that he decided to come to us.'

Sherlock Holmes shrugged, 'In order for you not to be surprised, and to understand the reason, you have only to remember our conversation on Tversky Boulevard.'

Without much trouble, we found Benkendorff House in which Kliukin's store was situated. We asked whether we could see the owner, to which the shop assistant pointed at a lean, dark-haired, middle-aged man sitting at a desk. The desk stood beside one of the display windows and was piled high with papers. We approached him.

'I had the honour of receiving from you today a letter addressed to me at the Moscow Grand Hotel,' said Sherlock Holmes with a bow.

The publisher immediately realized who we are. He shook us by the hand, asked us to wait a few moments and went into a back room.

'My son will be here in a minute and I would ask you to wait for his arrival,' he said when he returned. 'This is not the place to talk about such matters. With your permission, we will adjourn elsewhere, where you will be told in detail everything concerning my request for your presence.'

Holmes bowed silently. Only a couple of minutes passed and a young man, wearing a school uniform, walked in and Maxim Vasilyevitch Kliukin handed him a set of keys, meanwhile asking us to follow.

We followed Kliukin for a couple of hundred steps along Mohovaya Street and found ourselves at the Peterhof tavern. Up the stairs we went and along a corridor with private rooms along it. We passed several doors and entered one of the larger rooms in which, to our great surprise, a fairly large number of people were already waiting. Several rose to meet us when we came in, and Mr Kliukin introduced us.

I don't remember all their surnames, but I did remember Messrs Yefimoff, Karbasnikoff, Suvorin and others. All those present were either publishers or the owners of major book stores.

After the initial polite exchanges, Sherlock Holmes asked Mr Kliukin to come to the point without further ado.

'This is what it is all about,' Maxim Vasilyevitch Kliukin began. 'I speak at the request and on behalf of all those present. We are ten publishers and store owners from which a considerable number of books have vanished this past year. We have searched and searched for them but, so far, to no avail. I accidentally heard of your presence in Moscow and decided to tempt fortune, to ask you for help.'

'I am at your service,' said Holmes.

'You see,' said Kliukin, 'as I have already said, we have no direct evidence against anyone. Nevertheless, owing to certain considerations, we are led to suspect certain minor bookstore proprietors who are buying up goods stolen from us. So far, it is unclear to us who carried out the robberies and how, but we are able to give you the names of ten people who, we think, merit special attention.'

'You will let me write down their names?' asked Holmes and took out a notebook.

'Of course,' said Kliukin. He dictated the names of bookstores in various parts of town with their precise addresses.

'And this is all you have for me?' asked Holmes.

'Alas, yes,' said the publisher.

'Another question.'

'I am listening.'

'Do you sell your books in complete form, i.e. including bindings?'

'Of course, it would be strange if that were not the case,' said the publisher in surprise.

We discussed a few more trivial details and, having carefully written down the addresses of the stores that had been robbed, we bade the company farewell and left the restaurant.

III

For the rest of the day and evening Holmes worked his way with painstaking care through a reference book, occasionally going downstairs to use the telephone. At the same time he called for a courier and told him to order notepaper with the heading 'Ivan Ivanovitch Sergeyev, Publisher,' and this was to be done as a matter of urgency.

Early the next morning the notepaper was delivered by the printer. Again, Holmes got to work on the telephone.

At the same time, I had to find out from all the publishers we had met the previous day what exactly they published and which books were principally stocked in their warehouses during the period of the robberies. A few hours of work and we had quite a list before us.

'And now, Watson, we can get down to some real work,' said Sherlock Holmes with a determined air.

Sitting down to our desk, we divided between us those book stores which the publishers had indicated as under suspicion.

We had four shops each. We each kept a copy of the list.

It is necessary to note that, at the request of Sherlock Holmes, the publishers who had been robbed were asked to give precise figures as to which books and what quantities had been ordered by those under suspicion. None of the figures was considerable. Each had ordered between one and three copies.

'Remember, my dear Watson,' said Sherlock Holmes, 'we will have to visit all the shops and ask for precisely those books which have vanished at the same time. It goes without saying that, in every case, we will ask for a higher number of copies than those the firm ordered.'

I fully comprehended Holmes's thinking. Indeed, this was the only way of coming across any trace.

At the same time, an error was possible and I couldn't refrain from putting it before Holmes. 'It might very well be that, despite the absence of the goods we ask for, the firm would tell us to wait a few minutes while they send a messenger to fetch them from the requisite publisher.'

'Of course,' answered Holmes, 'your presupposition is more than possible. But we can always telephone the publisher and ask whether a messenger came, who sent him and how many copies he took.'

'You are absolutely right!' I had to agree.

'So, let's not waste any further time,' said Holmes, reaching for his hat.

A few minutes later we had left our hotel and each set out on his route. We had to hurry. The day was slowly drawing to a close and the stores were going to shut in a couple of hours.

Having been to four stores, I returned tired and bad-tempered, with nothing to show for my efforts. In all four I got either a direct refusal or I was offered a lesser quantity than I had asked for, though I was told that if I cared to wait, my order would be filled in no time at all.

Moreover, the book store owners, when I told them that I

was opening my own business, assured me that if they were to get the book from the very same publishers I would have to go to myself, I wouldn't be a kopeck worse off. The reason was that they were old customers, were given a sizable discount and they would pass the books on to me leaving for themselves a very small profit. But I'd be getting the books for the same price I'd have to pay the publisher. No matter how cunningly I tried, I could find nothing suspicious that could cast any light on the offer. Upset by my lack of success, I returned to my hotel room, took off my coat and lay down on the couch awaiting Holmes.

Darkness fell.

Sherlock Holmes returned at about eight. He came in with a bold step and from the look on his face I immediately saw that he was satisfied with his excursion.

'A man's eyes and face reflect his inner state,' he said, looking at me with a smile, 'and, hence, I am certain that you are angry at your lack of success.'

He hung his coat up and turned to me, 'But that's how it always is, dear Watson, we look for some item in ten places. It doesn't mean it is in all of them at one and the same time. It has to be somewhere in a single place, and if two or three people were to go in different directions, one of them will certainly find what has been lost, unless, of course, someone has moved it somewhere else.'

'From what you say, I conclude that your excursion has been, in any case, more successful,' I said, feeling better. 'No, really, Holmes, you're lucky. Luck, real luck, dogs your footsteps whichever way you go. I really get to feel jealous, just thinking of your successes. Now, then, isn't it just chance that on this occasion I got the four stores which had nothing suspicious.'

Holmes shrugged indifferently, 'In solving crimes, blind chance often plays a leading role.'

*

IV

'And, so, my dear Holmes, I hope that you will share with me the results of today's labours,' I said.

'With pleasure, dear Doctor,' he answered, sitting down in an armchair and stretching his long legs as was his usual habit.

'Fediukoff's store, which I went to first, proved to be without suspicion,' he began. 'But the second, belonging to a certain Nikanoroff, somewhat did confirm my suspicions There, I found some books I was after, and although the quantity I asked for happened to be considerably higher than their purchase from the publisher, nonetheless, I was handed the quantity I asked for. But most interesting was the fact that several copies were not bound and still in loose-leaf. Imagine my joy! Needless to say, not a single publisher would deliver for sale in such a form. And how could one explain that this sort of goods is being kept in a store, except that it wasn't bought directly from a publisher. To put it bluntly, the book in question must have been obtained directly from the printer and binder, who stole it page by page. I asked Nikanoroff how come the book was not bound. He became embarrassed, said the books had been delivered in a hurry, and offered me a considerable discount. I hope he is now in my grasp, and tomorrow we'll investigate him properly.'

'Is he young?' I asked.

'Well, no,' answered Sherlock Holmes. 'I'd say, forty, and from his outward appearance, not someone I'd like to meet at night in a secluded place.'

'What about the other stores?'

'The fourth, belonging to a Semionoff, made me think all was not in order. The books are all bound, but they are in suspicious quantities, though, of course, that should not be enough to cast suspicion. Semionoff could very well argue that he bought the books from different publishers accidentally, not suspecting them to be stolen. Any accusation would fall apart.'

V

It was still quite early when Holmes woke me next morning. Opening my eyes, I was quite surprised to see an unfamiliar man with red hair and a thick red beard, wearing greasy, high boots and a red calico shirt showing from under his waistcoat.

'What do you want?' I asked, for some reason taking him for a labourer from outside.

The big chap fell about laughing.

'Oh, damn!' I exclaimed, recognizing my friend from his laugh. 'By God, Holmes, you disguise yourself so well every time, the best detective wouldn't know you.'

'Yes, it happens to be one of my chief attributes,' he said merrily, tugging a greasy black cap over his red wig. 'I'm off this very minute on certain business and I'll be back in a few hours. While I am away, will you find yourself an appropriate costume, well, at least one like mine. You'll be more comfortable in it.'

He nodded and was gone. I began to dress. After breakfast I set off for Suhareff Tower and soon acquired all that was necessary.

Two hours later I was completely ready. I changed into my new costume, ordered a cold buffet with wine, and waited for Holmes. I didn't have to wait long. Holmes returned at about ten.

'Now isn't this a treat!' he said, looking at the table which had been set. 'On my way home, I was thinking of a mid-morning snack. We'd best fortify ourselves as we might not be able to do so for some considerable time.'

We had a leisurely breakfast-cum-lunch while Holmes expounded on what he had been up to.

'Yes, my dear Watson, you may compliment me on the wide circle of acquaintances amongst street bookstalls which I have made today. And getting to know the porter of the building in which Nikanoroff has his bookstore didn't get in the way of progress, either. And just imagine what I discovered!'

'Well?'

'Nikanoroff is not Nikanoroff at all. He is actually Gabriel Voropayeff. The book store is registered in Nikanoroff's name, but he is unknown to the smaller stallholders and is never seen there, not as Nikanoroff. Gabriel Voropayeff, the boss, is the chap I had the pleasure of dealing with yesterday and he is nick-named Gavriushka. I gather, from hints dropped by others, that he is a somewhat shadowy figure. Luckily, there is a third-rate tavern opposite his premises and from it we'll be able to observe who comes and goes in and out of it.'

He fell silent and set about polishing off the roast beef. Having eaten, we left the hotel, with the suspicious eyes of grand-looking porters and door-keepers examining us from head to toe.

VI

'Perhaps I am mistaken, but I thought your absence was over-long,' I said as we strode along.

'Yes, I did stop off at a few more places,' he answered. 'I hope you won't think it strange that as of today I am the assistant to the warehouseman of the publisher Dmitry Panfilovitch Yefimoff.'

'Whatever for?' I asked in surprise.

'I had to do it to familiarize myself with his employees. Besides that, I was able to drop in on Kliukin, Karbasnikoff and other publishers who had suffered losses. I may now proudly say that I can easily recognize each of their employees.'

Thus, talking shop, we got as far as the book store outside which a black-and-white sign proclaimed: NIKANOROFF BOOKS. We crossed the road into an unclean, third-rate tavern, took a table by the window and ordered tea. Three hours passed in utter boredom and I cannot remember a single day of my life when I drank so much tea.

Although Sherlock Holmes did appear totally at ease, I could see that he never dropped his eyes from the place across the road, examining with a close eye everyone who went in or out. We were going out of our minds from sheer boredom and finally left.

Not being familiar with the employees of the publishers who had been robbed, I couldn't tell whether any of them were the ones who had been to Nikanoroff. However, since Holmes was making little notes from time to time, he had probably found familiar acquaintances amongst the visitors.

Having left the tavern, we strolled about for an hour or so, returned to our observation post and again got to drinking tea. Sometimes, I still wonder how I managed to survive all that tea.

Little by little, darkness fell. At seven o'clock precisely the shops began to close down. An athletic-looking, dark-haired man with the face of a gangster appeared on the threshold of Nikanoroff's shop. Two employees appeared with him and the three began to put up shutters over windows and doors.

'Quite the sympathetic looker, not so?' Sherlock Holmes whispered ironically, indicating the athletic, dark-haired man with a nod of his head.

'I take it, from your previous account, that this is undoubtedly the owner of the store,' I said.

'Spot on! This is Gavriushka Voropayeff, whom we are yet certain to be dealing with,' answered Holmes.

Having locked up, Gavriushka stroked his beard as if he had all the time in the world and, having said something to his sales-men, made his leisurely way towards the tavern. I saw Holmes's eyes light up when the man came in. Fortunately for us, he sat down at an adjoining table and asked for tea. Some twenty minutes later, a middle-aged, crafty-looking man walked in. He looked round, saw our man, approached and greeted him, and sat down beside him.

'Well, then?' asked Gavriushka out of the side of his mouth.

'All right, everything's OK,' was the answer.

'Look out, Fomka, see that you take care. You know for your-self, there's new measures being undertaken. See that nothing comes out.'

The new arrival waved his hand cheerfully as if he did not have a care in the world, 'They got the wrong 'uns!'

Gavriushka Voropayeff grinned smugly.

They were so near that we could hear every word, even when they lowered their voices to a whisper. For a while they fell silent.

'I'm off to Petersburg tomorrow,' Gavriushka Voropayeff said at last. 'You tell the lads to get together in three days time. We'll meet in the same tavern, in the back room.'

'Done!' answered Fomka. 'Is something going on in Petersburg?'

'I don't just go for no reason. I'm simply tearing myself apart. Have to get to Petersburg and Nijni and Kharkoff. I am being summoned from all over.'

'That's it, you see. It is having a business that covers the whole of Russia,' said Fomka smugly.

'I'll manage,' answered Gavriushka.

They chatted for a few more minutes and left. We settled our bill and went after them. Out in the street, we saw that Voropayeff had said goodbye to Fomka, after which they parted ways.

'That chappie will have to be watched,' said Holmes, nodding his head in Fomka's direction.

We followed him at a distance. This time it was a longish jour-ney. Fomka must have been a man very careful with his money. He didn't even take a tram, and we had to follow him as far as Marina Grove.

Fixing the house he had gone into, we halted for a minute and then, as if by accident, came up to the gates. Holmes asked me to wait, vanishing into the courtyard. He returned a few minutes later, making a sign for me to follow. We met around the corner.

'Well, have you found anything out?' I asked.

'Of course,' answered Holmes. 'That ten-kopeck coin I slipped the yard man must've had magical properties. Actually, I suspect Fomka upset him in some way, since he cursed him up and down behind his back. Fomka's real name is Ivan Vihliayeff, but amongst the riff-raff he is known as Fomka Nikishkin. The yard man reckons he was in jug thrice and reckons it won't be long before he goes in again.'

We walked silently for some time. Holmes was deep in thought. 'My dear Watson,' he said at last, 'you'll have to go to Petersburg.'

'If it is absolutely necessary,' I answered, 'of course, I'll go.'

'And you have committed Gavriushka Voropayeff's face to memory?'

'Oh, yes!'

'In that case, you'll have to keep him under observation tomorrow and then travel with him, but I do beg of you not to let him slip out of your hands.'

'I think you can depend on me,' I answered. 'Long practice with you has taught me a thing or two and if all that is required is to follow a man, I should be able to carry out such an assignment successfully.'

We caught a cab and returned to our hotel. That evening we dropped in on Dmitry Panfilovitch Yefimoff.

'Do you believe in intuition?' Holmes asked him.

'Not really,' answered the publisher.

Holmes shrugged, 'Pity! But I do, and in my personal experience, there have often been occasions when my intuition has proved correct. Take now, for example. I have a feeling that tonight you will be robbed. I suggest you join us in setting up an ambush.'

'If necessary,' muttered Dmitry Panfilovitch Yefimoff.

'Right-o! It's late and all your employees are fast asleep, so we won't be noticed. Take a torch with you.'

Dmitry Panfilovitch disappeared and was soon back suitably dressed with a torch in his hand. Within a few minutes we were entering Bahrushin House, where his storehouse was situated. He began to undo the locks.

'Oho!' exclaimed Holmes, 'Five locks! Unlikely the thief will come this way. A better assumption would be that he is going to come through a passageway from a cellar next door.'

We entered and secured five locks after which Holmes lit a lamp and got to work. He meticulously examined all four walls.

'The cellar from the house opposite goes under Kozitsky Alley,' explained Yefimoff. 'My cellar is a couple of yards short of that.'

'That's very important,' said Holmes, approaching the wall.

His attention increased. But no matter which way he turned, no matter how many chinks he looked into, he found nothing. An hour of this, and Sherlock Holmes had to admit defeat. His efforts had been in vain.

'There must be a way, of that I am certain,' he muttered. 'But it is done too well. Well, there's no other way. We'll have to sit it out. The thief will show us where his burrow lies.'

And he began to indicate our places to us. As for himself, he placed himself along the side wall where the passageway was most likely to be found. Yefimoff was hidden by the door behind bundles of goods. I was placed in the middle. The hours crept by wearily, but, at last, a dull sound came to our ears. We froze and held our breath.

And this is when something happened that even Sherlock Holmes did not expect. The door lock clicked. Then a second, and a third, and a fourth and a fifth . . . and the door opened.

In the doorway of the dark warehouse, Fomka's figure appeared in outline. He looked round carefully and made a few steps forward, holding a large bunch of keys in his hand.

I looked at Holmes. He sat there hunched, like a cat waiting for a mouse, ready to spring.

Fomka advanced slowly in the direction of Yefimoff. And suddenly the unexpected happened and totally upset our calculations. The appearance of the thug must have frightened Yefimoff. And instead of calmly waiting, he suddenly sprang back like a madman and, at the top of his voice, yelled, 'Stop thief!'

Fomka sprang towards the door. Holmes flew out of his spot like an arrow, but it was already too late. Fomka was through the door, slamming it shut after him, while Holmes, unable to stop in time, careened into it forehead first.

By the time we made it to the street, Fomka was far away. We heard him jabber something as he was caught in a leash by which a student was leading a dog, saw how he stumbled head over heels, as did the dog, but that only delayed him for a moment. Ignoring the student's curses, he was up and away and soon was hidden from view. Willy-nilly, we had to return.

'And you just had to start howling,' Holmes said with reproach directed at Yefimoff, who, in the meantime, had come to and joined in the chase.

'It's all right for you to talk,' was the answer. 'This is the sort of thing that you're used to, while it's a first time for me.'

There was nothing to be done. The red-headed thug had vanished and after a few exchanges we went home.

VII

We spent the whole of the following morning taking turns in the tavern opposite Gavriushka Voropayeff's bookstore ostensibly owned by Nikanoroff. It was my turn when, through the window, I saw Gavriushka emerging. He spent a long time haggling with the cabbie and they were finally off.

I was after him and soon we were at the Nikolayevsk Railway Station. It was twenty minutes before the next train to Petersburg. I saw Gavriushka Voropayeff in the queue for third-class tickets and got an errand-boy to get me a ticket also.

The journey to Petersburg passed quickly enough and because I was travelling second class, I hardly saw Gavriushka. But then, at Tver, I was fortunate enough to see him go to the telegraph office and, standing behind him on the pretext, that I, too, was sending a telegram, I read his over his shoulder as he was so short. It was addressed to Panova's Book Store in Petersburg, personally to an employee named Seriogin. The text was short and to the point: ARRIVING THIS MORNING. MEET ME.

The telegram was a real find. Now, at least, I had some sort of key. Arriving in Petersburg, a fairly well-dressed young man approached Gavriushka Voropayeff on the platform. They greeted each other, spoke and made their way to the exit.

I left my case with its change of clothes in the station baggage room and followed them at some distance. At Liteiniy Prospect they turned right and soon we were over the Neva River. After some zig-zagging along the narrow alleys of the Viborg bank, Seriogin and Gavriushka went into a small tavern, whose customers must have been mostly cab drivers as there was a large cab station next door.

I waited five minutes and followed them in. There was no vacant table next to them, so I had to occupy another that was one removed.

Gavriushka and Seriogin were, evidently, deeply involved in their own conversation and though they kept their voices low, from time to time some words reached me. They were haggling. The greedy Gavriushka would raise his voice quite considerably whenever money was mentioned.

'No, fellow, I simply can't. You know yourself how things are. Isn't a quarter enough! You can check every penny on me, but that's all I have. All that'd be left for me would be ten roubles for a return ticket and a cheap meal,' he said heatedly.

But Seriogin wouldn't give in, 'As you wish, but I won't settle for anything less than fifty,' he said firmly.

'Then feel free to go to anyone else,' said Gavriushka angrily.

Seriogin shrugged, 'Well, then, so we will. You're not the only game in town. There's plenty more,' he said nastily.

They lowered their voices and renewed their haggling. Gavriushka haggled with such emotion that perspiration began to run down his face. But it appeared that he wasn't getting his way. As their argument became more heated, their voices rose and became more and more hoarse.

Gavriushka became completely transformed. His face grew scarlet. His greedy eyes shone as if he were mad and his fingers convulsed into fists. 'Just you wait then,' he shouted, unable to contain himself any longer.

Seriogin looked at him and jeered, 'Let's see – who of us will wait and whom it'll suit best is still to be seen, but I'll say it'll be the worse for you,' he said and laughed in Gavriushka's face.

'So that's how you intend to carry on,' shouted Gavriushka, leaping out of his chair. And before the onlookers, who had begun to be interested in their quarrel, could react, he picked up a saucer from the table and let fly at Seriogin with it. If Seriogin hadn't managed to duck, the saucer would have smashed into his face. But it had been thrown with such force that it hit the opposite wall and with a ring fell to pieces on the floor.

Seriogin, in turn, seized a cup of tea and threw the contents into Gavriushka's face. 'Freshen up with that and calm down, because I can smash all this china over your blasted head,' he said, looking at the panic-stricken Gavriushka, now wiping his scalded face with a table serviette.

The hot shower, it seemed, had its intended effect on Gavriushka. He threw a series of curses at his friend and sat down again, curtly dismissing the waiter who had appeared, saying to him, 'What are you doing here! Go about your own business! We have our own to look after and we know each other well enough. Don't bother us.'

The brief outburst also seemed to have an effect on Seriogin. Both began to give ground and before long I noticed that they shook hands in the friendliest manner.

'So, thirty-five,' said Gavriushka

'I'll be bringing the stuff to the station in four hours,' said Seriogin, 'and then that'll be that.'

Their haggling over, they ordered vodka and bits and pieces to eat and began to speak so softly I could no longer follow what they were saying.

Not wishing to arouse their suspicions, I left and walked my way to the railway station, where I waited for them to appear. There was still plenty of time to dine.

Soon Gavriushka appeared. An hour or so later he was followed by Seriogin in a cab with two sizable baskets. Gavriushka took the baskets and counted out thirty-five roubles. Judging by the expression on his face, he parted with the money only very reluctantly.

Seriogin left, while the thrifty Gavriushka, sitting on one of the baskets, patiently waited for a train. As soon as the train arrived, Gavriushka began to lug his cargo into the coach. Not one to spend so much as ten kopecks on a porter, he carried them in himself, perspiring from the effort, having also spent a good five minutes in a heated argument with the conductor who hadn't wanted to let him on board with such large-sized baskets.

Eventually the matter was settled and Gavriushka, heaving and blowing, managed to accommodate his cargo on shelves above the seats. I lost him on the way to Moscow, as we travelled in separate coaches.

Before departing from Petersburg, I managed to send Holmes a telegram and he met me in Moscow. I described briefly for him everything I had seen and heard, and asked, shouldn't we be watching Gavriushka further.

'Oh, no, there's no point,' answered Holmes. 'It goes without saying that he will take his goods to the bookstore, and we're better off dropping in on him in an hour's time, when he will be going through what he has brought with him.'

We hired a cab and drove back to our hotel, chatting and asking each other about the results of our endeavours during the last few days. Just as I had expected, Holmes had wasted no time during my two-day absence.

'My dear Watson, it would appear we are dealing with a fairly large and well-organized gang, operating under Gavriushka's leadership in major centres throughout the whole of Russia with the criminal, Fomka Nikishkin, graciously contributing to the success of the enterprise. They are meeting today and I have already taken steps by which I can enter into their conspiracy.'

'How did you do it?' I asked.

'Very simply,' said Holmes with a smile. 'Once you find one end of the thread that, in itself, is enough to unravel the entire ball of thread. On this occasion I undertook a very simple action. As you know, at least temporarily I am assistant warehouse manager at Mr Kliukin's place. That day, when we sat in the tavern opposite Gavriushka Voropayeff's place, I saw one of Kliukin's employees going in for some reason. I made inquiries, only to discover he hadn't been sent by anyone. This was enough for me to conclude that this employee must be on the best of terms with Gavriushka. Two days' work in the warehouse and I uncovered the fact that this chap, Ivan Buroff by name, also helps out packing cargo dispatched to the provinces. It was no problem for me to get to know him. An evening in his company in Zvereff's Tavern in Kozitzky Alley and we were fast friends.'

'You are, indeed, a wizard,' I exclaimed, listening to Holmes's account. 'And what did your friendship lead to, then?'

'First of all, we both got drunk, well, he more than I. He seemed to see in me a pack leader, and when I finally hinted that it would be mutually profitable to collaborate, he saw the point immediately. Finally, he showed his cards. He said he regretted I hadn't appeared earlier. He found it difficult to work on his own, but he assured me that working with him, what with me as an assistant warehouse manager, could lead to us both making quite a lot of money. On the third day of our acquaintanceship, we managed to drag away a hundred books, which we temporarily placed in a room I had set aside in the warehouse.'

'So far I am with you,' I exclaimed. 'But what about the conference?'

Holmes laughed merrily.

'You have to understand that I am now, so to speak, one of the gang, having been inducted by working for it and, of course, having full right to attend general meetings of this all-Russia enterprise.'

'Have you, at least, spoken to Kliukin?'

'Of course, though mind you, he hadn't even noticed the thieving that took place. He has so many books piled up in his warehouse that they cannot be properly sorted out and the only way to solve the crime is by a thorough stock-taking in the book-shop and warehouse. And that only takes place once a year.'

'What time is the conference?'

'At nine in the evening.'

At the hotel, we went up to our room and I lay down to rest. However short the journey, nevertheless it had tired me out and it was with considerable relief that I slept for a couple of hours on my soft bed.

VIII

I woke from my nap to find Sherlock Holmes out. With nothing to do, I began to read the papers, which took up the rest of the day and part of the evening. Holmes returned that evening at ten, somewhat depressed and dissatisfied with something.

'You look as if all is not well,' I asked, 'is that so?'

'Indeed, the day has not been much of a success,' he answered.

'Perhaps you didn't get to the meeting of conspirators?'

'I got to it, all right, except that Gavriushka turned out to be much more cautious than I anticipated,' Sherlock Holmes began. 'He noticed my presence at once, and although he was some-what reassured when Buroff announced that I had already taken part in their work, despite that he had me leave on the grounds that I was insufficiently known to him.'

For some minutes, Holmes paced up and down the room, deep in thought.

'We'll have to see Kliukin today. I want a sudden, unexpected inventory carried out. If he agrees, I shall also go to the criminal investigation department and ask for Gavriushka's and Semionoff's premises to be searched. Would you like to come with me, Watson?'

'With pleasure,' I answered.

Wasting no time, we dressed, stopped a cab and instructed the driver to take us to Vagankovsk Alley, where Kliukin lived. He was home and immediately took us through to his office and shut the door. Holmes gave him the results of his surveillance in a few words and asked whether he would like to turn to the investigation department with a request to make a sudden search of the shops belonging to Gavriushka Voropayeff and Semionoff.

'And so, I await only your consent to carry out a search,' said Holmes.

For some minutes Kliukin was deep in thought. 'All right,' he said at last. 'If you consider it necessary, so be it.'

'And I may make the request to the head of the criminal investigation department in your name?'

'Of course.'

137

On this, the business part of our conversation ended and we turned to other matters. We stayed till half past eleven and returned to the hotel. That night Holmes didn't sleep in the hotel and when I asked where he intended to stay the night, he said, 'Shared lodgings. Perhaps I'll learn something new and interesting from Buroff.'

I only saw him at two on the afternoon of the next day.

'Well, my dear Watson,' he said, entering our hotel room, 'on this occasion we didn't err.'

'What happened?' I asked, knowing perfectly well that a man like Holmes wasn't likely to waste a night and half a day in vain.

'I had a good time with Buroff in the tavern,' answered Holmes.

'And you found something out?'

'Not all that much. Yesterday's meeting was quite stormy. Gavriushka is very tight when it comes to money and he was nearly beaten up because of it. By the way, Fomka Nikishkin did land him one in the face. I suspect Fomka somewhat lords it over him.'

'And what were they talking about?' I asked.

'Much as what I had assumed. First of all, Gavriushka explained to his suppliers which goods were most likely to move quickly and asked them to be good enough to devote their attention towards acquiring just these goods. Next he proceeded to pay off some and asked that employees of publishers not yet in his hands should be invited to join the operation. At the end, there was the usual wrangling over money. Gavriushka wanted to lower his payments, but was nearly beaten up so he gave way. He got so upset that he went off and got drunk with Buroff and some other fellow. The trio got to meet some young lady, who lifted a hundred roubles out of his pocket.'

As if remembering something very humorous, Holmes burst out laughing.

'What on earth are you laughing at?' I asked in surprise.

'This is just the sort of thing that so clearly characterizes someone,' Holmes said cheerfully. 'Here is a man, Watson, who watches every penny, and from whom a hundred roubles is stolen. He only noticed the loss of the money after he got home with Buroff. It was a scene worthy of a great play. Imagine a man in the grip of such a state of rage that he forgot the presence of his lawfully wedded wife. "I'll show her," he yelled so loudly that he could be heard in every room. "I'll see the police get on to her. She stole a hundred roubles!" And he kept on yelling he'd have the police on her.

'So far his wife couldn't understand what was going on, so she asked, "Who stole what?"

' "What do you mean 'who'? That woman I visited."

'It was so funny, my dear Watson! Here he was, hopping up and down in sheer rage, and unaware he was letting on to his wife what he had been up to!'

Now suddenly Holmes became serious, adding, 'And, then, today, together with various ranks of the investigative police, we carried out a search of his and Semionoff's business premises.'

'And did you find anything?'

'Of course. Nine thousand roubles worth of goods. Kliukin was able to recognize some six thousand roubles worth that belonged to him. But Gavriushka Voropayeff remains untouched. The shop is in Nikanoroff's name and he's not in Moscow. We have to have weightier evidence before Gavriushka can be charged.'

He fell silent for a minute and then went on, 'Watson, if you were only to see the hatred with which he looked at Maxim Vasilyevitch Kliukin when the latter entered accompanied by members of the investigation department. I am sure that glance bodes ill and he will try to be avenged.'

'Undoubtedly,' I agreed.

'Which is why we cannot let him out of our sight for a single moment.'

'You are suggesting—?'

'We have to take our places at our observation point without delay.'

'I'm ready,' I said.

'In that case, let's change.' With these words, Holmes opened his suitcase, took out two well-worn suits and handed one to me saying, 'The wigs and make-up are in the travelling bag.'

Within a few minutes not even our closest acquaintances would have recognized us. Wearing untidy black wigs and in well-worn clothes, we looked like a couple of roughnecks. The difficulty was to get out of the hotel without attracting the suspicions of the staff. This was not easy. We looked far from presentable, and the presence of a couple of such ill-dressed men wouldn't pass unnoticed at the Moscow Grand.

But Holmes rose to the occasion. Included in his wardrobe were a couple of perfectly respectable overcoats and two English felt hats. Once we put them on, we looked fairly respectable. We hid a couple of fairly filthy peaked caps in our pockets and left our hotel room. But even so, we attracted the suspicions of the senior porter. 'Where are you coming from?' he accosted us roughly.

'Number forty-three,' said Holmes quickly. 'From that British subject, Holmes.'

Such an answer, so boldly pronounced, evidently satisfied the man. He probably knew Holmes's true profession and, deciding we were working for him in some capacity, let us pass.

In a quiet alleyway we changed our hats, substituting them for our torn caps and rubbed a little dirt into our coats. And now we could go to the tavern which was our observation post. At about five in the afternoon we were in place.

IX

Sitting by the window, we fixed our gaze on the window of the bookstore opposite. Gavriushka appeared at the window several times and looked as if he was anxious about something. We drank tea for the sake of appearance, while carrying on a desultory conversation.

Seven o'clock. No sooner had the hand of my watch reached seven than the tavern door opened and Fomka came in. He looked gloomy and sullen. He ordered tea and took a seat with his back to us in the most distant corner.

A few minutes later, we saw Gavriushka and two employees leave the shop and begin to lock up. This done, he cast a suspicious look round, said something to the other two, and made his way quickly into the tavern. He saw Fomka in his corner at once and went straight to him. Then, having made sure they were not under observation, he bent towards Fomka, whispered something in his ear and, quickly leaving the tavern, was lost outside amidst the crowd.

Fomka waited a few minutes, settled his bill and also left. We followed him at once.

At the Strastniy Monastery, Fomka jumped aboard a tram car going to the Ustinsk Bridge. We hailed a cab and instructed him to follow. At Yauza, Fomka jumped off and went into one of the cheap taverns along the banks of this smelly little river.

'We'd better wait for him here,' said Holmes. 'Our appearance is bound to raise his suspicion.'

In the meantime, darkness was falling and we had to get nearer the tavern not to lose sight of Fomka when he emerged. Nine struck from a clock tower. A little while later and Gavriushka's familiar figure appeared outside the entrance of the tavern. He looked round carefully, went in and a minute later emerged, accompanied by Fomka.

They turned right along the river bank. Luckily for us, there was no street lighting here, so we moved silently after them. Several hundred steps on, we found ourselves in a silent, deserted locality. The figures of Gavriushka and Fomka were now hardly discernable in front of us. They finally stopped and began to descend quietly down to the river.

'Crawl!' Holmes whispered.

We stretched out on the ground and, like snakes, followed for some twenty-five paces. The darkness helped us.

Gavriushka was talking to Fomka about something or other, but all we could hear were snatches of what he was saying: 'Tomorrow . . . the damned fellow won't get away . . . get nearer . . . Peterhof . . . you'll counterfeit Yefimoff's. . . .' From time to time he snarled in fury. He raved.

Fomka's replies, delivered in a cold tone of voice, were short and sharp. 'So, tomorrow at the Peterhof at three,' we heard.

Then they dropped their voices again and we only heard the end of their conversation. 'Everyone scattered . . . well, that's to the good . . . let them look for witnesses if they can.'

There was more whispering about something and then they climbed up to the river bank again.

X

'And so, my dear Watson, till tomorrow. At three in the afternoon we will most probably see something interesting at the Peterhof restaurant.'

Our adversaries had vanished and we followed them no further. Returning back to town, we made our way directly to Kliukin.

'You've probably come with something new,' he greeted us.

'I don't wish to anticipate events,' answered Holmes with a smile, 'and only came to ask you about one or two things.'

'I'm listening.'

'Tomorrow you will very likely receive, in one form or another, something connected with the Peterhof restaurant. Regardless of whoever speaks or writes to you about it, please be on your guard and do nothing and go nowhere without letting me know beforehand.'

'Is that all?' Kliukin asked with a smile.

'So far, yes. Regarding Gavriushka and Semionoff, I suggest that you immediately give instructions that any goods dispatched by them to any destination will be intercepted along the way.'

'I've already done that,' answered Kliukin.

'That's excellent! It will only confirm the evidence against them, not that it is likely any more evidence will be necessary after tomorrow.'

We chatted for a while, bade him goodbye and returned to our hotel. The senior porter, having already seen us in our get-up, let us through.

Back in our hotel room, Homes changed into decent-looking clothes and suggested I do the same. Puzzled, I did as I was told and we were soon ready.

Again we emerged from our hotel, called a cab and Holmes instructed him to take us to the Peterhof restaurant.

It was already after midnight and the place was full. We just about managed to get a table. We ordered a light supper, but I could see from the look in Holmes's eyes that he wasn't interested in it. Other things were on his mind.

Half an hour later and I detected Gavriushka flash by through the door leading to the private rooms. Holmes immediately went in pursuit, but was back a minute later, sat down calmly and said quietly, 'Now they won't get away.'

The restaurant was preparing to close down and, nothing having happened, we went out with the other diners. Gavriushka and Fomka emerged with us. We saw them hail a cab and go off quickly.

Holmes went back, rang the restaurant bell and whispered something to the porter who opened the door and admitted us. Holmes put a ten-rouble note in the porter's hand and we followed him along the corridor into one of the private rooms. Holmes switched on the electric light and began to examine the floor and walls. This took him half an hour. He proceeded to thank the porter, took me by the arm and we returned home where we fell fast asleep.

XI

At one in the afternoon there was a knock on the door of our hotel room. It was a messenger with a letter. Holmes opened it and read, 'I received an invitation from Yefimoff to present myself at the Peterhof restaurant at three this afternoon. I am informing you as requested. Kliukin.'

We threw our coats on, ran out and jumped into the first available cab, which took us to Mohovaya Street.

'I have no idea what this is about,' said Kliukin, meeting us with a smile.

'You'll know soon enough,' answered Sherlock Holmes, 'but let me warn you, be careful entering the private room . . . don't step into it right away.'

'Is this some sort of hoax or are you trying to mystify me?' exclaimed Kliukin in surprise.

'Whatever it is, you'll soon be thanking me,' Holmes answered solemnly. 'And I hope your wife will also be very grateful.'

'I don't understand.'

'You don't have to yet.'

Holmes looked at his watch and said it was time to make for the restaurant, adding that Kliukin had to go in a separate cab and not to show by so much as the slightest sign that we were following him. So that's what we did.

Some twenty minutes later, Kliukin's cab deposited him at the restaurant and we followed closely behind as if we were total strangers.

'The name is Kliukin. Which private dining-room is my invitation for?'

'Let me show you,' said the porter.

Kliukin followed him and we followed Kliukin as if we were chance strangers.

'Here you are,' said the porter, indicating one of the doors along the corridor, and left.

Kliukin opened the door, stepped over the threshold and stopped in utter perplexity. Gavriushka and Fomka seized him by his hands and tried to slam the door shut.

But this was not to be. Like an enraged beast, Sherlock Holmes threw himself forward. Gavriushka and Fomka froze from the unforeseen interruption and let go of Kliukin's hand.

Holmes threw himself at Gavriushka, gave him a mighty thump to the head, then seized his shoulders and pushed him in the direction of the divan. And now imagine my own surprise. Gavriushka vanished through an aperture that opened in the floor.

Holmes didn't give Fomka a chance to recover from his surprise at this turn of events. We bound his hands and legs and only then Holmes yelled, 'Police! Call the police!'

A quarter of an hour later the restaurant was full of policemen of every rank and sort as well as agents of the criminal investigation department, all of them warned in advance by Holmes.

Holmes led everyone to the open trapdoor and said, 'The villain has fallen into the snare which he prepared last night for Maxim Vasilyevitch Kliukin. This is what I learnt from the porter. He and Fomka locked themselves up all day in this private dining-room. Sawing through the floor boards wasn't much of a problem. Having completed their work, they fastened the trapdoor in place, waxed the slits and, of course, ordered that the room should not be let to anyone else. Gavriushka handed out a good ten roubles in bribes. In the space under the floor boards was where they would have strangled you. I can only wonder at the depth of hatred that could bring a young fellow like that to plan such a horrible revenge. Fortunately, I followed him and was able to discover his work, otherwise, Maxim Vasilyevitch, things would have been the worse for you. I congratulate you on your deliverance from the hands of these villains. I look forward to meeting you later this evening, but in the meantime, I trust you will permit me to take my leave. My task is not yet completed. I have yet to make certain other arrangements concerning finding more of your stolen goods in the provinces.' He then turned to the police. 'As for those two fellows, gentlemen, you'll have to hold on to them and to hold on to them tightly. One of them already has half a dozen crimes he has escaped answering for and, of course, it is unlikely he will escape this time.'

He shook hands with Kliukin standing there completely taken aback and we both left.

5

THE PEARL OF THE EMIR

P. Nikitin

I

That was the year the Emir of Bukhara visited Russia. Accompanied by a considerable retinue, he travelled displaying all the splendour and opulence of the East.

Having paid a visit to Petersburg, he was returning home, but decided not to travel by rail but along the Volga. The weather was fine, with clear sunny days which lured him out of his stuffy carriage to breathe the open air. Orders were dispatched from Petersburg to Nijni-Novgorod to prepare a ship exclusively for the Emir and the town prepared to welcome this important guest.

At the time, Holmes and I were travelling along the Volga and stopped over at Nijni-Novgorod for a few days. We delayed our departure because of the Emir. We had been about to leave, when we heard of his impending arrival and stayed on to enjoy the brilliant spectacle. He arrived on the appointed day. With his retinue, all in gold and jewels, he literally flashed through the town and vanished aboard their ship. Holmes and I, and a crowd of curious sightseers, accompanied them as far as the wharf and then went home.

Less than an hour passed. Holmes and I were chatting, I think it was about Eastern peoples, when the door of our hotel room opened slightly and the lackey who looked after our corridor poked his head through the door and told Holmes that he was wanted by the Bukharans.

'What's happened?' asked Holmes.

'The Chief of Police and some Bukharans wish to see you,' he said.

'How strange!' Sherlock Holmes wondered. 'As far as I know, I have never met a single Bukharan. Oh, well, show them in.'

The head was withdrawn and a couple of minutes later the Chief of Police, accompanied by a couple of Bukharans, one of whom was an interpreter, came in. Sherlock Holmes introduced himself, then me, and asked the reason for such an unusual visit.

'Not as unusual as it may appear to you,' said the Chief of Police. 'Something very unpleasant has happened to His Highness, the Emir of Bukhara. I was sent for to assist in the matter, but I, knowing that you are temporarily staying here, advised that you should be brought in, in connection with the matter. With your assistance, the lost item will be recovered ten times faster.'

'I am flattered,' Holmes bowed. 'Of course, I shall try to be worthy of your opinion, but surely you have enough qualified policemen of your own?'

'Hmm . . . how shall I put it?' The Chief of Police was clearly uncomfortable. 'Yes, we have more than enough, and if I were to include the entire membership of the Union of the Russian People, there'd be more than are necessary, but . . . how can I put it better? You understand . . . in the last few years much has been annulled by the revolution and they are all specialized to good effect where political investigation was involved, much to the

148

detriment of criminal investigation. But you are an expert in criminal investigation, never having touched political matters and, of course, are bound to be infinitely better, and this is why I pin more hope on you than all my underlings.'

'Every state has its own way of doing things,' said Holmes with an imperceptible little smile. 'By the way, what you say is true and I am willing to help to the best of my abilities.'

'That's wonderful!' exclaimed the Chief of Police. 'And now that this matter is settled, I can go. I have matters to which I must attend. My task was only to convince you to take this on. I have the honour of taking my leave.'

He bade farewell to us and the Bukharans and was gone.

II

Sherlock Holmes invited the two strangers to sit and tell him what was the matter. The older of the two was richly dressed in silk robes with stars on his chest. With a self-important air, he sank into a sofa and said something to Holmes in his incomprehensible tongue. Holmes heard him out with the patience of a statue.

When the Bukharan had finished, the interpreter took over. First of all, he announced that before us sat none other than a Minister of the Court of His Highness, the Emir of Bukhara, Hadji-Mehti-Mashadi-Mahomet-Sultan.

Next, speaking on behalf of Hadji-Mehti-Mashadi-Mahomet-Sultan, he came to business, heaping masses of praise on the famous detective, every possible flattering mention and thanks that Holmes had undertaken to help His Highness to find the missing memento of his mother, so dear to him. And only after having delivered himself of all this and given a few answers to Holmes's queries, at a sign from the Minister of the Court, the interpreter set about explaining the heart of the matter.

'It happened today,' he began. 'His Highness, having toured the town, made his way with his retinue to the wharf of the "Along the Volga" shipping line where the ship prepared for him was waiting.

'It must be said that His Highness has one precious item which he particularly cherishes. This is a ring with a huge black pearl in the form of a pear. This pearl came to him from his mother, whom he loved very much. After her death, he had it set in a ring, but as he was afraid to lose or damage it, he wore it only at official functions, and as soon as a function was over, he would take it off immediately and hide it. The black pearl is regarded as a gloriously beautiful rarity. Foreign notable valued it at a million and a half roubles in your currency.'

'Oho! That's worth going to some trouble over,' exclaimed Sherlock Holmes. 'Such an amount must be the size of a Bukharan state loan.'

'Of course,' agreed the interpreter. 'Today, in advance of his arrival in Nijni-Novgorod, His Highness placed the ring on his finger. He wore it as he rode through the town and when he went on board. When the first whistle blew, His Highness went to his cabin to change out of his offical dress and change into his travel clothes. There were guards outside his quarters. He was helped to wash and change. Before he washed his hands, he took his ring off and placed it on the washbasin. He sent away his valet and the Emir remembers that when the valet left, the ring was still where he had put it down. On his way out of the bedroom, His Highness neglected to put on the ring, but when he went out on deck, he remembered and returned immediately.

'Imagine his consternation when the ring was no longer there. The alarm was raised. The sentries swear that nobody else had followed His Highness in or out of his bedroom. The soldiers who came with us on this trip are the Emir's most loyal and faithful men. Moreover, they are so arranged that they watch each other. So there is no foundation for doubting their word.

Nonetheless, they were all searched, but there were no clues to indicate anyone had entered the Emir's quarters.'

'Strange,' said Holmes. 'Perchance the Emir put the ring somewhere and simply forgot where.'

'Oh, no,' was the interpreter's rejoinder. 'His Highness has a very good memory and, besides, values the ring highly.'

'What else has been done to find the ring?'

The interpreter addressed Mahomet-Sultan in Bukharan and listened respectfully to his reply, which he then translated for Holmes. 'The ship is ringed on all sides by Russian police and our sentries both on shore and on the water.'

'On the water, how?'

'Around the ship, on the Volga, there are boats with sentries.'

'How soon after the theft were the sentries put in place?'

'As soon as the Emir announced the theft had taken place, that very moment Mahomet-Sultan ordered the ship to be surrounded on all sides and nobody was to be permitted on or off without being searched.'

'But did anyone get off the ship after that?'

'No.'

'Do you know this for a fact?'

'Yes, but you had best ask the sentries.'

A brief silence ensued.

'Yes ... a strange occurrence,' Sherlock Holmes at last said thoughtfully, 'an occurrence that is actually beginning to interest me. I'll get everything I am likely to need this very minute and we'll go.'

The interpreter translated this for Mahomet-Sultan, who nodded his head in approval.

Sherlock Holmes fetched his travel case. 'My dear Watson,' he turned to me, 'I'd advise you to take a couple of sailor's uniforms, make-up and a weapon. It is very possible we might not be able to get back for a few days.'

I complied instantly. Within a few minutes I had everything

packed in a bag I could carry easily and was ready for any more instructions.

'You'll have to carry our things,' Holmes said to the interpreter. 'I am going to call a cab. Our things shouldn't be a problem. We'll travel light and neither you, nor anyone, must reveal anything about us.'

Sherlock Holmes called the cab himself, escorted the guests out and they took our baggage and two pieces of hand luggage.

III

'Well, my dear Watson, time for us to start moving,' said Holmes after a few minutes.

We made our way to the wharf. On the ship, alarm showed on every face. The interpreter met us and told Holmes he had been assigned a separate cabin in case he had to cross-examine or talk to anyone privately.

'You did very well,' said Holmes. 'Are our things there?'

'Yes.'

We were escorted to the cabin.

'Now it's necessary for me to have full access everywhere,' said Holmes.

'This has already been arranged,' answered the interpreter. 'You and your friend have already been pointed out to the sentries.'

'In that case, leave us alone for now,' said Holmes.

The interpreter bowed and departed.

'Stay here for now, Watson.' Holmes said to me. 'I'll go over the ship, look at one or two things and return to fetch you.'

'Very well,' I replied.

He left and I was left to myself. He was back a quarter of an hour later.

'Let's go, Watson,' he said shortly.

A few steps along the corridor and we were outside the Emir's quarters. The sentry at the door admitted us. The Emir's quarters comprised four cabins with doors between all of them, and a reception room, which had been a first-class dining room. The Emir's office was to the left of the entrance, then his bedroom. To the right were the sitting room and a parlour. Holmes and I turned left into the office and then the bedroom. The floors here were covered with thick, luxurious carpets.

Holmes paused at the threshold and began to scrutinise the premises closely.

This scrutiny appeared to penetrate every little nook and cranny. Then he squatted down and crawled along the floor, examining it through his magnifying glass. Then he examined the divan, bed and washbasin, carefully looking behind them; next he knocked on the walls and shook his head in perplexity. Finding nothing in the bedroom, he went into the office. One after another he examined the other rooms, but there were no clues anywhere.

Suddenly he smacked himself on his own forehead. 'Now, now, Watson! We haven't yet lifted the carpets.'

I smiled involuntarily, 'I don't suppose you think someone is sitting under them?' I asked.

'Not entirely, but . . . you see, Watson, I haven't the slightest doubt that the thief didn't come in through the door. The sentry would have seen him. Nor would the windows have been of any use to him. They are seemingly locked from inside, while the putty around the pane shows the glass was installed some time ago. This means the thief must have found a hidey-hole on the ship . . . and if that so, he is still aboard.'

We moved the furniture around now here, now there, one after another, and lifted the carpet, carefully examining the floor underneath. We did all this in total silence, even walking on tip-toe.

Suddenly Holmes uttered a triumphant cry. 'Have a look,

Watson,' he whispered and motioned for me to come near. I crawled up to him.

Holmes suddenly lifted the corner of the carpet by the head of the bed, 'The first thing that struck me was that the corner leg of the bed was not pressing down on the carpet,' he whispered.

I looked at the floor under the carpet and all the same noticed nothing.

'You don't see it?' smiled Holmes.

'Absolutely not,' I replied.

'And all the same, it is so simple.' Holmes still smiled and said softly, 'Look at the floor boards. In all the other places where we examined the floor, you noticed, of course, that the cracks between them had been filled with paint and where the paint cracked, dust and other dirt particles had collected. It's different here. The cracks are not filled with paint and there is no dirt, which shows that these floorboards are not immoveable.'

Holmes produced a thin spike, stuck it into a floor board and gently raised it. The board shifted.

He moved it just a little and then replaced it. He then covered it with the carpet and moved the bed so that all four legs pressed down on it. 'Now the entrance is sealed,' he said, getting up. 'The most important is done. There's only trifles left to be attended to now. The criminal is on board, because he has nowhere to go and the sooner the ship moves, so much the better. Watson, let's go to Mahomet-Sultan.'

We left the Emir's quarters and went on deck.

IV

We found the Minister of the Court standing with the Emir and quietly conversing with him. We waited till he looked in our direction and Holmes gave him an imperceptible sign. He indicated with his eyes that he understood. He ended his conversation with the Emir and, accompanied by the interpreter, made his way to Holmes's cabin. We followed.

'The sooner the ship leaves, the better,' Holmes said to him. 'Rest assured, the thief will not escape.'

'Really,' exclaimed the Minister joyfully, when he heard this announcement from the interpreter.

'Yes,' said Holmes. 'He is on board and, of course, won't risk escaping as long as the ship is ringed by sentries.'

'Oh! Oh! In that case I will inform His Highness at once!' the Minister exclaimed through the interpreter and the two Bukharans ran out of the cabin.

The second whistle sounded a minute later. A few minutes later, the third whistle sounded, sailors rushed about the deck, the military band thundered and the ship began to move gracefully away from the wharf.

'Now, then, my dear Watson, we have to become sailors,' said Holmes, opening his travel case.

But first, before changing, Holmes went out of the cabin and, returning after a little while, said, 'Splendid. Everything's done. The interpreter has asked the ship's captain to instruct the bosun to sign on two more sailors who will now appear before him. So, look lively, Watson, change and let's go to meet our new chief. And to look younger, a new fair-haired wig for you, into which rub wood-oil instead of pomade.'

I obeyed therewith. In twenty minutes we were ready. The interpreter arrived just then. Holmes told him briefly what he had noticed and advised him to get the Minister to assist him in switching the Emir's bedroom and office and place sentries there for security. When all this had been said, the interpreter left and we were off to see the bosun.

The signing-on ritual was short and simple.

We were shown our places, our watch was assigned, our surnames written down, Holmes as Gvozdeff and I became Panshin. After that they let us go. By a fortunate coincidence our watches coincided. There were still three hours before our first watch, so we wandered up and down the lower deck.

Holmes wanted to pay special attention to that part of the ship lying under the Emir's quarters. But to carry out any substantial observation of this part of the vessel was completely impossible, because here the whole of the lower deck was filled with the baggage of the Emir and his retinue, the chests being solidly packed from the deck to the ceiling. This discovery put Holmes in an especially good mood.

'Undoubtedly, there is a way of getting between the chests to the Emir's bedroom. The thief isn't going to stay there for long and, one way or another, will emerge,' he said, having finished his inspection. 'But he has to have an accomplice on board. The accomplice blocked this particular area with chests in such a way that nothing could be checked between them. My dear Watson, let's find out who supervised the loading.'

'That shouldn't be too difficult,' I answered.

'If that's what you think, you do it,' said Holmes.

V

Without a word, I made my way to the bottom deck where those sailors who were not on watch took refreshments and rested. And as soon as I appeared amongst them, I began to abuse one of them, 'How the hell did you stow away the luggage, so that nobody can get through or even crawl through!'

'And what the hell are you barking at me for,' he bit back. 'Wasn't me indicated what to put where.'

'Then who was it?'

'Who? That new fellow, Skalkin, or whatever his name is!'

Hearing his name, an older, bearded sailor looked at me intently and said angrily, 'Well, it was me, and what got in your way?'

'The devil take you!' I yelled. 'I can't get through.'

'No need for you to get through there,' he muttered. 'So shut up or I'll bash your face in.'

I managed to smooth over the quarrel, went to Holmes and told him everything I had discovered.

'Splendid!' exclaimed Holmes. 'That means he is new. It's worth knowing and he will have to be watched.'

Three hours passed and we reported for our watch. Holmes's watch was on the lower deck. I was on the upper, by the wheel. My watch began at eight and passed quietly. But when I had completed it and went down to meet Holmes, who had completed his, from the look he threw at me, I realized something unusual had happened.

But it wasn't possible to have a discussion. We weren't alone and could be overheard. We went down to the sailors' quarters, undressed and went to sleep.

It was still completely dark when Holmes woke me up. He slept beside me and a slight touch from him was enough to bring me to my feet. I yawned several times and tossed and turned as if to show that I had slept enough and began to dress. We went up unnoticed and crept into our cabin.

With intense curiosity I waited for what Holmes had to tell me. 'And so, in a couple of hours, the situation should be clear,' he said softly.

'You've found something out tonight?' I asked.

'Yes,' he answered. 'It was just before eleven o'clock at night. I was on my watch and observed Skalkin carefully emerging from the sailors' quarters. I pretended to be dozing. He looked at me suspiciously, but was apparently reassured and dived in amongst the luggage. There was nobody there. I sat with my back to him, watching intently through a mirror which I had taken the precaution of hanging up on the wall and which he hadn't noticed. Thanks to this mirror, I could see everything behind me. He threw another glance at me, was still reassured that I wasn't watching, and carefully approached one of the chests. Pushing it aside, he quickly disappeared in the gap that appeared. I leaped up from my place, carefully approached and put my ear to the edge of the gap he had created. It was just as I expected. Out of the pile of chests I overheard a conversation.

' "It's dangerous to come out," whispered one voice.

' "I know," said another.

' "Low water at the Jiguli sector of the river would be best. Are the fellows ready?"

' "Yes, they're none of them locals. They unload barges offshore. Nobody knows us. Is the cofferdam in order?" you probably know, Watson, that's the compartment that separates two bulkheads.

' "Yes, it's fine," the other assured him. "Nothing else?"

' "Nothing. Be off."

'I heard a rustle and rushed to my place, keeping up the pretence that I was dozing. Skalkin moved the chest back to its previous position and went to the sailors' quarters.'

'But what does this conversation signify,' I asked.

'I don't know exactly,' Holmes shrugged. 'But Jiguli is not far and there is some sort of sandbank, not far from which a barge will be unloading on shore. That's where you and I, Watson, must keep our eyes peeled. That's where the thief has to vanish, and it would be a great shame for us if we were to let him slip through our fingers.'

'And according to you, what's all this about a cofferdam?'

'I don't know,' Holmes said thoughtfully.

VI

While we were talking, dawn had broken. We left our cabin and, unnoticed, descended to the lower deck to go our separate ways. At eight o'clock in the morning our watch began.

This time Holmes was by the wheel, while I was instructed to stand on the upper bridge, nearly next to him. I had to transmit certain instructions and wave signalling flags when we met other ships, which in those busy days sailed up and down the Volga one after another.

Our ship was sailing along the Jiguli sector. Carefully scrutinizing the river banks, I still kept on looking stealthily at Holmes. He stood there turning the wheel like a seasoned sailor.

Suddenly, as I looked at him, with his eyes he was indicating something at a distance. At this point the Volga widens. I looked at the side Holmes was looking at and there, on the right bank, men were working on a barge. We were nearly parallel to it. It was probably being unloaded.

I was hardly able to get a good look at it, when I heard a noise from the bridge, 'Where, where are you going?' It was the captain and in an unnatural voice he was yelling, 'Turn the wheel to the left, to the left!'

The wheel began to spin madly. But the ship, instead of turning left, continued straight on, if anything, more to the right. The helmsman and Holmes appeared anxious and lost. The captain himself leaped to the wheel and began to turn it in a frenzy. But the impossible was happening. Instead of veering left, the ship headed straight for the sandbank.

'Stop! Back! Back!' the captain yelled through the megaphone at the engine room.

But it was too late. A crackling noise came from beneath our feet, we felt a light shudder, and our ship ploughed up the sandbank virtually at full steam. There was an incredible rumpus. The engines were put into reverse, but did not obey. No matter what the captain and his crew undertook, the ship wouldn't budge.

'Watch out!' Holmes whispered.

The captain now gave orders for distress signals to be raised. These were seen from the barge by the shore. Soon enough, a crowded longboat glided away from it in our direction. As it approached, Holmes began to count the number of labourers aboard it coming to help. There were twenty-three of them, ordinary porters, and the overseer.

The captain and the men in the longboat agreed on the remuneration and the overseer ordered twenty of the men up on the ship. The longboat was by the right-hand ladder. Holmes and I scrutinized carefully everyone coming on board, but nobody excited our suspicion. This is when the interpreter came up to me.

'Be prepared,' Holmes whispered to him. 'Point me out to the sentries and order them to obey my orders. Prepare to lower a boat. The outcome is at hand! Hurry!'

The interpreter rushed off to do as he was told.

In the meantime, work on the ship went on at a furious pace. After two hours of intensive effort, the ship somehow shifted from the sandbank and the barge labourers began to go down the ladder to their longboat. I began to count them again. One after another, twenty men went down that ladder.

And suddenly Holmes whispered anxiously, 'Look! Look! There's twenty-four leaving.'

I hastily recounted the number of men in the longboat. To my amazement, I noticed there was just that one extra man aboard. This was all the more surprising, because I had personally counted that out of the twenty-three originally in the long-boat, twenty had come up and twenty had gone down.

'Yes! Yes!' Holmes whispered anxiously. 'He got out from under. That's what the business with the cofferdam was all about. Under water there must be an exit leading into a cofferdam affixed to the bottom of the ship. He went out through that!'

And turning round, he shouted loudly, 'Arrest the sailor Skalkin. Guard! Into the boat!'

The alarm was raised. Skalkin was instantly seized, tied with ropes, while a minute later, together with the sentries, we were speeding in pursuit of the longboat on its way at a fast clip. The heavy longboat began to slow down. With every minute, the distance between us lessened.

'Halt. Or we fire!' yelled Holmes.

I thought there would be a riot on the longboat, but the threat worked and it stopped yards from the Jiguli shore.

In that moment, we saw a figure leap into the waist-high water and move towards the reeds.

'Shoot him!' commanded Holmes.

The man dived, came up and dived again. Shots rang out but missed their target.

'Dammit!' yelled Holmes, beside himself. 'Follow me!'

With one leap he was in the water and flung himself towards the fleeing man. 'Arrest the crew of the longboat. Five men follow me!' he shouted.

Knee deep in water, we chased after the unknown man. Holmes, revolver in hand, was in front. Now the fleeing man, in water a little deeper than his ankles, suddenly stumbled and an inflated ox bladder flew out of his hand.

'Get the bladder!' shouted Holmes without turning round. I grabbed at it.

The escapee made a gesture of total despair, as if the loss had been of everything at stake. He reached into his pocket and out came a revolver. All of a sudden it went off twice at Holmes and the man vanished into the reeds. Holmes shot thrice and then he, too, vanished amongst the reeds.

A few minutes later, their figures appeared atop the steep bluff above us and from which we heard more shots.

Then, as we stumbled upwards, we saw the two opponents fall on each other and heard Holmes cry out, 'Kartzeff!'

And the end came. No matter how long we searched for Holmes, no matter how loudly we hailed him, the deserted river bank remained deaf and dumb to us. Holmes and his enemy had vanished and we even couldn't establish where they had gone.

VII

Tired and despondent, we returned to the ship after a four-hour-long search. 'What's this?' asked Mahomet-Sultan through the interpreter, pointing at the bladder in my hand. I handed him my wretched trophy and something rolled around inside. Intuitively, I took back the bladder, tore it apart with my bare fingers and suddenly a huge black pearl rolled round our feet.

What happened to Holmes, I know not. All I know is that I went no further. I stayed at the scene of this sad occurrence with four sentries but a three-day search yielded no results.

From the papers, I was later to learn that the sailor Skalkin was the escaped prisoner, Foma Belkin. He confessed to being an accomplice of the notorious swindler and burglar, Kartzeff, in the theft of the pearl aboard the ship. An inspection of the ship revealed that under its right side there was some sort of coffer-dam, through which the thief had crept out through an exit below the water line. The barge overseer was another member of the gang, but the barge labourers were completely innocent. Apart from all this, on the right-hand side of the ship, a cunningly attached rudder was found. It was this that Kartzeff had been able to operate, to bypass the ship's rudder, making it plough into the sandbank.

6

THE COMMERCIAL CENTRE MYSTERY

P. Nikitin

I

This happened in 190*.

Sherlock Holmes had come to Nijni-Novgorod partly on holiday, partly to acquaint himself better with faraway Russia, of which the English have only a vague notion. Although there were no professional reasons for his visit, nevertheless, it was still noted locally. No matter how hard he tried not to be noticed, to remain aloof as he strolled around the town, he was followed by a bevy of curious citizens and heard his name whispered behind his back. Of course, he thought that all this attention was idle curiosity, but things turned out otherwise.

He was staying at the Post Hotel (by the Black Pond). On his third day, returning to his room, he was told by a porter that a gentleman had asked for him, and when told that he was out, had requested that he leave a message to indicate at what time he would be available for consultation.

'When is he coming for my answer?' asked Holmes.

'This very evening,' the hotel porter answered.

'Splendid!' said the detective. 'I wasn't intending to go anywhere in any case.'

The porter went off and Holmes stretched himself out on the settee with a local newspaper.

Here it must be said that the famous English detective had once spent two years in Buenos Aires, where he had boarded with a family of Russian émigrés. This close association with them resulted in his being fluent in Russian, both as regards knowledge of the language and pronunciation. Of course, he could never get rid of his English accent, but he spoke with such clarity, and his knowledge of the language was so profound, one would have thought he had spent an uninterrupted ten years in Russia.

Having read one newspaper, he picked up another, but soon his lids grew heavy. He covered his face against flies with a newspaper and dozed off.

II

A light tap at the door woke him. He must have slept for some time, because it was already dark outside. He rose, changed swiftly and said in his resonant voice, 'Come in!'

The door opened and a thickset, middle-aged man came in. He was a man of some presence, wearing a summer coat cut in the latest fashion. In one gloved hand he held a felt hat and a silver-handled gold-monogrammed cane. He bowed courteously and asked to be excused for having called without an appointment.

'You must be the gentleman who called earlier,' said Holmes.

'Indeed I am! I was here some hours ago but, unfortunately, missed you. I do beg of you to hear me out—'

'I am at your service,' Sherlock Holmes bowed. 'I presume

that you need my assistance in some matter, but I am surprised how you found out who I am, and that I am here at all.'

'Oh!' exclaimed the stranger. 'The whole town is talking about you. In any case, your fame has crossed the sea and it is not surprising that, hearing of your arrival, I immediately decided to meet you.'

Flattered by such a response, Sherlock Holmes smiled and bowed. 'Do take off your coat and make yourself comfortable.'

The guest threw off his coat and approached the detective, 'Allow me, then, the honour of presenting myself. Ivan Vladimirovitch Terehoff,' he said, giving his name, patronymic and surname. 'I am a local merchant and a member of the First Guild.' He gave a little bow.

'Very pleased to meet you,' answered the detective. 'How can I be of service to you?'

Terehoff sank into an armchair, lit a cigarette and began his story. 'I sell linen, lingerie and fashionable goods of every sort. My father and grandfather were also in the same line of business. Ours is an old and well-established family business. Usually, I trade in town, but every summer we have a fair. Our fair dates from the thirteenth century and traders come from Central Asia, Siberia and many, many other faraway places. For the period of this Great Fair I rent premises in the Commercial Centre. That is where I now have a shop, along the right-hand side of the arcade.

'Up until this year everything went well, and I had nothing to worry about. But this year, a whole series of unusual events have shocked not only my employees, but also my prospective customers who, by the way, are already gathering for the fair.

'Before the shop was ready to open, my three assistants and I were putting away merchandise on the shelves and decorating the display windows. We had worked by the light of electric lamps. I had opened the shop myself and locked it up myself, first having switched off the electric lights when we were done for the day. I put the locks on the door and the metal grill over the windows. I turned to go, when the senior shop assistant leapt to my side. His face was as pale as our linen. He was trembling.

' "What's happened?" ' I asked in alarm.

' "For God's sake," ' he whispered. ' "For God's sake, look in the display window." '

'I looked, and stepped back in horror.

'Some sort of creature resembling a human figure wrapped in a shroud danced as if possessed inside my shop, shaking itself all over as it danced.

'The two other shop assistants were struck dumb. They were as terrified as my senior assistant and I were at that moment.

'We stood there for several minutes, rooted to the spot.

'I'm not timid by nature. I've been educated abroad, and I'm a university graduate. I'm not one to believe in black magic.

'But even I was a little afraid. Not for long, though.

'I recovered, took myself in hand and began to undo the locks.

'But just in case, I sent one of the shop assistants to fetch a policeman and ordered the senior assistant to watch the apparition through the window.

'Hardly had I taken the second lock off, when he yelled out, "Gone! God preserve us sinful creatures."

'He said that it had vanished all of a sudden and the shop was plunged into darkness again.

'The policeman now appeared with the assistant sent for him.

' "There is someone in the shop," I said to the policeman. "Come in with me and let's look."

'I unlocked the door, switched on the lights and with great difficulty persuaded the assistants to follow me inside. The shop was exactly as we had left it. There was no trace of the apparition, no sign of revelry. The five of us searched every nook and cranny. We searched under the counters, in drawers and boxes, turned over the entire stock. A mouse would not have eluded us.

But . . . all our exertions were in vain. Was it a figment of our imagination? I decided that that was the case.

'Evidently my staff thought otherwise.

'The next day we continued with our work.

'But in the evening, just as I locked up the shop, the entire incident was re-enacted.

'The pale apparition shook and pranced about. Now I had a chance to look at it. There was no face, just a skull and a set of terrifying bared teeth.

'The apparition skipped in a paroxysm on the same spot, threatening us with a long knife, which it held in one bony hand.

'We trembled in terror. We wanted to run.

'I made a superhuman effort and again unlocked the shop. That very instance the apparition vanished.

'Inside, it was as if nothing had happened.

'My employees fled and a crowd of people from neighbouring shops gathered round me. The whole of the Commercial Centre was there. Everyone was terrified, confused, bewildered, dismayed. Some of those present had caught a brief glimpse of the apparition. They were now describing it to the others who, in their turn, were torn between fear and curiosity.

'Someone said to sprinkle holy water inside the shop and conduct prayers.

'The more courageous went in with me and, again, the shop was searched. And yet again, nothing and nobody.

'The third day was the eve of the opening of the Great Fair.

'Ignoring my pleas, my employees flatly refused to enter the shop. Holy water had to be sprinkled, religious rites had to be carried out, before they relented. I had also taken the precaution of asking the help of the Chief of Detectives. Two detectives were assigned to the shop. They searched it thoroughly before I locked up, tested the floor and walls, but found nothing.

'It was only after I switched off the lights and put the locks on the door that the two detectives themselves and my employees stepped back in horror from the display window through which they had been peering.

' "It's a corpse!" someone screamed in an inhuman voice.

'My hair stood on end.

'There in the shop, I saw a large coffin, inside which a loathsome skeleton sat, holding on to the edges with skeletal fingers. The others told me that I had missed the part when the lid of the coffin fell open and the skeleton sat up.

'The shroud no longer covered it.

'And then the skeleton suddenly bounded out of the coffin, and once on its feet, began a frenzied dance. Next, a thick column of smoke blew out of the coffin and everything vanished as if by magic.'

III

Ivan Vladimirovitch Terehoff fell silent and asked for a drink.

'A drop of port is just what is called for,' said Sherlock Holmes, and poured him a drink.

Terehoff reached for the glass and drained it.

'Your story intrigues me more and more by the minute,' said the English detective. 'Do go on.'

'I think I got to the point where the apparition vanished,' Terehoff resumed his account. 'My employees made themselves scarce. I screwed up what little courage I had left and, together with the two detectives, we re-entered the shop.

'This time we actually raised the floor but, again, found nothing suspicious.

'It was midnight before I returned home. I felt beaten, racked by evil forebodings.

'My wife, thoroughly frightened by all these happenings tried, for the third time, to convince me that the place was cursed, that it would bring bad luck, and I should move my shop elsewhere.

168

'The appearance of the coffin she regarded with superstitious awe.

'As for me, I have to admit that I found it all horribly oppressive. All through the night, I was pursued by nightmares in which countless coffins appeared. In my waking hours, I was distracted by melancholia. My heart ached constantly.

'I hated the thought of abandoning the familiar surroundings in which I had traded so long.

'Those of us whose business lies in the Commercial Centre can depend on regular trade there. Anyone would have to look long and hard and yet not find anything as well suited for that purpose.

'There was a vacancy at the other end of the arcade, but it was too small for me and, besides, surrounded by smaller stalls that all but hid it from view. The rest of the Commercial Centre was occupied by well-established firms. It was unlikely any one of them would be available in time for the opening.

'I decided to sit it out.

'My old shop assistants flatly refused to continue working for me. I had to find new ones.

'I found only two fellows brave enough to work for me, and they demanded double wages. Since I didn't know them personally, I had to make enquiries about them.

'One of them had worked a year for some major manufacturer, but had been dismissed for bring rude. His name was Simon Reshkin. The other was an Englishman, Smith Copton. He had worked for a Russian bank some time ago, but resigned in high dudgeon. A large sum of money had gone missing and he had objected to being searched. Quite a few employees had been searched and they'd not made a fuss over it. But this proud Englishman had taken umbrage. He had been held in high esteem by his superiors, who had tried to talk him into staying, but he left nevertheless.

'Since then things had been hard for him, but he preferred to eke out a living from the little money he had saved. Anything, not to work at a job in which he would be treated badly again.

'He was particularly recommended by the director of the bank in which he had been employed.

'The Englishman didn't immediately agree to work for me.

'It was only when I told him the whole story of the apparition, that he announced, with a grin, that he was drawn out of curiosity and a desire to earn his fare home.

'The Great Nijni-Novgorod Fair opened.

'We opened up in the morning and had just taken our places, when all three were forced to flee as though driven mad.

'It was the smell.

'Not just an ordinary sort of stink. This was a loathsome, acidic smell which caused our heads to spin and bile to rise in our throats.

'It wasn't that the smell was strong. Its effect was awful, so awful that we couldn't stay inside the shop, nor even stand beside it in the arcade. It seemed to have penetrated every nook and cranny. It filled the air.

'Customers approaching the shop or walking past it seemed to break out in some kind of paroxysm followed by headlong flight, holding on to their noses, cursing.

'Our neighbours, reacting to the fuss, ran out of their shops and then, at a distance, yelled at us to lock our jinxed shop and get the hell out of there.

'The fuss grew by the minute.

'At the risk of passing out, I got to the door, slammed it and locked it shut.

'The noise brought the police. The senior of them, when what had happened had been explained to him, lost his temper. "What's going on here!" he shouted. "Everyone else is behaving normally but here, as if on purpose, there's all these senseless goings-on."

'I tried to justify myself, but he refused to listen.

'I unlocked the door for him, but before he could go in, he backed away as if scalded, holding his nose. "What are you up to?" he screamed at me. "What have you been sprinkling inside?"

'But I could only tell him what I knew.

'Both shop assistants confirmed my story and the police officer drew up a protocol.

'To determine what the odour was, a chemist and a doctor were summoned, but the moment they poked their noses inside, they rushed out, as though driven mad.

'Retreating some distance from the door, they stared at each other with bulging eyes, spat and finally announced they had never come across such a foul smell in either chemistry or medicine.

'Neither of my assistants being prepared to enter the shop, it became necessary to call out the fire brigade. They smashed the windows leading out on to the street. When the air inside had cleared somewhat, they came in to determine the source of the foul odour. Even though the shop had been ventilated somewhat, they couldn't stay long. Emerging, they said that the odour came from the outer facing of one of the counters. The counter was then smashed and the pieces thrown out. But there were horses outside. They began to breathe hoarsely and then took to headlong flight, dragging their carriages with them ... followed by the curses of the coachmen.

'The assistants now informed me that they couldn't work here any longer. "It's not your apparition that scares me," said Smith Copton. "I just don't want to breathe such foul air. You're being pursued by some evil genie. It would be best for you to move. Do so, and you'll get good staff. Stay here, you won't survive the week."

'Both left, wishing me all the very best.'

Terehoff fell silent again.

Sherlock Holmes listened to him attentively, very taken by the story. He refilled Terehoff's glass and handed it to him. Terehoff drank.

'How did it all end?'

'After that last incident, my wife renewed her pleas even more forcefully for me to change premises,' answered Terehoff. 'Finally, I gave in and took the only premises left in the Commercial Centre.'

'And then?'

'As soon as I had vacated my premises, I still kept an eye on it. I think the apparition must have gone on strike. For a while the place remained vacant, but then some Greek called Alferakki took it over. He trades in eastern delicacies and fruit, both wholesale and retail.'

'And how are things with him?'

'He doesn't know of any apparition and laughs at me when someone brings up my misfortunes,' Terehoff said angrily. 'Personally, I don't believe in the supernatural. I am sooner likely to suspect some human trickery. In a word, I'm mentally confused. Then I heard that you are in Nijni-Novgorod and decided to seek your advice. Supernatural or otherwise, I want to get at the truth. I am prepared to pay you five thousand roubles.'

Sherlock Holmes smiled, 'That would amount to five hundred pounds sterling.'

'Absolutely so!'

'In that case I am at your disposal. For me, as an Englishman, time and every action are measured in monetary terms. Although I took a lively interest listening to your story, I wouldn't spend any time over it, unless I was remunerated. Please draw up a contract and . . . who knows? Perhaps I'll be able to restore your former premises to you, but without the evil presence.'

The detective and the merchant sat down and began to draw up a contract.

IV

Several days passed. It was late on 27 July. The shops had long since shut for the day. The drunken revelry for which the Nijni-Novgorod Fair was famous was in full swing. The old times are gone forever, as are the old music and dancing. It wasn't so in those days. No sooner did the shops shut for the day, than the merchants hurried to the restaurants from whence music and women's voices were raised in song. To the sound of them (part singers, part prostitutes), business deals were transacted. Mirrors were cracked. Then was yet the time, when drunken merchants still beat up waiters for any minor blunder.

That evening, the weather was terrible. The north wind blew all day. The rain poured in buckets. It was close to midnight, and everyone had taken shelter in restaurants.

Two men emerged from one of the restaurants in the park opposite the Commercial Centre. They made their way past the Flatch clock tower towards the Oka River wharf. Despite the pouring rain, the two men did not hurry. Engrossed in conversation, they spoke in undertones.

Following them out of the same restaurant, but at a distance, was a man in a hooded waterproof cape. This was Sherlock Holmes, the famous London detective. Three days and three nights spent at the fair were beginning to yield results. He had noted a few things here and there, and now wouldn't let the two men out of his sight.

He sat down behind them on the ferry, but didn't pick up anything useful. The two men were deep in conversation, but they were only discussing the Great Fair and the prices that had been established for certain goods. They disembarked at the Krashinsky Wharf, where they parted. Sherlock Holmes managed to overhear a phrase dropped by one of them, 'And so, congratulations on the start of work. Goodbye.'

At this moment a dark figure approached Sherlock Holmes.

This was Dr Watson, who accompanied him everywhere. 'Well, what?' he asked softly.

'Let's go; I have to talk to you,' said Sherlock Holmes.

'What about those two?' asked Dr Watson.

'They'll keep. I'm not interested in their doings when they're apart.'

They took a coach and returned to the Post Hotel. Having locked the door, they began to share their findings.

'I haven't found out anything. I don't even know the names of the pair you have been watching,' said Watson sadly. 'Just as you suggested, I spent two nights in the taverns along the Bentakurovsky Canal. Lots of suspicious types there. Two men entered Tarakanoff's tavern while I was sitting there. What confused me is that they seemed alike in build to the pair you were interested in who were at the fair.'

'Describe them?' Sherlock Holmes interrupted.

'One was dark, the other ginger haired. Both lean. Both with moustaches, but otherwise clean-shaven.'

Sherlock Holmes jumped up in excitement, 'That's them all right, the devil take them. Do go on, I beg you. Your efforts were not wasted.'

'They sat down at the table adjoining mine and ordered an expensive wine,' went on Watson. 'This tavern didn't have the brand they wanted. They insisted it must be sent for. They kept on repeating that there was some job they had to get under way, otherwise they could miss out on all this money intended for the fair. Nothing suspicious in that. But when they'd nearly got through the bottle they had ordered, one of them said, "If only we could get under way! After that, we're all right on our own, and as for him—" Following this, they dropped their voices, though I did hear them mention the Bentakurovsky Canal several times. I suppose you know, Holmes, that this particular canal has an evil reputation. It passes through the distant coun-tryside, along its banks are the taverns with the worst reputation, the police often find corpses in its waters, in which quite a few crimes have been concealed.'

'Yes, indeed, what you have to say is of great significance,' Sherlock Holmes said thoughtfully. For some time he sat in silence, except for drumming his fingers on the table. His brows were knit in thought. Finally, he lifted his head.

Watson, anticipating that now Sherlock Holmes would relate what had happened to him, prepared to listen.

V

'There's not much for me to tell,' said Sherlock Holmes after a long pause. 'It was sheer chance that led you to the pair I was following.'

'And they are—?'

'The Englishman Smith Copton and the Greek Alferakki.'

'Not the very same one who rented Terehoff's shop in the Commercial Centre!' exclaimed Watson, looking puzzled.

'Indeed, the very same.' Holmes nodded. 'I began to watch the two of them, and soon enough I discovered a close connection between the new owner and the unemployed assistant. This was an important discovery and, as far as I am concerned, if Smith Copton really needed a job, his friend Alferakki would have given him one. After all, the Greek had hired another assistant with a poor reputation. But since he didn't take on Copton, it could only mean the latter was not in need of employment.'

'Damn it, your observations are, indeed, very interesting,' said Watson.

'Hold on,' Sherlock Holmes stopped him. 'It would appear that Copton's claim to be in financial need was pure invention. But since they always met in secret, I came to the conclusion that they have some enterprise in common. Now put the following facts together: an apparition appears in Terehoff's shop, Copton goes to work for him, the simultaneous appearance of a foul smell, forcing the shop to be cleared and ... Alferakki, who knows Copton well, occupies the premises.'

'Indeed!'

'This is how I see it, then,' explained Sherlock Holmes. 'For some reason, Alferakki and Smith Copton need Terehoff's shop. There is a mystery here, and in the end we will solve it. I think a major crime is in preparation.'

'Is that what you presume?' Watson interrupted.

'I am certain of that. And so they decided to squeeze out Terehoff, come what may. That's why they did all those horrible things. I haven't yet examined the old premises, but I presume that the trick was all of an optical nature, which means they are skilled. Utilizing the power of superstition, they got rid of the employees. But Terehoff was still being stubborn. That's when Copton appeared, and his task was to create the final outrage, which forced out Terehoff.'

'So what did he rub into the wood?' asked Watson. 'I smelt it. Despite the passage of time, the odour had survived. I nearly went out of my mind, sniffing that wood at the police station.'

Sherlock Holmes smiled, 'I was able to place that odour instantly. I came across it in South Africa some ten years ago. A tribesman wanted to get out of being a guide to a British detachment. He didn't want to desert, which meant facing a firing squad. And so, one day, when he entered the camp, everyone nearly went out of their minds. Tethered horses tried to break away. Oxen tore through the camp and brought down tents. The men cursed and ran in all directions. That same odour came from him. The guide calmly paraded up and down the camp, claiming he had rubbed himself with an antidote against mosquitoes. He was ordered to get the hell out of there, or else.'

Watson laughed, 'How very droll! And what was the antidote?'

'Juice squeezed from African gorse. The plant only grows in southern and central Africa, and even so, rarely. But to continue. Copton was hired as a sales assistant, brought a jar of this foul liquid and rubbed some of it into the wood without being noticed. And achieved his aim.'

'What then?' asked Watson.

'Then,' answered Sherlock Holmes, 'when Terehoff left, Alferakki immediately took over, while Copton left Terehoff's employment for whatever more substantial task awaited him.'

'Your conclusions are certainly logical,' said Watson.

'It is very likely that, by themselves, the pair cannot cope with the matter at hand,' Sherlock Holmes went on developing his thoughts, 'because there is talk of a third person. But they don't want to share with him and, for some reason, consider him a danger to themselves. They probably promised him the earth to come in with them and, having used him, they'll get rid of him. I can see another crime taking place here.'

'Do you really think so?' asked Watson.

'Of that I am certain. I have a strange premonition of an irreversible tragedy.' Sherlock Holmes was silent for a little while. 'And so, my dear colleague, keep an eye on Copton while I do the same to Alferakki. We part now, but we must get under way early tomorrow morning. Some mysterious plot is being hatched before our eyes. It would be a shame if we don't put a stop to it.'

'With you on the case, success is bound to come!' said Watson warmly. 'Meanwhile, I'll take your advice and get a sound night's sleep to make sure I am full of energy in the morning. A very good night!'

'Good night!' Sherlock Holmes rose and shook his hand.

They parted, having first agreed on prearranged recognition signals and where to meet.

*

VI

Soon after noon on the following day, a middle-aged man with a long dark beard and the looks and conduct of a merchant of average means entered the Commercial Centre of the fair and made his way slowly along the arcade. Outside Alferakki's shop, he examined the sign above the door and then the goods in the window. He scratched the back of his head and went in.

'Would you be wholesalers?' he asked the owner standing by the till.

'Wholesale and retail, both.' The man locked the till and approached the customer.

'So,' said the latter, stroking his beard, 'and where are your goods manufactured? Russia?'

'Never,' said the owner smugly. 'Our goods come from Turkey, Greece and Italy. Allow me to ask whether you trade in such goods, too?'

'Yes,' said the visitor. 'My business premises are in Yeltze and Orla, from where we export to other places. Kromi, for example, Karacheff, Griazi.'

'Very glad to make your acquaintance,' Alferakki smiled and bowed. 'I am sure our goods will give you satisfaction. Do look for yourself.' And with a broad gesture he indicated the counters and shelves.

'Won't buy unless I try,' smirked the buyer. 'I take it, you're in business, not just for idle chatter.'

'Goes without saying,' said the owner.

The buyer began to examine and try the goods, making observations that showed his familiarity with the business. He went round the shop slowly, from time to time asking to see this or that item from the shelves. He then asked for samples of a quarter pound in weight of each item. He paid, promised to return in a few days, and left.

Who would have recognized Sherlock Holmes in this buyer!

Leaving the shop, he glanced at his watch and made his way to one of the restaurants in the park opposite the Commercial Centre. Watson was already there, at a table by the window.

They shook hands and asked the waiter to show them to a private room, where they ordered lunch. They were on their own there and could speak freely, though they had to keep their voices down.

'Have you been following Copton?' asked Sherlock Holmes.

'Yes,' answered Watson. 'He met Alferakki today. Part of their conversation was inaudible. Part incomprehensible. But I did manage to catch one phrase. Copton asked Alferakki if he'd managed to remove the cinematograph—'

Sherlock Holmes jumped at this word with a look of pleasure on his face. 'Hurrah!' he exclaimed. 'So that's the use to which this appliance was first put in Russia!'

'I don't understand,' said Watson, looking puzzled.

'Oh, haven't you read anything about this remarkable new invention. It's a so-called living and moving photograph.'

'I've read about it,' said Watson, sounding aggrieved. 'What's it got to do with the matter at hand?'

'You'll see,' said Sherlock Holmes smugly.

[For the information of readers, the cinematograph had already appeared elsewhere, but in Russia it wasn't widely known yet.]

'Did you not note, Watson, a metal box nailed to the door of Alferakki's shop?' asked Sherlock Holmes.

'I did see it,' answered Watson. 'I presume it is a ventilator or an electric meter.'

'That's what anyone is likely to think,' Watson nodded. 'Who would think that a projector, as yet unknown in Russia, is hidden inside. This is where a hole was knocked through the wall for a ventilator and it is through this hole that the light passed from the appliance in the metal box. From what Terehoff had to say, the shelves at the back of the store were covered with a large linen sheet at night. This sheet was the screen. All those demons, prancing skeletons, coffins, were projected on it.'

'But how did they get the appliance to work?' asked Watson.

'It works automatically; the tape winds automatically. I remember now, traces of electric wires on the box to get the mechanism going. Well, my dear Watson, you certainly didn't waste time and effort today. Keep on at it, do, and I'm sure you'll come up with more of interest.'

'Oh, no,' answered Watson. 'That's all that I have for you. Now it's your turn.'

'My pleasure,' said Sherlock Holmes. He lit up a cigar, drank a glass of Benedictine and, chasing it down with black coffee, began to speak.

VII

'I examined Alferakki's shop closely today. Even a cursory examination caused me to reconsider the whys and wherefores of the box you took for holding an electric meter. Thanks to you, all became clear, but I won't labour the point. I was able to look over all the counters, but especially the shelves, and I made a significant discovery. The wall along the left side of the shop, with the exception of a little section at the back, is totally concealed by a huge cupboard filled with shelves. But, if you look at the depth of the shelves and the sides of the cupboard, its back does not touch the wall. The depth of the shelves, judging by the sides, is considerably less than the depth of the cupboard. What it means is this. There is a gap between the back of the cupboard and the wall, and you can get into that gap by way of the left-hand back corner of the shop.'

'Hmm! That is, indeed, some discovery,' exclaimed Watson.

'But that is only the first part of what I discovered,' said Sherlock Holmes. 'The major discovery is that behind the wall of the cupboard there are building works in progress.'

'What sort?'

'Going through that shop, I glanced at the floor under the furniture supports. Someone had brought tiny bits of brick and mortar in on their shoes. There were more of these behind the counter, especially to the left and behind. Our friends are working on that wall to get at something. There is a textile shop to the left, but . . . hmm. We have to find out what's going on no later than tonight, or we will be too late.'

Sherlock Holmes lapsed into a deep and thoughtful silence. 'Well, Watson,' he said finally, 'time for you to change and check the taverns along the Bentakurovsky Canal. I, too, have one or two places to check up on. I'll be in Vertunoff's tavern in two hours. You'll know me by the torn boots I'll be waving about.'

They parted, each going his own way. It was six in the evening when three men entered one of the taverns along the Bentakurovsky Canal. There was the Greek Alferakki, Smith Copton and Alferakki's sales assistant, Ivan Veskoff. They were followed along the canal by a typical vagrant, waving a pair of boots about. Right by Vertunoff's tavern, he was joined by a porter. These were Sherlock Holmes and Dr Watson, who had changed their appearance so that nobody could recognize them.

'They're in there,' Sherlock Holmes indicated the tavern door through which the three men had entered. 'Ivan Veskoff is nine sheets to the wind already, and the other two are pretending to be, too. Watch them closely. In the meantime, let's go inside.'

They stood outside, made a show of swearing at passers-by, and went in. But the men they sought were not there. They'd probably taken a private room. They sat down for a little while and Sherlock Holmes gestured to a waiter, 'Hey, there, lad, find us a proper stall!' His voice was rough and hoarse.

The waiter looked at them with questioning eyes, 'Not enough space for you hereabouts?'

Sherlock Holmes grinned and winked slyly.

'Don't be difficult, you little pipsqueak. I've enough to grease a palm, and I feel crowded here,' he said smugly.

The waiter's attitude changed instantly. He was used to vagrants and thieves and knew that if a thief was celebrating, something would rub off on him.

'Money up front!' said Sherlock Holmes, still smugly.

This definitely convinced the waiter that these guests were all right, and had carried off some piece of business. He got positively friendly.

The tavern had three separate small rooms, which the tavern-keeper called cabins and the vagrants referred to as pigpens.

Sherlock Holmes followed the waiter. From one of the cabins they heard voices. Naturally, they took the adjoining one. They called for a bottle of vodka, food and beer. And they, too, began to celebrate. They spoke loudly, roared out songs at the top of their voices and swore. But they listened attentively to every word from the adjoining-room.

Alferakki and Copton were encouraging Veskoff to drink up.

Veskoff had drunk quite a lot already. He yelled, sang at the top of his voice and carried on in the most boisterous manner. Suddenly, Veskoff yelled, 'To hell with it all! Just one more swing with a crowbar and a little push with the saw . . . and we're rich, rich, rich!'

'Shut up, fool,' hissed one of his companions.

At this moment Sherlock Holmes sang drunkenly. Curses sounded from the other side of the wall. Sherlock Holmes was silent. The drunken sales assistant tried to say something, but his companions wouldn't let him. They poured more wine and cognac down his throat.

It grew dark. Night fell. In both cabins the conversation went on. Now the conspirators fell silent, and snores came from their room.

Copton, making out he was drunk, summoned the waiter, 'Give us the bill!' There was an argument over how much had been consumed. The waiter collected the money and returned with their change.

Watson ran out and settled with the cashier. When he returned, there was a row going on next door. The drunken sales assistant wasn't able to come to, breathed heavily, groaned while his two friends tried to get him out. It sounded as if he was being forcibly dragged out by his armpits.

Half a minute, and Sherlock Holmes and Watson followed on silent feet. Outside it was so dark, you couldn't see a human silhouette two steps ahead.

VIII

Both pairs moved slowly along the shore of the Bentakurovsky Canal. It was quiet, except for the occasional vagrant making noises in his sleep. There were no streetlights, no police. At this time of night, hardly anyone ventured here. With every step it got quieter and quieter and grimmer. Suddenly, out of some pit, came a hoarse, sleepy voice, 'Someone's coming. Let's at 'em.'

Footsteps sounded. Sherlock Holmes stopped Watson and, bending close to his ear, whispered, 'The vagrants recognize strangers. There's going to be a fight.'

Hardly a minute later, and the same hoarse voice yelled harshly, 'Stop, or you're dead.'

For about five seconds, the silence of the grave. Then the sound of bone-shattering blows. Two bodies fell to the ground and their groans echoed up and down the canal.

'Got your bit, have you?' came Copton's sarcastic voice. 'Lie still. Won't take much to finish you off.'

And the first pair moved off. Holmes and Watson followed, shortening the distance behind the others to ten steps. Now the footsteps in front of them were silent.

'Here's OK,' came the very quiet voice of Smith Copton.

Holmes and Watson froze, hands on revolvers. The two in front of them carried out a whispered consultation, but in the silence of the night their voices carried.

'One blow and he's finished,' said Alferakki.

'What for? I hate shedding unnecessary blood,' answered Copton. 'He's drunk and I've slipped him a Mickey Finn. Just toss him in. He'll drown.'

'And if he wakes?' asked Alferakki.

'For heaven's sake, do you think I'm doing this for the first time?' said Copton impatiently. 'A pail of water would be enough. Shove his head in it and hey presto. It's not as if he can move.'

'You sure?' asked Alferakki, sounding sceptical.

'For sure! Come on, into the canal with him. It'll be daylight any minute. The staff will be there at ten, and we've got to be well away by then.'

There were careful footsteps and the noise of a body being dragged along.

Holmes whispered so softly Watson hardly heard him, 'Stay here. Follow them. As soon as they've tossed him in and fled, fish him out. With luck it won't be deep. Resuscitate him. Take him to the nearest police post. Then hurry to the branch of the State Bank at the fair. Ask for me.' He gave Watson a gentle shove and stood waiting.

There was a heavy splash. Then all was still except for the sound of hastily retreating footsteps. Sherlock Holmes followed some fifteen steps behind. But when streetlights appeared, he fell back. All he wanted was to see the direction they took.

Seeing that Alferakki and Smith Copton were heading in the direction of the Commercial Centre, he turned and swiftly made his way through a side street. Outside a handsome residence he rang the bell at the main entrance. The policeman on point duty rushed over and glared at his dirty bare feet, 'Who are you?'

'Quiet,' was the answer. 'Can't you tell CID?'

Nevertheless, the policeman wanted to see some ID, and on being shown identification, calmed down. Holmes, of course, as soon as he had undertaken the job, had gone to the police and had been issued with the requisite documents.

In the meantime, a voice came from the other side of the door, 'Who's there?'

'Sherlock Holmes, the detective,' answered Holmes.

'Who else?'

'It's me,' said the policeman. 'I'm on point duty here. Open up, Ivan, it's OK.'

Ivan, the valet, evidently knew him well enough to recognize his voice and opened the door. 'What's going on?' he asked, letting them in.

'Is the director here, the director of the State Bank's fair branch?' asked Sherlock Holmes.

'Yes. What's happened?' asked the valet anxiously.

'So far nothing, but I need to see him on an important matter,' Sherlock Holmes interrupted him sharply. 'And if you go on trying to indulge your curiosity instead of announcing me, I'll make sure you get the blame.'

The frightened valet asked Sherlock Holmes to wait in the sitting room and went off.

The bank director appeared a moment later. He'd been entertaining all night and was fully dressed. He was middle-aged, sturdily built. His hair was an iron grey and he wore a Vandyke. He looked thoroughly perplexed. Probably warned by the valet, he didn't seem bothered to see a barefoot vagrant.

'What's the matter?' he asked anxiously.

'Does anyone else know I am here to see you?' asked Sherlock Holmes.

'No, nobody. This room is only for official visitors. But why are you here?'

'Your bank is under threat. I am asking you to telephone and order two armed men to be sent there. You have to get hold of the cashier or whoever holds the keys to the strongroom and follow me. I'll explain along the way.'

The director had his wits about him. He didn't ask further questions, but picked up the telephone. Orders were swiftly given. The valet ordered a horse and carriage.

The director and Sherlock Holmes set off for the main entrance of the Commercial Centre of the fair. This entrance was shut to the public, because the office of the provincial governor, the offices of the State Bank and other government departments were on the top floor.

'Did you take a revolver?' asked Sherlock Holmes as the coach moved off.

'Yes,' said the director, 'but you did promise to explain.'

'With pleasure,' answered Sherlock Holmes. 'The matter is very simple. A temporary branch of the State Bank is opened for the fair and very large sums of money are kept in anticipation of the fair.'

'Indeed,' said the director.

'Well, a couple of men decided to do something about it. Just under the floor of your premises there are two shops. A manufacturer and Alferakki, ex-Terehoff.'

'Indeed that is so,' confirmed the director.

'No doubt you have heard of the mysterious goings-on at Terehoff's.'

'Of course.'

'It's like this, then,' said Sherlock Holmes. 'Alferakki and his colleague needed that shop, because it is right under your storeroom and safe. I determined that as soon as I paid a visit to you. By means of trickery, they managed to get rid of Terehoff and to take his place. They've already knocked a hole just under the safe between their ceiling and your floor. According to my calculations, the break-in should take place today.'

'Oh, my God!' said the director.

'That's why our appearance at the bank must be carried out as quietly as possible,' added Holmes.

The coach, by this time, had arrived near enough to the main entrance to the Commercial Centre. Sherlock Holmes ordered the coachman not to pull up, but to go a little further. They got off quietly and opened the door. Inside, they went up the stairs to the security guards. 'There's a major crime being planned here,' the director addressed the head of security. 'To prevent it, we need absolute quiet. One of you has to let me into the store-room. As soon as you hear a whistle, bring the sentries with you. We'll wait inside. The door must be shut but not locked.'

'Yes, sir,' bowed the officer.

The cashier, three policemen and Watson arrived, all summoned by telephone. 'All our own people,' said Holmes. 'Everyone, take your shoes off. We must not be heard.'

The whole party entered the bank. The door to the storeroom was unlocked, the seal taken off the strongbox containing the money. The director was made to sign a receipt.

Holmes switched on the light. They were inside a small store-room. The walls were of thick stone. Metal leaf was nailed down to cover the floor. In the middle of the room, a large metal trunk was fixed to the floor. It had a flap with a metal grill nailed over it.

Sherlock Holmes shook his head. 'They'll have to work at getting to the money.' He placed everyone in position. He and Watson hid behind the strongbox. The others were told to wait outside. 'If you hear me whistle,' he whispered, 'rush inside and if you don't see me, go for the strongbox.' By way of explanation he added, 'It is likely, and more than likely, that the thieves have sawed an aperture into the storeroom from below the strong box, and nobody would see it from any angle.'

'Indeed,' said the director, looking at the proceedings with great interest, and awe at Holmes's part.

Holmes looked around, 'Well, sirs, take your places and not a sound. The slightest noise, a cough, a movement of the hand or leg, and all is lost.'

Everyone did as they were told. Holmes asked the director to unlock the strongbox. The director then left. Holmes and Watson were left alone in the strongroom.

IX

Left alone with Watson, Holmes opened the strongbox. It was filled with gold and bank notes. They dropped down behind it and switched off the lights.

Everything was still. Placing their revolvers beside them, they lay down silently on the floor. Time dragged on leaden feet. There wasn't a sound from down below to give away the presence of the thieves. Nearly an hour passed.

But then, at last, somewhere in the distance, from under the floorboards, a slight rustle came through. At first it didn't come through very clearly, but after a while, more and more. At last a light creak came through, as if someone had stepped on the precarious step of a ladder. This sound came not so much from under the trunk laden with money, but as if from a corner of the storeroom. Then the sounds ceased for a few moments.

Sherlock Holmes bent right up to Watson's ear and whispered very softly, 'There is a passageway through the wall, and then it goes between the floor and the ceiling.' He was silent again, and pressed his ear to the metal flooring to pick up the slightest sound.

Someone moved softly under the floor, and from under the trunk laden with money, a tool scraped. Then, another. Under the trunk, two people were working purposefully.

Sherlock Holmes crawled towards the trunk and placed his palm over the bank notes to feel any movement beneath them.

Below them, two people were filing away uninterruptedly. Approximately another hour went by. It was very likely that the files were constantly oiled. That's why the sounds were so weak.

And that's why the watchman outside could hear nothing.

But now all was still again. It was still for a couple of minutes, but then there was a rustle under the floor, as if mice were scurrying about. And then, all of a sudden, Sherlock Holmes felt the money under his palm shake and begin to go down. He realised at once what was happening.

He touched Watson gently on the shoulder, took his hand and shoved it into the trunk. 'The moment I pull you by the sleeve, jump right into the trunk,' whispered Holmes.

He rose quietly to his feet, bent over the trunk, using his palm to monitor its descent together with the money. The very moment that the upper layer of money was down to the level of the surrounding floor, Holmes tugged at Watson's sleeve and with one quick movement switched on the light. Both leaped into the trunk.

A sharp whistle sounded the alarm.

That very moment, the bottom of the trunk, which the thieves were lowering with their hands, collapsed under the weight of Holmes and Watson. The thieves were caught by surprise from the weight of the two bodies. Unable to hold the metal floor on which the trunk had stood, they let go and fell in different directions.

All this took two or three seconds. Now events followed one upon another with the speed of lightning.

The drop was not far. It was a mere three feet or so between the floor of the upper storey and the ceiling below. It was only the suddenness which stunned thieves and detectives, and then only slightly. A moment, and both sides had recovered so that a life-and-death struggle began in that narrow space.

X

As soon as Sherlock Holmes and Watson felt they had fallen on something solid, they drew their revolvers and threw themselves on Compton and Alferakki. Those two, in their turn, thought there were only two in pursuit. So they, too, threw themselves at their adversaries. Several shots rang out.

But at this moment help arrived from above. Three policemen and the full complement of guards were already clambering through the aperture, rattling their arms.

The thieves realized the game was up as far as they were concerned. They fired a couple of shots at random, to stop their adversaries for half a minute, and threw themselves through the passageway in the wall, hoping to make their escape through the shop below.

Watson, wounded in the arm, fell with a groan.

Alferakki was already at the entrance, but Sherlock Holmes brought him down with a flying tackle, while a couple of soldiers piled on top of him.

Compton was less lucky. Lightly wounded in the leg when the shoot-out began, he fell behind his companion and for a moment was surrounded by his pursuers. Seeing that there was no way to save himself, he decided to sell his life dearly. With wild curses, he thew himself into the thick of his opponents and laid low two soldiers with three shots. But at this moment, one of the Centre's watchmen, driven by the ferocity of what was happening, stuck a bayonet in his face. The blow was so fierce the bayonet went through his skull and he fell dead.

Alferakki was tied up. Guards were placed over the scattered money and a cashier assigned to count it. The criminal was led off to the police station.

The news of the attempt on the bank was all over the police station, and Sherlock Holmes was accorded a hero's reception. Thanks were heaped on him.

The third member of the gang, the cashier Veskoff, was also brought to the police station. He had fainted, but a doctor had been summoned to bring him to, and when he was told how his partners-in-crime had intended to deal with him, he made a clean breast of things.

Alferakki and Veskoff were placed in shackles and led away to await trial.

The very same day, Sherlock Holmes stopped by to visit Terehoff at home. 'Your old premises are available again and it is unlikely any apparition will appear,' he said with a smile. 'But you'll have to repair the wall.'

And he told the merchant the whole story. The happy Terehoff instantly laid out the promised sum of money, saying he'd pay Watson too. And he hastened to the Commercial Centre.

XI

A search of Alferakki's apartment only confirmed Holmes's suppositions. A projector was found, tools and correspondence which led to a whole gang of criminals being apprehended.

But a search of Compton's apartment led to an unexpected finding. The 'poor' Englishman had 60,000 roubles hidden in his mattress and proof that he was directly responsible for the theft of money from the bank in which he had been employed. The stolen money was returned to the bank, which presented three thousand roubles each to Sherlock Holmes and Watson as a reward.

Watson recovered from his wound in a matter of days.

And a month later, the police were able to establish the identity of Alferakki. It turned out that he was David Gabudidze, an escaped convict, a brutal robber, once the terror of the Caucasus.

7

THE MARK OF TADJIDI

P. Nikitin

I

The search for a major criminal brought Sherlock Holmes and me to Kazan. We spent approximately a month here, returning by way of a two-berth cabin on a boat owned by a company called 'The Flying Service'. We intended to sail along the Volga as far as Yaroslavl and catch a train to Moscow from there. It was peaceful sailing on the river. The weather was good. We spent all our time on deck, admiring the beautiful shores of the Volga.

Sherlock Holmes grew more cheerful and his ill humour at times vanished. I looked at my friend and was glad for him from the bottom of my heart. Several days passed in this way.

The boat sailed past Nijni-Novgorod and a day later we arrived at Kostroma. Here we were to load a large cargo and the captain announced we could rely on being there a good two hours.

'Would you like a stroll through the town, my dear Watson,' Sherlock Holmes suggested as our boat was made fast.

I readily agreed and we set off. But there was nothing of interest there, and after we had strolled about less than an hour, we
returned to the pier.

Here all was bustle. A score of stevedores, carrying heavy
bales, filed aboard the boat, bearing cargo from the warehouse
on the pier.

We stopped at the entrance to the warehouse and silently
watched all this activity. Twenty minutes or so went by. A few
words, suddenly uttered behind us, caused us to prick up our
ears and turn our heads.

The foreman was talking to a representative of the shipping
line, '—hasn't been collected for a while. I turned up yesterday –
terrible smell. Couldn't figure out where it came from. Seemed
to come from some corner . . . This morning I turned over the
whole warehouse, all the baggage, and found—'

'What was it?' asked the representative of the shipping line.

'It came from a basket,' answered the foreman. 'Unbearable
stink. A large basket sent as baggage to Kostroma from Kazan. It
was unloaded five days ago, but the recipient hasn't collected it.'

'Let's take a look,' grumbled the representative of the shipping line unhappily.

Some instinct pulled us after them, and we followed them into
the warehouse. The stink was something awful.

The representative of the shipping line made a face and spat
frantically. 'The devil knows what it is,' he swore. 'Turf out this
disgusting basket. It's probably full of rotting meat. A formal
protocol will have to be drawn up, the river police called in and
it has to be thrown away. Be a good chap, get the river police.'

The foreman ran out and was back soon with several river
policemen of different ranks. The shipping line representative
announced that the basket contained putrid cargo, that it had
made the air in the warehouse foul, and that the basket would
have to be opened. Interested in the goings-on, we approached
the group. The basket was untied and the lid taken off. A loath-

some smell came from it.

Inside the basket, a bale was tightly wrapped in a heavy tarpaulin. The tarpaulin was cut away on three sides and lifted off. Everyone jumped back in horror.

A corpse, chopped into pieces, was packed into the tarpaulin. There was no doubt that it was a human corpse. A wrist, sliced away from the corpse, lay on top.

'The devil!' said Sherlock Holmes, approaching the basket. 'A cargo that's been around for a while.'

'I'll ask you to get the hell out of here,' a police officer, just noticing us, threw the words at us somewhat fiercely.

'And why not simply say, "leave"?' said Holmes lightly.

Such simple words maddened the policeman, unused to being reproved.

'Just you wait and I'll have you down at the police station,' he yelled, and for some reason opened his briefcase, as if about to prepare a charge sheet.

'You're quite in order to do so,' answered Holmes calmly. 'Would you like my name? Sherlock Holmes.'

What a picture! The police officer was hopelessly embarrassed, confused and began to utter embarrassed apologies. As for the others, hearing the name of the famous detective, they silently examined him with wide-open eyes, forgetting all about the basket and its grisly contents. As if nothing untoward had occurred, Sherlock Holmes turned on his heels and left the warehouse without a word. I followed.

II

We returned to our boat and went to the dining room, intending to have a bite to eat. But hardly had our waiter approached us when the local Chief of Police, two policemen, and the police officer who had come down on us in the warehouse came hurrying in. Someone must have pointed us out, because the Chief of Police came straight over to our table.

'I would like to proffer my deepest apologies for the slight lack of tact on the part of my subordinates,' he said politely, addressing Holmes, 'but in the heat of the moment and under similar circumstances, a man may lose his composure.'

'Precisely what a policeman ought not to do,' Holmes shrugged. 'In England it is a severely punishable offence.'

'You are completely in the right,' agreed the Chief of Police. 'But I do beg of you most earnestly to overlook this untoward occurrence.'

The Chief of Police sat down at our table and spoke so pleasantly and in such a friendly manner that Holmes finally gave up. 'Very well, then. Consider it long forgotten. After all, travelling through Russia, if I were to remember every slight large or small, to which we English are subjected and to which we aren't used – why, I would've had to leave long since.'

The atmosphere changed and the conversation turned to the crime. However, at that moment the third whistle was blown and we had to bid each other farewell. We left Kostroma and, a day later, were already in Moscow. But the events which had taken place continued to interest us very much. The newspapers gave daily reports, but the news only revealed that the investigation wasn't progressing and the outcome was unlikely to be a positive one.

The investigation was simply unable to establish a motive for the murder. Nor was there any clue as to the identity of the victim, though it was hoped that would be discovered: the perpetrators had mutilated, but hadn't had the time or simply hadn't thought of destroying his clothes.

It was eventually established that the dead man was Count Piotr Vassilievitch Tugaroff. He owned a small estate in Kazan Province and a house in the city of Kazan itself.

When the newspapers had published news of the murder and

described his clothes, it was expected that relatives or someone near would respond. The victim, as Holmes and I had anticipated, was identified by his wife, the Countess Tugarova. She had seen reports of the murder and had written a letter full of despair saying that her husband, living with her in Oriol, had vanished three weeks earlier. What little description there was, fitted him. Judging by the material from which the clothes were made and the gold chain round his neck, it was possible to assume the victim came from the moneyed classes. All else was a mystery.

Some days later, matters improved somewhat. But even this fresh information did not lead to any results. The investigation continued to tread water and there was no further progress.

III

That evening, Holmes and I had just returned from a stroll, and he was sitting down to write a letter to England, when there was a knock at the door.

I said, 'Come in!' and a lady dressed in elegant black with black crepe from head to toe came in.

She was about 20 or 25. She had a beautiful figure, dark complexion with regular features and black hair. She did not look Russian at all.

She looked us both over, bowed with a sad look on her face and addressed me. 'Might one of you be Sherlock Holmes?' she asked.

I gestured toward my friend.

'Won't you sit down, madam,' Holmes said.

She sat down without further ado.

'I am the Countess Tugarova,' she said softly. Her accent didn't sound at all Russian. 'I was in Kostroma, where my husband's body was found, and heard of you by accident. I was told you had gone to Moscow and this is where I finally found you, with the help of the local police.'

Sherlock Holmes gave a little bow.

'Forgive me,' she said. There was entreaty in her voice. 'I've heard so much about you, so it isn't surprising that I turn to you for help. As far as I can see, the investigation is hardly moving forward—'

She broke off what she was saying and began to speak English. 'You must help me! Once, you and I were citizens of the same country. I owe so much to my husband, I am determined, at all costs, to bring the evildoer to justice.'

As soon as she began to speak, Holmes smiled, 'Undoubtedly, you are of mixed race. From which side?'

'You're right,' said the countess simply. 'It was my mother who was English.'

'Forgive me for the interruption,' smiled Sherlock Holmes, 'but I shan't interrupt any more unless it is absolutely necessary. I am all ears. If you want me to take up this matter, you must tell me everything in order, not omitting the slightest matter.'

He made himself more comfortable in his armchair and repeated, 'I am ready.'

IV

'We came to Russia some time ago,' began the Countess. 'But if you must have a full account, I must begin with my own life story. I am now 21. My husband was 45 a little while ago. Originally, I was a foster child. On several occasions he told me that while travelling through India, he stopped off at Bombay, where he rented a small private residence. That's where he got me for a present. To put it at its simplest, I was abandoned and left to him when I was 3. His first thought was to place me with the local police, because of the difficulty for a grown man of dealing with a child. But he changed his mind and decided to take me home to show off as a curiosity. I repeat this, as he told it to me himself, when sharing his own past with me. He was 23, when I was abandoned. During his stay in Bombay I was looked after by an old Indian woman who, naturally enough, told one and all of his intention to take me home. Before he left, the count received a letter from my father. In it, he said that he was of mixed race, and his wife had been an Englishwoman, who died in childbirth. But he was very poor and decided to foist the child on the count in the hope that, in good hands, she would have a better future than with a poor mulatto. He didn't give his name. The count took me along on his travels, and when he returned to Russia handed me over to the old woman who had been his own nurse. That's when, for some reason, I was brought up to call him "Papa". Having handed me over to his nurse, he vanished again for several years and returned when I was 9. But in his letters to his steward and to the nurse, he often mentioned me and showed his concern for my education—'

Sherlock Holmes gestured for the countess to stop and asked, 'Tell me, please, where exactly did the letters come from?'

'I was too little then to be interested in such things, but later I discovered that the greatest number came from India, and two letters were stamped in Tonkin,' she answered.

'Thank you,' Holmes bowed. 'Pray, continue.'

'Returning to Russia, he saw me,' the countess continued. 'At the time we were living on his estate. He was always affectionate towards me, was very satisfied with the progress I made in my studies, and at times examined me himself. But he never let me leave his side. This time he stayed a year in Russia, and I became very attached to him. Once, it was at the end of summer, he came to me pale and full of anxiety. 'Irra,' he said to me, 'there's a madman in the vicinity. He attacks people, bites and kills them. That's why you mustn't leave the house without me. I forbid it.' I was terribly frightened. After that we always stayed together, even going out in the garden. Nurse told me that Father was afraid for me. He hired four watchmen and guard dogs were chained in the yard. Nurse told me he frequently got up at night and went round the estate with a gun. Once, as evening was approaching, I wanted to pick some fresh roses. I went to look for Father, but not finding him, decided I'd go by myself. I put on a kerchief and went out through the yard and into the garden. I don't know what made me do this, probably because I was frightened by the count's warning, but I didn't open the gate straight away. So first I peeked through a chink in the fence. And there, behind a shrub, was a human head. I screamed and ran back without so much as a look at the face of the man in hiding. Hearing my outcry, the count rushed out of the stables. I told him what had happened. He went for his gun and, as if crazed, rushed into the garden. I hid in my room, frightened to death. He didn't find anyone and came back very upset and angry. For a whole hour he upbraided the watchmen, and the very same day hired four more and armed them. That evening he told me that we were leaving. He collected his personal belongings and papers himself, and ordered me to pack only three dresses, six changes of underwear and my favourite knick-knacks. Till the very last minute, none of the staff knew we were leaving. At eleven he ordered the best troika to be harnessed to the largest carriage and spare horses to be tied to the back.'

The countess paused and asked for a drink. With the agility of a young man, Sherlock Holmes jumped from his armchair and poured a glass of very good wine with water.

'Thank you,' said the countess, taking the glass.

She drank a little and smiled sadly, 'I hope I'm not boring you.'

'On the contrary,' Sherlock Holmes exclaimed with animation. 'It is utterly romantic and intrigues me more and more. If I were a writer, I would turn it into a novel. It would create a sensation.'

'In that case, I shall go on,' said the countess sadly.

V

'And so, by eleven o'clock that night, all was ready,' the countess began again. 'But first, the count called together all the watchmen. He ordered them to make a circle around the estate and move out in a radius. Half a kilometre away, they were to fire a shot.

'When the watchmen had gone off, the count summoned his steward, gave him a packet with instructions and announced to all that he was leaving. At this moment, we heard shots fired in the distance. That was the watchmen scaring off whoever it was, on the orders of their master. Our belongings were loaded and secured. With the staff looking at us in bewilderment, we drove through the gate and tore along the road as if we were crazed. The count personally indicated the route to be taken. We turned at the first crossroads and sped ahead, turning right and left by the minute, as if to cover our tracks. We covered about seventy kilometres, allowing the horses only a brief respite. When the horses were too weak to go on, the count ordered the spare horses to be harnessed and we sped off again. As the morning wore on, the coachman begged several times for the horses to be allowed to rest (the first troika we had set out with had simply been abandoned along the road), but the count was adamant. We sped on till the shaft-horse collapsed. The count ordered the coachman to mount one of the others and find, for any amount of money, the best possible horses. The loyal coachman (he'd served the count's father) galloped off and an hour and a half later was back with three horses of lesser quality and their owner. He was happy to accept two of our exhausted horses with three hundred roubles in exchange for his. Our dead horse was left on the road. The horses were changed and we flew like the wind. At about five we heard a whistle and soon got to some railway station. You should have seen the count's look of joy when he saw a train. I remember neither the line nor the name of the station. The count jumped out of the carriage, ordered the porters to unload and then wrote something on a piece of paper to which he affixed his seal. Then, I remember, he called the coachman and said, "Listen, Dimitri! Go where you wish, but remember, this girl's life depends on your silence. Rest here for a while, feed the horses, and go anywhere, where you can sell the carriage and horses. This note and your passport formally attest that they are yours. And here's another two hundred roubles. Go to your native province of Orlov. I know your village and I'll get in touch with you there. Should anyone ask after me or the girl, don't say where you dropped us off. Say nothing about us. Farewell." '

'That poor coachman. It was such an unexpected gift. He threw himself at the count's feet. But at this moment the train drew into the station. We bought tickets, handed in our luggage and got into a separate compartment. We travelled for two, maybe two and a half days. The count calmed down at once and became gentle and cheerful. In this way, we arrived in Kharkov. We put up in a hotel for two days, at the end of which the count announced to me that I was enrolled in a really good boarding school where he would take me. The next day he took me to Madam Beckman's boarding school, where he bade me farewell, asking me to behave and study well, so that he shouldn't have to blush for me. And then he left. Nobody knew where. I didn't see him till I was in the seventh grade. Nobody visited me. I had no relatives. During school holidays I stayed with one of my schoolmates. The count paid the school fees meticulously. He sent me affectionate letters and so much pocket money I was thought to be one of the richest pupils in the school. Up until the fifth grade I thought he was my father. But once, suddenly, when I was already in the fifth grade, he revealed in a letter what I have told you about my origins. Except he added that, God grant, my fate would soon be changed and I would find my real parents. He also enclosed his portrait. The letter disturbed me considerably and I wept over it night after night. I was astounded by the thought that the count, in effect, was a total stranger where I was concerned. We southern girls develop too early and it was possible that even then I began to think as a woman. But at the time, I was not aware of it. I kept on looking at the portrait the count had sent me. The count was a very handsome man. Another two years passed. I was a good student and already in the seventh grade. Once, I was summoned to reception. There was the count! My first instinct was to throw myself round his neck, but suddenly it came to me, he is a man and a stranger. I stopped in confusion. But he looked at me in rapture, as if astonished by what he saw before him. Even then I understood that glance. After that, his visits became more frequent. He behaved like a relative, and yet, like a stranger also. At Christmas he came to fetch me and we went to Paris. We travelled about for a month and he brought me back. I finished seventh grade. Some decision had to be made as to what to do with me. The count avoided his own estate and never even mentioned it. As for me, I was at a loss; what was I to do? But just before I graduated, my fate was decided. After the final exam, I was allowed leave. I remember that day as if it were now . . . we took a picnic basket and went out into the country. In a little forest glade we spread a carpet, lit a fire, and cheerfully set about preparing lunch. After lunch, seeing that there was just the two of us, the count sat down beside me and said seriously, "I have to talk to you, Irra." My heart began to beat faster and, involuntarily, I dropped my eyes. He began, "I don't want to keep you in a state of uncertainty, Irra. Soon we have to part forever." I screamed and fell unconscious. When I opened my eyes, the count was bending over me. Oh! His eyes gazed at me with such silent love, that everything within me began to quiver with joy. I threw my arms round his neck and covered him with kisses, begging him not to leave me, swearing I was ready for anything! He asked very solemnly, "Do you love me, Irra?" "Yes," I said. "And I love you too," he said passionately. "That means we will be man and wife. But so that you shouldn't reproach me in the future, I must tell you everything and the reasons why I wanted to part from you. I am being dishonourable. First, I should have returned you to your parents. Nor am I as good as you think I am. I have one sin on my conscience, a very considerable one—" But here I placed my hand over his mouth and asked him never to bring such matters up again. In the end, we decided to get married first and then, some time, to visit my parents. "Believe me, there is nothing mercenary in my seeking to marry you," said the count to me. I burst out laughing. Two months later we were wed and lived happily in total harmony. That's the story of my life. Not long before his death, the count got a letter from somewhere. It plunged him into such a fit of anxiety that for some time he went about as if he had been driven mad. Then suddenly he announced that he had to go to Kazan to sell the house and estate. "Whatever happens to me, don't worry," he said to me on parting, "Whatever happens will be for the best." And away he went. That's all I can tell you, Mr Holmes.'

The countess fell silent and large tears appeared in her eyes.

VI

Sherlock Holmes listened in silence, only raising his head when the countess ended her story. His brows were furrowed, his lips tightly pressed together. There was an enigmatic look in his eyes, which neither the countess nor I could comprehend. Suddenly he rose and began to pace the room nervously, occasionally stopping to look out of the window to cast a thoughtful look outside.

'You didn't see the letter which came to the count?' he asked the countess.

'No,' she answered. 'All my life I felt that there was some mystery involved. But since the count said nothing to me, I didn't feel I had the right to ask questions.'

'But did you notice whether, prior to his departure for Kazan, he set anything down on paper?'

'Most probably he did. He spent half the night in his study.'

'What did he say on leaving?'

'I've already told you. In addition, he told me that he might be away for some time. Then he repeated several times that whatever happened to him, I wasn't to worry.'

The countess opened her eyes wide as if a thought had struck her, 'Do you know, Mr Holmes, it just came to me. Every time he repeated that phrase, he would stress it.'

For a moment only, Holmes's eyes flashed. 'So what do you think?' he asked.

A ray of hope shone in the eyes of the countess, 'Could he still be alive?' she asked, her voice shaking. 'Is this some sort of machination on somebody's part?'

'What about the scar on the left leg? And the clothes?' Sherlock Holmes said thoughtfully.

'Yes, yes, it's so,' the countess whispered, confused and bewildered. 'There is no doubt that the leg belongs to him.'

'In any case, we must hurry,' said Holmes firmly. 'Where are the count's remains?'

'As soon as the authorities had finished their investigation, they gave them back to me. I took them to Oriol and had them buried in the Trinity cemetery,' answered the countess sadly.

'You still have an apartment in Oriol?'

'Yes.'

'In that case we go there by the very next train.' Holmes turned to me. 'Would you look up the train timetable for Oriol, my dear Watson. When is the next train?'

I looked up the timetable and said we had three-quarters of an hour.

'Oh, we have enough time,' Holmes exclaimed. 'Countess, can you meet us at the train?'

'Of course, I have only to stop at the Northern Hotel to collect my things.'

We set off.

VII

We were in Oriol the very next day.

'My dear Watson, will you escort the countess home,' Holmes asked me, as soon as we stepped off the train. 'I'll explore a little and join you presently.'

He wrote down her address and her husband's burial place, but prior to leaving us asked, 'When did the funeral take place?'

'Two days ago,' answered the countess. 'As soon as the funeral was over, I set off for Moscow to find you.'

Holmes set off in one carriage and the countess and I in another. Our carriages parted by the Mariinsky Bridge.

The countess's apartment wasn't very spacious, but furnished richly and in great taste. I waited while she changed and we had tea together in the sitting room.

Sherlock Holmes joined us a couple of hours later. He didn't say a word about where he had gone. He ate some pastry, drained a cup of tea quickly and without further ado asked to be taken to the late count's study.

'Nothing has been touched since the count left,' said the young widow, leading us into a fairly large study. There were bookcases all round the walls, massive furniture, armchairs covered with dark yellow hide. Holmes stopped and silently examined the room. I, too, examined everything with great curiosity, seeking to penetrate whatever mystery was concealed here.

Evidently, the count had a wide range of interests. Several

works on a wide range of subjects by famous scholars lay on the desk. A naval globe stood on a large stand in one corner. Maps of different countries hung on stands, with handwritten notes on some of them, probably in the count's own handwriting.

But what attracted most attention was the back wall of the study. A huge, fluffy carpet, evidently of Indian make, covered the entire wall. Over it, different weapons were arranged in beautiful order. The weapons consisted of ancient arrows, bows, quivers, tomahawks, shields of rhinoceros hide, halberds and boomerangs. Between them were unusual little axes with long handles, the official swords of the English, French and German navies, Japanese weaponry, revolvers, and different sorts of firearms, many of which were official weapons of various armed forces.

In the corner, touching the edge of the carpet, there were two tall, though not very deep cupboards with inlaid decorations. Inside them stood largely scholarly books.

Sherlock Holmes, having made a superficial examination of the study, began a detailed examination of the papers on the desk. The side drawers were unlocked, but held nothing out of the ordinary.

Once he had finished with the desk, Holmes began to examine the floor. He moved the furniture, shelves, poked about under the bookcases with a stick, bringing out papers and all sorts of rubbish.

He examined every bit of paper with especial interest. Suddenly, he gestured me to come close. 'Please look at this,' he said, handing me a torn envelope. This was an ordinary envelope, of average shape and size, addressed to the count from Calcutta. The address was written in English. The handwriting was poor, but the writing instrument had been pressed hard on the paper. There was a British colonial stamp. But what hit the eye was a strange seal on the envelope. It was elliptical in shape, just over an inch in length. In the middle, there were three left legs, with long lines below the knees on every single one.

'What does this seem to you?' asked Holmes.

'A very strange seal,' was all I could say.

'And you find nothing about it to tie it to the count?'

'Absolutely nothing.'

'There were three of them,' said Holmes, deep in thought.

'Three of whom or what?' I asked.

'Three people with scars on their left leg,' Holmes answered seriously. 'Those long lines across the legs evidently stand for scars. But then, the late count also had a scar on his leg—'

For a minute he was deep in thought, then suddenly exclaimed, 'Tadjidi!'

'What's that?' I asked in surprise.

'Oh, it's all fully come back to me. In India, my dear Watson, there is a small tribe called Tadjidi. They live not far from Bombay, and are distinguished by their bloody rites. Blood accompanies every rite of passage in their lives. At birth, the baby's ears and nostrils are pierced for decoration. Bride and groom, on marriage, have symbolic signs of loyalty cut into their skin. At burial, the widow is burnt alive on a pyre, and so on. There is a ritual, which consists of an oath not to reveal mutual secrets. Those who undergo this ritual of mutual secrecy have to cut long and deep gashes on their left leg. The count had been in Bombay at some point and it is very likely that he is bound by oath with two other people, of whom at least one belongs to the Tadjidi tribe.'

Holmes placed the envelope in a notebook and resumed his searches.

For some time he stood before the cupboards examining the inlays, looking at the cupboards from all sides. Next he tried to open the drawers in the desk that were locked, using the master keys he always carried with him. He failed and stepped back. 'Well, enough for today,' he said and went up to the countess. 'Before leaving, I have a question.'

'I am at your service,' answered the young woman. She had paid minute attention to his every word.

'What was your maiden name?'

'Benaliradjewa,' she answered.

Sherlock Holmes and I both looked at her in amazement.

'What an unusual surname?' muttered Holmes. 'You and the count carried different surnames and till his letter arrived, couldn't you have guessed he was not your father?'

'Strange, isn't it,' said the countess. 'I was far too naïve, and I'd never heard the count addressed by his surname, only by his first name and patronymic. I just assumed we had the same surname. The other pupils didn't seem to know anything. The headmistress probably knew, but said nothing.'

'Aha!' mumbled Holmes and made his farewells.

VIII

Leaving the countess, we strolled along Bolhovsky Street, booking into a hotel. Holmes asked for stationery and sat down to write letters to someone. He then went to the post office and when he came back, said to me, 'My dear Watson, there's night work for us today and every day this week. I hope you'll agree to accompany me, if only to be a witness to the solution of one of the most mysterious murders ever committed.'

'That would give me great pleasure,' was my reply.

'Splendid!' Holmes nodded his head. 'In the meantime, we must find a library or a reading room which not only subscribes to English newspapers but keeps them for reference.'

We went out in search of such an institution. But wherever we went, either English newspapers were unavailable or they were only kept for a year or two at most. Holmes was in despair.

But in one of the libraries we were advised to look up an elderly Englishman called Dewlay, who had spent most of his life in Oriol. He had been a chemist, and then opened a chemical dye works, which allowed him a good income. We got the address and made our way to him. Very soon, quite unceremoniously, we introduced ourselves to him, much to his joy.

When we told him what we needed, old Mr Dewlay nodded smugly. 'Oh, in rereading our old newspapers, I find consolation in this barbaric land,' he said with pride. 'I've been getting *The Times* for twenty-eight years, and not a single page is missing.'

His apartment was in the same courtyard as his dye works. He took us there, introduced us to his wife and had the old newspapers brought to us.

The Times newspapers for each year were neatly arranged separately, which made Holmes's search so much simpler. Holmes thought for a moment and asked for those newspapers which had come out nineteen, twenty and twenty-one years ago.

Our gracious host ordered whisky and soda and we helped ourselves to an Englishman's favorite tipple, while Holmes delved into the yellowed newspapers.

Over an hour passed. And then Sherlock Holmes joyfully struck the heap of newspapers with the palm of his hand. 'That's it!' he exclaimed happily. 'Come here, my dear Watson. Let me show you something very unusual, even though this newspaper is all of twenty years old.'

I hastened to his side.

'In your opinion, my dear Watson, who could our beautiful client possibly be?'

'The countess?' I asked, my curiosity excited.

'Yes!'

'How am I to know?' I shrugged my shoulders.

'I expect you to say, a poor girl of mixed race, adopted by the count.'

'Of course.'

Sherlock Holmes smiled enigmatically. 'It would be a great mistake to think that,' he answered. 'Just imagine, Watson, that in her own homeland hers was a much higher status, and that she would have been infinitely richer, despite being a countess here, than the count's fortune.'

'Damn me, if I follow what you are saying!' I exclaimed.

'All this I discovered very simply,' said Holmes imperturbably. 'Surely, Watson, in listening to the countess's account of her origins, you must've sensed considerable strains and gaps.'

'Of course I have,' I admitted. 'But, then, what can a woman say who knows nothing about herself and can only describe her past from someone else's account.'

'You are quite right,' Holmes agreed. 'But doesn't that mean that whoever told her of her past, lied. If he hadn't lied, her story wouldn't have suffered from such defects.'

'True.'

'That's just it! Listening to the countess, it immediately occurred to me that the greatest doubt came over me only when she gave her maiden name, Benaliradjewa. Isn't it strange, to give such a name to a child who is to be taken away to Russia, baptized and given a Russian education? Besides, the surname is a genuine one; it wasn't made up. I remember too well the name which resounded up and down India in its time. And here it is again. Let me read something to you from days gone by '

Holmes lifted a yellowing newspaper sheet and read:

Telegram from the colonies.
India. Bombay.

The local population is tremendously upset by a particularly audacious theft which took place not far from Bombay from the palace of the rajah, Ben-Ali. Ben-Ali, much respected by all, famed for his riches and influence over the local population, went hunting, leaving his year-old daughter at home. Rajah Ben-Ali, a handsome man, is married to an Englishwoman from a good family. This is why Irra's skin is more European than Indian. Irra, an only daughter, was worshipped by her family. When Ben-Ali was setting off for the hunt, Irra and her nurse were walking in the palace vicinity. When the nurse and baby hadn't returned for some time, the alarm was raised. The nurse was found by the roadside, stabbed to death in her bosom. The baby had vanished. Now a full alarm was raised. Thousands of horsemen and men on foot were sent out in all directions, but in vain. Irra had vanished. The rajah returned, widened the search and offered a huge reward for his daughter's return, but to no avail. The British police joined in the search.

Sherlock Holmes lowered the newspaper and looked at me. I was visibly upset.

'And you think—' I began, but Holmes interrupted me.

'Little Irra, daughter of Rajah Ben-Ali, kidnapped twenty years ago near Bombay, is found. The sole heiress of one of the richest men in India has become a Russian countess.'

Holmes fell deep into silent thought. Then, 'Indeed, my dear Watson, we have to act with great care. There is a mystery attached to the life of this young woman and our task is to resolve it.'

Having spent a half-hour in the company of Mr Dewlay, we bade farewell to our cordial host and left.

IX

But we didn't return to our hotel. Outside, Holmes seemed to consider something. 'First of all, we have to fortify ourselves with a good portion of roast beef or something else. Let's find a restaurant, Watson, before night falls.'

We found a restaurant, where we ordered cold roast beef and

fried chicken with rice. Our appetite satiated, Holmes turned to me, 'I shall ask you, my dear Watson, to spend the night at the home of the countess. Say nothing of our discovery. Watch the yard and street with great vigilance. I am off to the cemetery, and shall join you at the countess's in the morning. She will have to tell the servants that you are a close relation of her husband and that you come from some other town.'

We parted. I carried out Holmes's instructions to the letter. For some reason, it did appear to me that the countess was being watched, and I advised her to change her bedroom for the time being, to the other end of the apartment. She did as I suggested and moved into a small sitting room, which only opened into a second one.

At eleven she retired. I switched off all the lights, tested the locks and placed myself on watch. I took off my shoes and moved silently from room to room, diligently watching the yard and street.

I wasn't the only one doing guard duty. Outside, there were two sizable Alsatians that could have handled a bear. During the day, they were chained up, while at night they were let loose. They let nobody pass, except the count, countess and the cook, who fed and chained them up or released them as necessary.

I passed from room to room, looking out for anything suspicious. The street was like any street. An occasional late passer-by disturbed the silence and finally all was still. Dawn began to break and carts from the villages broke the stillness on their way to market. Morning, and the town took on its usual appearance.

Holmes appeared at eight. I could see from his face that he had achieved nothing. I reported that I, too, had seen nothing. He announced, however, that he was persevering with his original plan and suggested we catch up on our sleep at our hotel.

No point in describing the next four days in detail. They were all the same. Holmes spent day and night at the cemetery, while I stayed in the apartment of the countess. She acceded to

Holmes's advice not to leave the house, confining herself to a brief turn round the yard.

X

Came Saturday. It was the fifth day of our uninterrupted watch, and I felt somewhat tired. Evening approached. All these days I had only slept in fits and starts. It was with less than pleasure that I looked forward to another sleepless night. Moreover, the young countess was beginning to look as if she was weary of our futile efforts. She had even begun to scoff at Sherlock Holmes's genius. Yet more and more her voice held notes of sadness.

That evening she read some French novel and retired early. I was about to switch off the lights, when I suddenly heard her voice. 'Mr Watson! Mr Watson!' she cried out anxiously.

I hastened into the sitting room beside her bedroom. She stood in the middle of the room, pale and trembling, dressed in a pale blue housecoat which she had hastily thrown on.

'What's happened?' I asked.

'Were you in my bedroom?' she asked, looking me in the eye.

'Whatever for?' I asked in surprise.

'What about Mr Holmes?' she asked.

I shrugged. 'Mr Holmes was here at the break of dawn today. He merely said a few words to me and left immediately,' I said.

'And nobody, but nobody else, entered the house?'

'I can confirm that.'

She raised her beautiful hand and proffered me a small unsealed envelope. 'In that case, you may be able to explain what this letter means and how it came to be on the pillow on my bed.'

Bewildered, I accepted the letter. The address was typewritten.

'Countess,' wrote its anonymous author, 'although you don't know me, nonetheless I am your friend. Circumstances, which came about because of your husband's trust in me, have entangled me in your family secrets. I beg of you, by all that's sacred, please listen to me. You are in the most terrible danger. Don't leave the house, not by so much as a step. Not even in the yard. And always carry a weapon. Just in case, beware even of the servants. I know that some detective is living in your house. Please tell him to be more careful and not show himself so openly at windows. He can watch over you just as well with dimmed lights and drawn curtains. Have courage. All will be for the best. Your well-wisher.'

I had hardly opened my mouth to say something, when I was shaken to hear a noise at my back. The countess screamed and held on to a chair for support. I turned quickly. Sherlock Holmes was standing in the doorway, a look of glee on his face.

'Dear God, how you frightened me!' exclaimed the countess, recognizing him.

'Forgive me, but there was an important reason why I came in without ringing the doorbell,' he answered.

'But how did you manage to get in?' wondered the countess.

'No need for any special talent,' answered Holmes with a shrug. 'My friend Dr Watson does not possess the talent of a detective. Here he is guarding the house, yet he left a window open in the corridor. Anyone could get in easily from the street.'

I was too disconcerted to say anything.

XI

'There we are, then!' exclaimed the countess. 'At least I now know who entered the house and slipped a letter on my pillow. Mr Holmes, you did that most skillfully.'

A puzzled look appeared on Holmes's face. 'Do I take it that

you are insinuating I was here and slipped you a letter surrepti-
tiously?' he asked.

'So you weren't here?' the countess asked sarcastically.

'I don't suppose you'd let me have a look at the letter,' Holmes
said, a solemn note in his voice.

I handed him the letter. Holmes examined every line carefully,
then looked again through a magnifying glass and for some
reason even gave it a lick with his tongue.

The countess and I watched him with curiosity.

'Whoever wrote this letter, wept over it,' he said suddenly.

The full meaning of this sentence hadn't penetrated when
suddenly Holmes looked at the countess fixedly and said slowly,
'This letter was written by . . . your husband.'

A piercing scream burst from the young woman's bosom. And
if I hadn't managed to get to her side in time to support her, she
would have collapsed on the floor.

It took some minutes to calm her. As soon as she had recovered, she asked, 'My husband? My God! For God's sake, explain
immediately what you mean by that.'

'Nothing more or nothing else than that he is alive, that
nobody cut him into pieces,' said Holmes speaking with great
clarity.

The countess pressed one hand to her heart and with the other
frantically seized Holmes by the hand, 'It can't be! For God's
sake . . . it's about time you told everything.'

'First of all, calm yourself and sit down,' Holmes said.

The countess obeyed and sank into a chair in agitation.

'And so, listen,' Holmes began speaking seriously. 'I don't
know the details, but I shall relate the whole course of events
to you in general terms as I am sure they happened. Watson, do
listen, but at the same time watch the street. Extinguish the
lights and let's move to the dining room. And so, I begin,' he
started again as soon as his instructions had been followed and
I had sat down by the drawn curtains, while he and the count-

ess sat down beside me. 'Unlike the count, I see no reason to make a secret of your origins. Twenty years ago, you, the year-old daughter of the famous Rajah Ben-Ali was kidnapped by three evildoers, one of whom was the count himself.'

'Oh, no!' moaned the young woman.

'Whether the count was an evildoer or fell into their company inadvertently, we'll soon know. All I know is that the count was bound by oath to the other two, one of whom belonged to the Tadjidi tribe. Of course, I could be wrong but, judging by the weapons with which the count's study is hung, he had something to do with pirates. Those little axes with the long handles are their favourite weapons for fighting at close quarters.'

'Oh, God! Oh God!' wept the young countess.

'Oh, there's no need to upset yourself so,' Sherlock Holmes tried to calm her. 'After all, what I am saying is mere supposition. In addition, the extent of the count's guilt is not clear at all and, for some reason, it seems to me that he suffered some great sorrow in his life, which vindicates him. Today's letter demonstrates that he fears for you and has been doing all these things because he wants to save you, but not to escape justice, else he would have referred to the detective with hatred.'

Hope and joy now came into the voice of the young countess as she murmured softly, 'Of that I am sure! He is too noble.'

'And so I continue,' Sherlock Holmes resumed softly in the darkness. 'Bound by oath, they kidnapped you. How you fell into the hands of the count, I don't know. But the very fact that you were with him aroused the jealousy of the others, and they decided, at all costs, to take you from him. It is probable that the count received a letter with the seal of Tadjidi and one of the other two members of the enterprise sought him out in Russia. The count refused to give you up and decided simply to kidnap you. You were then already 9 years old. But the count was fortunate enough to escape this person, carrying you away on that memorable night. Seven years went by and the count, having given you an education and turned you into an exceptionally cultivated young woman, wanted to return you to your parents, but he fell in love. Love, and the fear that you might not wish to surrender yourself to him, that's what caused him to conceal the mystery. He married you and decided to visit your parents when you had finally grown close to each other. Their status and wealth was of no consideration to him. Mind you, he must have known that after your disappearance Rajah Ben-Ali had offered a reward of ten thousand pounds sterling, the equivalent of a hundred thousand roubles, to whoever found you. Five years later, the unhappy father doubled the reward. It is very likely that the possibility of earning such a huge reward gave no peace to the other two, which is why they didn't give up their search for the count. The count got a letter and then vanished. One of the invisible enemies arrives in Russia and the count kills him—'

'What are you saying!' exclaimed the countess.

'He kills him, having lured him into a trap,' Holmes continued imperturbably. 'He dressed him in his own clothes, killed and placed him in a basket, having first mutilated his face and knowing full well that going by the gash on the leg and the clothes, the corpse would be taken for him. Why? Evidently, he reckoned that the third villain would fall for this. The death of the count would be trumpeted everywhere by the newspapers and the third one would come here to kidnap you. Of course, thinking the count dead, he wouldn't be so careful—'

'Sssh,' I whispered at this moment, seeing the dark silhouette of a man walking back and forth across the road.

Sherlock Holmes abruptly stopped his account and ran to the curtain.

*

XII

'Now, then, my dear Watson,' he whispered, 'redouble your attenton.'

To the extent that the darkness allowed it, we saw that the man appearing to wander aimlessly opposite the house was above average height, well built, wearing a light well-fitting suit. Twice he walked past the countess's home, stopped and turned his head to the right, peering into the darkness.

A couple of minutes later, a wagon, the kind used to transport furniture, drove from around the corner. It stopped some way from the house, and a man came from it and approached the man standing on the pavement.

The two exchanged a few words, after which one returned to the wagon, while the other remained standing on the pavement.

There were no passers-by.

'Look! Look!' whispered Holmes. 'Look at the fence opposite.'

I looked in the direction he had indicated. A dark, half-rounded silhouette crawled over the top of the fence.

'Someone is watching the man on the pavement,' I whispered.

'Yes, indeed!' answered Holmes. 'Slip off your shoes in case we have to move quietly.'

Meanwhile, the man on the pavement looked carefully on all sides and then swiftly crossed the street. Now he was under the window next to ours.

We froze, listening for the slightest sound, taking our revolvers out of our pockets, just in case. The poor countess sat there, more dead than alive, her heart beating loudly in the stillness. We now heard the noise of a cut being made.

'Diamond cutter,' whispered Holmes.

The sound was repeated several times and the glass cracked. The curtain billowed as the air blew in and we heard a rustle. Holmes jerked me nervously by the sleeve. I looked out on the street and saw a silhouette waist-high by the fence. The silhouette froze and a shot rang out.

The man on the windowsill gave a loud shriek and we heard his body collapse heavily on the pavement. At this moment, Sherlock Holmes swiftly flung the window open, leapt out and made for the fence.

I couldn't very well leave him, so I threw myself after him, shouting to the countess, 'Call the servants! Tie up the man lying outside if he's lightly wounded! Send after that wagon!'

A moment later we were over the fence in pursuit of the killer. We were so quick that he was unable to run as far as the opposite end of the yard before we caught up with him. But to my surprise, he didn't point his gun at us. On the contrary, he turned the barrel down towards the ground, waiting for us proudly, evidently not intending to defend himself.

Holmes aimed his revolver with one hand, and with the other took a torch out of his pocket and pointed the beam at the face of the criminal. The man who stood before us was of noble bearing with a handsome open face. He was pale as a sheet, but looked at us with the calm look of a man who had fulfilled his duty. It was the look of a man who had killed an opponent in a duel for insulting someone close or wounded his honour.

'Count Piotr Vassilievitch Tugaroff, I arrest you,' said Sherlock Holmes loudly and clearly, lowering his revolver.

'I surrender,' answered the count, 'but I would like to know who I am dealing with.'

'Of course,' said Holmes, 'I am Sherlock Holmes and this is my friend, Dr Watson.'

The count's eyes lit up joyfully, 'I am glad that it is you I have to deal with,' he exclaimed. 'You will understand me better than most. Let's go to my house and should you still have any doubts about me, feel free to summon the police. I only ask that you hear my story before I am led away to prison.'

And he threw his weapon down.

'I do believe you,' said Holmes unexpectedly. 'Let's go. As for the police, they're bound to be here any minute.'

We made our way to the count's house. The shot had already disturbed the quiet street. In the distance we heard the trill of a police whistle. At the front door Holmes gave a strong pull at the bell.

'Who's there?' asked the countess.

'Holmes and Watson,' answered the former.

The door opened and we entered the well-lit hallway. Seeing her husband, the countess started back, then, with a loud sob, threw herself at him. He embraced her silently, while tears cascaded from her eyes.

XIII

It was a good half-hour before the countess calmed down.

'I would like to tell all first and then I shall ask you to summon the police,' said the count at last. 'But where is the man I shot?'

'He is heavily wounded and we've carried him inside,' answered Irra.

'All the better,' the count nodded his head. 'But let Irra be the first to know her past.'

'I already know,' she murmured and blushed.

'How?' he answered upset.

Holmes gave a brief account of his investigations.

'Hmm! Your fame still doesn't do you justice,' said the count, staggered by what he heard. 'But what convinced you it wasn't me in that grave?'

'That was very simple,' explained Holmes. 'I dug up the corpse at night and tried your boot on its leg. Moreover, a swarthy man came to the cemetery watchman and asked to see your grave. I saw him. He read the inscription on the tombstone and when he was convinced that you were buried there, he smiled happily and left. A minute later I saw you flash through the greenery.'

'That's true,' said the count solemnly. 'But let me begin at the beginning. To explain my connection with these two men, I have to tell you that I was orphaned at 17 and set off to travel. For over a year everything went well, but towards the end of the second year, when I was sailing from Calcutta to America, we were attacked in the Indian Ocean by the corsair Daudalama. During the attack, I fell into the sea. Luckily for me, the leader, Daudalama of the tribe of Tadjidi fell with me. He had a severe head wound and would have gone down but, driven by pity, I held him up, not knowing I had saved the life of such a villain. The pirate ship came by and fished us out. For having saved the life of their leader, I was allowed to live. Daudalama, who seemed to be like a cat with nine lives, soon recovered. He promised that my life would be spared, but with this proviso, that I was to swear an oath not to reveal his misdeeds. Otherwise, I would die. There was one other prisoner. He was a proper villain himself. He actually asked to be admitted as a member of the pirate crew. What was I to do? I decided to accede to the demand and escape at the first opportunity. The oath and the slashing of the legs was administered. I, Hammer (the other prisoner) and Daudalama swore to be blood-brothers. I spent two years with the pirates. Unfortunately, my passport was with me and the pirate discovered my name. He attacked ships and killed everyone on board, but that wasn't enough to satiate him. I was present but did not take part. I was closely watched. Daudalama had a deadly enemy. This was Rajah Ben-Ali, who had hanged his father, also a bandit, after whom his son took. And so the pirate decided to avenge himself. The rajah worshipped his daughter, little Irra. Daudalama's idea was to kidnap the little girl, hold her to ransom and then, having dishonoured her, to return her to her father. He told me I was to be his partner in this conspiracy. Hoping to escape, I agreed. And

so, Hammer and Daudalama and I set off for Bombay. The rest
of the story you know. On the way back, at night, I escaped with
the little child. For twelve days we were at sea in a plain Indian
boat till a ship picked us up. To what authority was I to hand
over the child? In any case, I was sure Daudalama would kidnap
her all over again. That's why, returning to Russia, I sent a letter
to the rajah telling him not to worry about the child. I intended
to bring her up and then return her to her father, hoping that by
that time justice would overtake the pirate. As for me, I kept an
eye on his whereabouts and misdeeds. That's how it was till Irra
was nine. But now Daudalama, by some twist of malign fate,
discovered my whereabouts. Together with Hammer, he arrived
in Russia to kidnap little Irra and carry out his revenge. He
warned me in a threatening letter, saying I had best give the lass
up voluntarily. But I didn't answer. And so they appeared, lying
in wait for her like beasts on the prowl. Hammer gave himself
away when Irra was approaching the gate. I managed to put a
bullet through his side but, despite the wound, he escaped. I
suspect Daudalama didn't want to leave his wounded partner
behind. Nobody else knew what had happened. When Irra grew
up, I wanted to return her to her father myself, but I . . . I fell in
love. I was so afraid to lose the woman I loved I didn't dare tell
her her real name. Besides, I was afraid of the publicity and the
fact that the world would ascribe mercenary ends to me. After
all, the rajah was rich beyond the dreams of avarice. I thought
the bandit had vanished, when the blow fell. Daudalama found
me a second time and sent Hammer here. He wrote to me,
saying that unless I give up Irra, his vengeance would fall on me
too and, in any case, Irra would not escape dishonour. This was
the second letter carrying the mark of Tadjidi. So I thought of a
trap. I set off to meet Hammer in Kazan, where he was to arrive
after going through Persia and the Caucasus. We met in Kazan.
I told Hammer that I intended to give up Irra and asked him to
write to Daudalama to this effect, that we were on our way to

THE MARK OF TADJIDI

Oriol to fetch her and would he join us there. Hammer's clothes were too light for the Russian climate, so I gave him mine. I lured him to a spot I had prepared, killed him, cut him up into pieces, put the remains in a basket and hid myself away. Everything was as I expected. Daudalama read of my death in the newspapers. On the one hand, this reassured him. On the other, he was at a loss as to Hammer's whereabouts. Perhaps he'd fallen into the hands of the police! Daudalama thought it through and decided he had nothing left to worry about. Running into me was no longer a risk. He could walk about freely and was getting ready to make off with Irra quite openly, which was why I was able to put a bullet into him.

The count fell silent.

Noises came in from the street.

The count spoke again, 'And now, for the final proof.'

He went into his study and opened a secret compartment in one of the inlaid cupboards by pressing on one of the stones.

'Here is my diary,' he said, handing Holmes a thick notebook. 'You will recognize that it was written long, long ago from the handwriting and ink. Here are the bandit's letters, and here is my last will and testament, made ten years ago, in which I reveal Irra's real name and leave her, in the event of my death, my entire estate. And now, I ask you to hand me over to the police.'

Sobbing, the countess fell at the feet of her husband and embraced his knees.

We stood there, not knowing what to do.

XIV

A month passed. The trial was over and he was found 'not guilty!'

The wounded pirate was forced to confess to all his crimes. He was handed over to the British authorities and his life ended on the gallows.

Soon enough, Rajah Ben-Ali was told of his daughter's fate. His joy knew no bounds. He sent quite a deputation to fetch his daughter and son-in-law.

Sherlock Holmes and I received generous rewards and for some time corresponded with the count and countess, till time and other concerns distanced this enigmatic affair in our memories.